My Side

Tara Brown

Copyright © 2013 Tara Brown
All rights reserved.
ISBN:- 10: 0991841174

ISBN-13: 978- 0991841172

Just to see if I could

ACKNOWLEDGMENTS

Thank you to Katy Austin, she is a person I cannot live without. She is the first stranger who believed in my crazy stories and me. I love you Katniss-Spicypants!!!

Ruthi Kight (Roof) and Amanda Engelkes (Mani) are both an integral part of the team that has helped me along the way, love you ladies. Thank you to my Nators, too many people to list. I am the luckiest author ever. I have the best of the best for a street team!!

Thank you to my family for supporting me through all of this craziness, I swear one day I really will take a break from it all.

I love you Nick!!

Thank you to my amazing editors, Andrea Burns and Rhiannon Nicks. You want to correct so many of the little things that I swear are words. Tots is legit, it's tots legit.

Thank you to Steph at Once Upon a Time Covers, who else is up at midnight when I suddenly need a cover? No one!! You got my back and are always on call for the millions of novels I seem to have on the go and I love you for it!!

There are too many bloggers and reviewers and people to thank. I am blessed and I love you all!!

Thank You!

This is My Side

Chapter One
Handcuffs and bear spray

Knots didn't twist in my stomach as the plane landed. I wasn't as excited as I had thought I would have been. There was a level of freedom, mixed in with my emotions, that was taking over everything else and giving me a feeling of blissful peace.

The guy behind me pressed against me in the lineup to deplane. I moved forward into the lady in front of me, trying to escape the mouth breather. The plane, that had been far too cool in the air, was now a sweaty pit of anxious people ready to leave the confines of the narrow walkway.

I lugged my carry-on to the baggage pick-up when we finally started walking. The people surrounding me looked either tired or excited. Only a few seemed like they were unsure of what to feel, like me.

I dragged my white-blonde hair back into a ponytail. The mouth breather was watching me from across the baggage-claim area. I reached into my carry-on and rubbed my hands against the mace in my shorts pocket. I brought it with me everywhere.

I would mace mouth breather's ass in a heartbeat.

Danny, my brother, had bought me a special blend of bear spray that was supposed to be lethal. I watched the mouth breather with hatred filling my eyes. I wanted him to think again about watching me. I stared him down until he slunk back into the shadows. I wasn't becoming a skin suit. I saw Silence of the Lambs. I knew about the lotion on the back.

Bags started to go round the conveyor belt when I finally tore my eyes from his hiding place. I reached and heaved mine off when I recognized the pink bow my mom had tied on it.

My shoulder burned within seconds of carrying it to the exits behind the herd of people leaving.

"I can get that for you. Give you a ride to wherever you're going?"

I sighed and prepared myself to grab the mace as I turned, surprised to see a young guy with a red beard.

I grinned, "Thanks, but I have a ride."

He nodded at the middle-aged mouth breather with the sweat stains and the greasy, fat face hiding behind a pillar. "Stay away from that guy over there; he was staring at you and muttering some creepy shit when we were on the plane."

I looked at the disturbing fat guy and weighed my options. If he was on the bus with me, he could follow me and find my house. If I caught a cab, he could follow it with another cab. My guts said that the redhead was the better option. I handed him my bag, "Okay. Let's go."

I could take this guy, maybe. He was thinner and more coffeehouse mellow than mouth-breather, skin-suit-wearing stalker. Either way, there was panic and instability flying through my brain. I had to take deep breaths.

My mind whispered traitorous lies, like I had made a mistake or I wasn't as brave as I was pretending to be. I knew it wasn't true. I was brave. I had proved that already once. Maybe more than once.

I followed the redhead to the short-term parking lot. He turned back, "Name's Mick."

I smiled, "Nice to meet you, Mick. I'm Erin." I glanced at my watch. I wanted to be at the apartment by four in the afternoon. It was 3:54; that gave me six minutes. I scowled as he looked at me. "Student?"

I nodded, starting to worry. What if he wasn't the nice, red-bearded young man he seemed to be?

He beamed, "Me too. I'm in the marine bio master's. You?" Never mind, he was a student. I felt a bit better until I thought about the fact that he had a beard. Divers rarely had beards—right? "Law."

"At Northeastern?" I nodded and he nodded back, "Cool, me too." He walked to a black truck, "This is me."

I slung my bags in the back, "I really appreciate this, Mick."

He shook his head, "I got a sister, dude. If she ever got ogled by some fat fuck like that, I'd choke his ass."

I chuckled and climbed into the truck.

"You know Boston?"

He nodded, "Yeah, I did my undergrad here. I'm from Colorado originally." He started the truck and laughed, "I can tell by the paranoid wild eyes on you that this is your first trip, huh?"

I did up my seat belt and shook my head, "I came with my family in the summer for orientation." I didn't want him to think I was completely at his mercy. I had come for orientation and for my father's marathon years before. Of course, both times all I had done was read and wander the city looking at old buildings. I hadn't actually paid attention to anything.

He backed out and drove off, a bit too fast for my liking.

I studied him for a second, "You allowed beards in marine bio, what with the diving?"

He shook his head and stroked the long, scraggly bush, "Nope. Gotta shave in a couple weeks when school starts." He scratched and ran his hands over it, "Had a bitch of a time in Bali this summer 'cause of it. My passport picture has no beard."

I started to relax. He seemed like a stoner. "What's your sister's name?"

He gave me a sideways glance, "Lisa. She's a total bitch. She's sixteen and completely running the whole house. I went home for a week, and I was ready to murder her." He chuckled, "Sorry. I'm not... like a serial killer. Ha, wrong thing to say to a random chick."

I giggled nervously and looked at my watch; I was only going to be a couple minutes later than I expected. My Google map on my iPhone showed us nearly there.

"What's the address?"

I started to panic, "Oh... it's in my phone." I zoomed in on the apartment and picked a close by restaurant, "You know where Cappy's Pizzas and Subs is, by Hemenway?"

He nodded, "Yeah, for sure."

"Right near there."

It wasn't exactly near there, but it was better than ending up a skin suit.

He chatted and I looked out at the river basin. It was amazing. So much more amazing than Grande Forks, North Dakota.

The ride was over in exactly fourteen minutes. It was faster than the map gave us during regular afternoon traffic.

He pulled up in front of Cappy's. The red brick buildings everywhere were awesome. The street was old and cool, but with modern touches, somehow blending in. I felt tiny, and yet, somehow powerful among it. I would be an official law student in a couple weeks. That was powerful.

He dragged my bags out and passed them to me, "If you don't recognize me at school, it's the missing beard," he chuckled and slapped me on the arm, "See ya, Erin."

I grinned, "Thanks again, Mick."

He shook his head, "Stay away from creepy dudes." He waved and climbed into the truck and merged.

It was late afternoon, but the traffic wasn't too bad. I pulled the handle out on the bags and started the short trek to the apartment on Hemenway. The building was white brick and clean. I sighed, seeing it. It looked like the picture on the internet. If the inside was what I had seen in the pictures, I would be in heaven. I fished the key from the bag and hauled everything into the brown, old-fashioned, wooden doorway. The door had to be older than anything I had ever really touched.

I fingered the carved wood and tried to settle the leaping excitement inside of me.

I was sweating and ready to just leave the bags at the bottom of the stairs, when I saw the old staircase.

No elevator.

I grimaced and started the huge walk up the stairs. It was worth the climb. It was my first house, my first stand as an adult. Everything was fitting into the plan too perfectly. Minus the elevator. That made me nervous. Things never went perfectly.

When I got to the fifth floor—the top floor, I took a minute to catch my breath. The bags were too heavy.

I crossed my fingers as I wheeled everything to apartment 521. My hands trembled when I put the key in the hole. Everything was too perfect so far. I prepared for the worst.

I turned the lock, opened the door, and just stared. I expected it to be a disaster; Murphy's Law said it should have been, but it too, was perfect. White, crisp walls with a light-beige sofa and a white love seat. There were armchairs and beautiful sofa tables. The clean lines and simple colors carried into the kitchen, where white cupboards with glass inlays and a pale, marble counter awaited me. Everything was modern and clean. The only thing I hadn't noticed was that the dishwasher was stainless steel, where the rest of the appliances were white. It was an odd thing to see, it sticking out against all the white. I would have noticed it. It had to be new. New was good.

The floors were dark hardwood and brand new. Everything was glass and white and clean and crisp, except the dishwasher. It was exactly the apartment I wanted it to be. It was almost completely the picture from the Internet.

When did that ever happen to people?

I took it as a good omen. Like I was on the right track. I was finally getting my dream.

I set my stuff inside and closed the door, locking all three of the locks, and leaned against the door. The sigh that left my parted and completely peaceful lips was cut short by a noise. A girl moaning maybe?

My head lifted when I heard it again.

My hand slipped into my pocket, clutching the mace. I walked farther into the apartment, looking around for the source of the noise.

Were the walls thin? Was it coming from another apartment?

I tiptoed down the hall to the first bedroom. My heart was pounding as I rested my hand on the cold, metal knob and waited for the courage to open the door. I turned slowly, not making any noise.

The room was a bit stale, but it was empty. I sighed and closed the door.

I did the same in the bathroom, but again, it was empty. The new glass tiles and beautiful four-piece bathroom made me happy. But the sound of people moaning and a girl giggling didn't.

I left the bathroom and walked to the end of the hall, where the last bedroom was. I gripped the mace as I heard the sound again. I clutched both it and the door knob. I turned the knob slowly, cracking the door open only a bit.

Feet moved, squirming on the end of the bed, pushing beautiful beige covers to the floor.

Two people mauled each other, sliding against one another. A strong male body with tattoos and lean muscles was grinding against a slim, overly-tanned female with bleached hair.

My heart felt like it was going to explode. I pulled my cell phone and dialed 9-1-1 as I sprayed. Screams rose from the bed as I hosed them in mace.

"WHAT THE FUCK?" the guy screamed.

I turned and ran down the hallway to the bathroom. I closed the door and locked it. In a low tone, I whispered, "Hi, I need the police. I live at seventy-three Hemenway Street, Apartment 521. There's someone here. Intruders. Please hurry."

I turned off the phone and sat on the edge of the bathtub. My heart was pounding, my mouth was dry, and my hands clutched the mace so tight, I couldn't feel it in my grip anymore.

Hands started pounding on the door. Shouts and screams and footsteps were everywhere, making the small bathroom so tiny it felt like a coffin. I closed my eyes. Names were called, sentences were screamed, but I didn't stop rocking and clutching the mace. The door sounded like it was going to be ripped off the hinges.

I looked at my phone. I wanted my parents. I wanted Danny. I wanted anyone who would solve the dilemma and make it go away.

My brain taunted me. It almost laughed at how right it had been. How I had made such a mistake. How I wasn't strong.

"YOU OPEN THIS GOD-DAMNED DOOR AND GET THE FUCK OUT OF MY HOUSE! CRAZY-ASSED, STALKING BITCH!" the guy screamed.

I trembled but then I heard it, the sounds of rescue. The sounds of people shouting for them to get down on the ground. I started to cry; tears of joy streamed down my cheeks.

I got up and banged on the door, "I'm in here. Is it safe?"

A man shouted at me, "Miss, are you the one who called?"

I turned the lock on the door and nodded.

A police officer greeted me in the small crack space I let the door open, "Miss, you okay?"

I started to cry heavily, "Noooooo."

I let him open the door all the way and pull me into his arms, "It's okay. You're safe now."

He led me from the bathroom to the living room where two half-naked people were cuffed and on their bellies on the floor.

The guy turned. His face was puffy and red from the mace. He glared, "SHE'S CRAZY. THIS IS MY HOUSE. JESUS. YOU IDIOTS ARRESTED THE WRONG PERSON. SHE'S IN MY FUCKING APARTMENT. WHAT THE FUCK? DO YOU KNOW WHO I AM? SHE'S A STALKER."

The cop gave me a look. I ran to my bag and fished out the lease agreement that I had printed out.

"See—my house," I said defiantly.

The cop looked it over and shook his head, "She's got a lease, man."

The girl was crying on the floor with no shirt on, and her obviously-fake boobs holding her up in the air, like she was doing 'upward dog' without hands.

I looked at my watch; it was 5:00, and I wasn't on schedule the way I wanted to be. I wanted to be running and unpacked by 5:30.

Chapter Two
Roomies

I felt considerably worse when the tattooed guy produced a lease agreement, identical to mine, from a cupboard. He ranted and pointed at me, cussing up a storm when the cops removed the cuffs from him and the girl. They tried to calm him down, shaking their heads and muttering, "This is a civil issue. You need to hunt down the property-management people."

The guy rinsed his eyes at the sink in the island and pointed his middle finger at me, with water dripping from his red face, "This is bullshit. I want her escorted off the property. Use the cuffs."

I felt sick. My whole plan was taking a huge turn down a road I hadn't been prepared for.

The cop shook his head, "It's as much hers as it yours—in our eyes."

One of the other cops motioned for the guy to come over, "Lochlan, can I get you to sign this?"

Why didn't he want my signature? I was the one who called? Maybe it was a witness statement for his defense, and I didn't need one 'cause I had called. I hugged myself and paced the living room.

The sobbing girl ran and grabbed her shirt. She slapped the dark-haired guy when she left.

The guy took the hit, staring daggers at me, "Guess there'll be no happy ending at the end of that meal." I noticed the red was starting to lighten in his eyes, flashing dark-blue hatred at me. I hadn't noticed his eyes were blue before. They had looked black—with hate. The way he furrowed his brow took away all the light from his eyes.

The cop laughed with the guy and pocketed the thing he signed, "This is pretty funny. You have to admit. You being you and whatever."

The guy didn't look like he felt like laughing. He looked savage. I didn't feel like laughing. I hugged myself and dialed the property manager's office… again. When I got the answering machine, I felt homicidal.

The guy pointed to the door, "Well, now that we've determined this place is both of ours, can y'all leave and let me and her figure it out before we get evicted? And I'd like to get my shirt on." He dried his dark hair with a tea towel. His ripped and tattooed body had droplets of water running down it. I tried not to look, but he was incredible to look at, like watching athletes or seeing a celebrity. He had a rough edge but there was so much beauty.

He caught me staring at him. I quickly changed my look of awe to annoyance. He gave me a half-assed grin, shaking his head.

The cop nodded at me, "You guys okay, alone together?" he almost joked, as if he was implying something. I ignored his weird comment and clutched my mace in my hands. I looked at the tall, angry guy next to me and sighed, realizing that there was no way out of it. I nodded, "I'm fine." The guy left the room and came back with a shirt on. He rubbed his eyes, "My eyes are still fucking burning."

The cops laughed again and left us standing in the living room, staring at each other. There was a darkness about him that scared me. He was stunningly beautiful but looked angry, like he might not be able to control it.

His murderous stare didn't lessen when he lifted one side of his lips into a cocky grin, "You want a beer?" He sounded annoyed still but I caught something, a twang in the way he said beer. I could still see the hostility in his eyes. They were beyond expressive.

I nodded and sat on the couch. Angering him further wouldn't help the situation. I pinched the bridge of my nose and took deep breaths. When I felt better, I looked up at him, "Since it's your house too, I'm really sorry for spraying you with mace." I really wasn't though. The girl looked like a hooker. I didn't want hookers in my house. The thought of it made me want to clean everything. Yuck. My mother would have had a fit.

He gave me the same cocky half smile and pointed at me, "I call bullshit on that. I'm gonna bet you feel pretty good about hosing me with it. You seemed to enjoy it."

I bit my lip and nodded, "I probably saved you from paying for whatever that was going to cost you, and whatever STD's you would have gotten."

He brought me a beer and sat across from me on the white couch against the wall, opposite me, "Funny. So where you from?"

I frowned, "Not here, obviously." I wanted to unpack, clean my room, and make everything feel like home. I didn't want to be having small talk with a sleazy, tattooed stranger, beautiful or not.

"You here for school?"

I nodded and took a sip of the beer, tapping my finger against the bottle, "So, you rented from T&N Property Managers as well then?"

He nodded and took a long pull from his beer.

I ran my fingers through my hair and had a small sip of the beer. I processed it all as I wiped my mouth, "Who was the guy you spoke to? Tom?"

He shook his head, "Lady named Leslie."

I crossed my arms and sat back, "So we spoke to two different people about renting the same place? Clearly a miscommunication."

He gave me a look, "Obviously."

I laughed, "Sorry, I have to say it out loud; it helps me figure it out. How much did you pay?"

"Fifteen hundred a month, all in, except my own cable and phone. But everything else is included."

Tapping my fingers against the bottle, I nodded, "Me too."

He winked at me, "Cleary this is a mistake; I'm sure they'll find you a nice place somewhere else."

A frown crept across my brow, "Why do you assume I'll leave?"

He drank till it was empty and then sighed like he was refreshed, "Because my lease agreement was signed before yours."

I had no argument for what he'd said. Technically, his contract would be the one that was valid. A sickening feeling was creeping around inside of me, when my phone rang.

"Hello?" I snapped it up fast.

"Hi, Erin, it's Tom Banks at T&N. I got your message. We definitely have an issue. We don't have anything in that neighborhood or anything that is that nice." His voice was annoying, or maybe it was his words.

I winced, "Can I put you on speaker? The other tenant is here as well."

"Sure thing."

I pressed speaker and held it out. He cleared his throat, "Like I said, Erin, we don't have anything for rent that would compare. Can you two hang tight for a couple weeks until something comes up? It's a two bedroom, no different than having a roommate."

My eyes shot up at the dark-haired guy. He shrugged, but I shook my head, "You can't expect me to live with a stranger?"

The dark-haired guy smirked, "My name's Lochlan, Lochlan Barlow." He said it like I might know him.

I scowled at him and sat upright, "Tom, you have to fix this. I came all the way from North Dakota. That's a long way to come for this level of unprofessionalism. I signed a lease for a two-bedroom apartment, overlooking the park. I signed for this specific apartment. You can't possibly think that we can just live together." My heart was racing. "He could be a pervert. I can't share a house with him. He's already had some strange woman here; I think she was a hooker. He's probably on drugs or something."

Lochlan's dark eyebrows went up, "Whoa now. Hold on. I don't need some prissy little girl calling me a pervert, Tom. That hooker-looking girl happened to be a very friendly server at Cappy's." He gave me a cold stare, but I caught the slightest bit of amusement in it, "Now, I signed the lease before she did. I rented this before her. If she's gonna be calling me names and shit, or macing me again, well then, I think she has to leave."

Tom sighed loudly, "Look, you two, it's the start of the new semester. We never have anything for this time of year. I am very sorry. We will throw in this half-month for free and next month. So August and September will be free. If you can just adjust and be okay with a couple weeks together, we are bound to find a few suitable place. I will reimburse the rent you've paid for August and September. Then, starting in October you will only have to pay half of your rent for each of the months that you're together. Surely a compromise is possible. Act like adults for God's sake. I'll send over new contracts for this month and we will go month to month from there, until you're comfortable signing a full-year lease together or we find another apartment. Lochlan, your lease will supersede hers still, though. I'll have something added that if you forfeit on the new leases, the old ones are reinstated. I don't know what else to suggest."

I was about to lose it, so I stood and paced, "This is unacceptable. I'm a law student; I don't need some hood rat bringing home women. I paid the money, and we have a contract. I could sue you…"

Lochlan cut me off, "I'm in. I want my rent back; I'm in for sure. I've always liked having a roommate. Least this one's easy on the eyes, Tom."

Tom chuckled into the phone, "Well, good luck with that, Lochlan, not that you'll need it. Goodbye Erin, let me know what you decide." With that he hung up.

I stood there staring at the phone, wondering what in the hell had just happened.

I dropped back onto the couch, "This can't be happening."

He rolled his eyes, "It's alright, princess. You'll get by. It's six—maybe eight weeks tops, like the man said. How hard can it be? Surely you had roommates in North Dakota."

I felt a loss of control. I didn't like that feeling. I stood up abruptly and walked to the hallway to get my bags. I snarled, "I guess I'll take the other room, since you already had a friend sleep over."

He put his hands up but never stopped smiling, "Hey, I got here today too. She wasn't my friend, and she didn't sleep over. She was my waitress. Now since you ran her off, I'd be more than happy to let you take her place. You can pay me back for macing me." He winked and gave me a one-sided smile.

I growled and lifted the mace again. He put his hands in the air, "It was a joke, princess."

I made a guttural noise, "Stop calling me that. I'm not a princess." I turned and dragged my crap to my room. When I closed the door, I felt like everything was spinning out of control.

How had this become my reality?

I plunked on my bed and texted my brother.

'I have an issue.'

He didn't respond. I felt my lower lip creeping out as the pout took over. Instead of being a baby and letting it get me down, I started unpacking. I could control this space. This was mine.

I set up everything and checked the bed to ensure it was actually clean. Part of the payment of the damage deposit had been professional cleaners and fresh linens. It had been the ideal place to rent. I sat on the bed and sighed. Everything had been perfect for five whole seconds. But now I couldn't let myself get too comfortable. The blue-eyed devil with the cocky grin was no doubt getting this place. I would be packing and moving all over again.

A knock startled me. I looked at the door confused, did he want us to talk and be friends... like he wasn't stealing my home. "What?"

He opened the door, "Come with me," he said it expectantly.

I felt myself pulling backwards, farther into the bed, "What?" I asked disgustedly.

He put a huge hand out. I noticed the callouses on the tips of his fingers, "Come with me. I have an idea."

I looked at his hand, like he was holding something dangerous out for me to look at. I stood but didn't move towards the door. He laughed and stepped back so I could walk out. When I got into the hallway, he just looked down on me, like he was studying me. Being close to him in the hallway made me clutch my mace and try to ignore how hot he was.

His look turned shady as his eyes traveled every contour of my face. I sneered, making him smile. "Hmm," he made a sound and walked away. I followed him to the front door with my key in my pocket, and mace in my hand, in case he got any funny ideas. But he left first and locked it when I stepped out.

I walked in his shadow and tried to ignore how tall and big he was or how good he smelled.

He was the enemy. The sexy enemy.

I grinned bitterly, "You know the gentlemanly thing to do would be to let me stay."

He looked back and winked, "I know; that's why I am."

I hated him, even if he smelled good and looked like sex on a stick. He was tall, six-foot-two maybe, with a thickness to him that made his tee shirt tight in the chest and arms. But he wasn't bulky. He was lean and strong looking. His dark hair was cut and styled in a fohawk, with some of it hanging in the back almost like a mullet, but somehow on his cocky, sexy body, it was hot. I noticed a huge, sun tattoo at the base of his neck sticking out the top of his shirt. His back flexed as he walked. I mentally slapped myself. It was hot in the stairwell, and I hadn't had sex in a while. That's all it was. I didn't sleep around, and not with guys who had already done it once that day with someone else. I shuddered, imagining it.

We walked down the street, not talking. It was awkward and annoying. He slowed down when I fell behind, waiting for me, "You hungry?"

I shrugged and walked next to him. I had wanted to be done my run and drinking a smoothie, or whatever cool dinner I had made myself. He was messing with my plan. For some reason, I didn't mind as much as I was protesting and acting like I did. I felt safe being with him. He was capable. I let him lead me around. It was an odd new experience, and I didn't even know why I was doing it. I rationalized that we needed to get to know each other, but I knew I didn't care about that. He was too close to me, smelling good and hovering. I liked it and I could rationalize the devil out of it, but something about him made me want to take my shirt off.

He stopped at a dingy restaurant and opened the door for me. Cool air blasted from inside. I scrunched up my nose and stepped in. He walked ahead of me, when I stopped and stared at the décor. I followed him, gazing all around me, stunned at the smells and scary-looking people.

I looked around as we neared a table. "We just seat ourselves?" I asked, a little confused. He laughed and plunked into the booth. I sat down slowly, trying to see if I was sitting in anything. It wasn't my kind of place. I wasn't a total snob; my favorite foods were truck foods like on Eat Street, but this was like a truck stop. The greasy-haired people seemed seedy, and I felt like I stuck out.

"Relax, princess. They won't bite you."

I gave him a look. He winked, "I might though."

We were interrupted by a waitress with big boobs and huge blonde hair. She was instantly sexing him up with her stare. He enchanted every inch of her, too. Some people had behavioral ticks; Lochlan's was sex appeal, a charm that made me want to touch him or be near him. The waitress noticed it; ladies on the street noticed it.

He played with the salt shakers, glancing up at her through his thick lashes, "We'll have two mugs of draft and," he paused and looked at me, "You eat meat?"

I nodded, feeling completely confused by him.

"And two of the house burgers with fries, please."

She giggled and left, "Sure thing."

He held my stare for a minute and then sat back confidently, like he was taking me in, "What's your deal?"

I thought I misheard him for a second. I was still waiting for my menu. I looked at the back of the waitress and then him, and shook my head like I was losing my mind, "Did you seriously just order for me?"

He folded his arms and tilted his head, licking his lips. He didn't answer.

I leaned in, "Are you insane? Who just orders a stranger food?"

He blinked his long, dark lashes at me flatly, "My name is Lochlan Barlow. I'm from Tennessee. I'm a Scorpio, and I don't really like long walks on the beach or romantic movies or anything like that. I like to shoot pool, hang with my friends and drink beer." His voice dropped, "You wanna know a secret? I find gardening therapeutic, and chess with my grandpa."

I had nothing. He was clearly insane and a sarcastic, entitled asshole to boot.

He waited for me to respond but I had nothing, so I looked around the restaurant—if you could call it that. I smiled at the waitress when she brought the beers, "Thank you." She ignored me and grinned at him, "You aren't really Lochlan Barlow from Thin Ice, are you?"

He nodded his head once, "I am." He said it like he might toss his fohawk about any second. She looked like she might pay him to do it. Thin Ice? I racked my brain, but I didn't know what it was. Was it a show? Was he a movie star? He looked like one.

Her eyes widened, like she was going to have a heart attack. She gushed, sliding a napkin at him, "Can you sign this?" Her voice was a squeak.

He chuckled, "What's your name, darlin'?" He was very Tennessee when he said darling.

She bat her chunky, black lashes at him, "Darla."

He gave her a subtle smile; it was sweet and sexy as hell. "Darla, that's pretty darn close to darling." She giggled again. I watched in horror. But he took the pen and scrawled some kind of chicken scratch on the napkin.

I drank my beer, shaking my head slowly at the spectacle. His cocky shit attitude was somehow appealing to this woman for whatever Thin Ice was. She hugged it to her chest and ran to the back of the restaurant.

His charm shut off when he looked at me. I could see a difference in the way he spoke to me and looked at me, compared to her. He nodded, "What's your deal?" He was almost rude to me.

I shook my head. I was completely confused, gripping my beer for fear I would throw it in his face.

He flashed me a sarcastic smile and leaned forward, "This is not going well, I mean, as far as first dates go. You seem really tense. Maybe we should have a couple shots first." He waved the waitress back over.

"Two shots of Jack. Make `em doubles."

She winked at him. I had thought he was being charming to me, but after seeing him lay it on thick, I realized the way he was with me was his natural state. With her, he seemed to be trying at it.

My mouth was hanging open, stuck on his comment, "This isn't a date, and I don't drink shots. Look at that girl two booths over; she's watching you like she hopes you might show up any second on her plate. She literally spotted you and then put lipstick on. You buy her shots and I guarantee, they'll go farther than they will with me."

He gave me a funny look, "I bet I can get farther than you think."

Arrogant bastard.

I tried to stand but he grabbed me, "Don't leave." The way he said it made me sit, like I didn't want to. It was real. He was being genuine. The charm and arrogance were shut off. He had the strangest effect on women, me included. He was like our own brand of kryptonite.

I sat back down and watched as he looked over his shoulder at the girls in the booth. He gave them a wave and turned back to me, as if none of it had happened, "You'll drink these shots. You'll like it, trust me." He ordered for me, made me stay, and now was going to force-feed me shots.

I almost stayed just to see what weird thing he was going to do next. His eyes were so blue suddenly, they took my breath away.

"Kryptonite," I muttered.

He gave me a weird look. The server delivered the amber liquid shots. Instantly, my skin crawled.

He lifted his.

I frowned, "I'm lost. You want me to drink with you, and hang with you, and we're vying for the same apartment? I don't mean to be rude, but I really think you should go drink with those girls over there. I don't want to drink. I'm being polite drinking this beer because you ordered it, and it's not the server's fault you're an overly-confident piece of work. I don't like to drink, but if I do, I drink red wine."

He held the glass up, completely ignoring me, "Have a shot, Erin. It ain't gonna kill you." He said it 'keeeel' with a laugh and a smile that melted a tiny bit of my hard exterior. He wasn't going to relent. His eyes made me feel something I didn't want to. He was force-feeding me my feelings too. Except dislike. I couldn't dislike him. He could have sold me a shit popsicle, and I would have sworn it was my favorite flavor.

I relented after he didn't stop holding his in the air. I lifted the other shot, skipped clanking it against his, and drank it back.

I shuddered, making him laugh, "See? That was easy. Now drink the beer. Jack makes it taste better. Maybe it's not red wine, princess, but it's better than just straight draft beer."

His mocking tone was driving me insane. I slammed the glass down, "My name is Erin Benson. I'm starting school in a couple weeks. I'm studying law; obviously, I want to be lawyer. I'm from North Dakota. I am a Gemini and I do like long walks and romantic movies, but I prefer books. I like men who treat women with respect and have more than two brain cells making desperate attempts at a fire in their thick heads. I don't like being called princess, and I hate people who presume to do things for me, like they know me better than I know myself."

He winked and smiled, "Now, how hard was that?"

He was insufferable. I swallowed some beer and nodded, "You want to steal my house. It was hard. I don't want to talk to you. I want to scream at you but that's the wrong response. That's not civil."

He pointed at me, "It's mine, and I'll tell you what. If they find one just as nice, similar area and same rent, I will be the one to move out. Until then, we make the best of this and not be shitty to each other or mace anyone. Unless it's a girl who won't leave in the morning. You can mace them." He offered me one of his big hands, "Deal? And I'm not kidding. If I end up with some clingy broad, I hope you'll go as hard as you did today. Maybe even a little extra."

I blocked out the annoying dribble coming from his lips and noticed how long and strong, but still slender, his fingers were. The ends were completely calloused. They didn't look like they belonged on a movie star. But the waitress had asked him for his autograph? Maybe Thin Ice was a band or something like that.

I placed my hand in his and let him shake for us both, "Deal, but your clingy women are your own problem. I might warn them before you get them down the hall."

He laughed, "Fair enough."

I felt the roughness of the fingertips and frowned, "So, you're on a show or in a band called Thin Ice, or is that something else?"

He beamed, "I am the new lead singer of Thin Ice."

I pulled my hand from his, "Singer?" I said it with a boatload of distaste.

He lifted the glass and nodded, "Yup. I play guitar, piano, and bass too. I'm learning the fiddle right now."

I bit my lip, watching him, "For a living? This is your job that's paying your half of the rent?" I asked and sat back more.

He scowled, "If you want, my job can pay all the rent, and you can pay me back with massages and fetching me beers."

I shuddered. Of course he was in a band. The carefree attitude, calloused hands, girl in his bed, charming smile and ridiculous good looks. Of course he was a singer. Only something that perfect, could be so flawed as to be creative, chaotic, and an artist. Had he been a businessman, I would have told him to try out for the Fifty Shades movie casting call. He looked just enough like David Beckham with his strong, athletic body and tattoos and cocky attitude. I could see him as someone as smug as CG in a movie.

I ignored his taunting and mocked him back, "So a singer in a band. What made you do that?"

He shrugged, "I've never been in a band before, and I thought, why not?"

The waitress came with our burgers. They were massive. I ignored her, not intentionally, "You've never been in a band before?"

He shrugged and pointed at my plate, "No. Don't worry. I'll eat what you can't."

I cocked an eyebrow, "I can eat it all."

He rolled his eyes, "Yeah, okay."

Still unable to comprehend him or his 'career' choices, "How do you know it's going to work with this band, and you'll be able to pay rent and live?"

He gave me the sparkly smile from before, "Princess, don't worry about me. Worry about that plate, because if I'm done before you, my hand may creep across the table for whatever is left."

I laughed and lifted the burger, "I'm not paying your rent ,and you're not eating my burger." I watched him take the first bite and inspected mine. It was bacon, cheese, lettuce, tomatoes, double patties, and slathered in a sauce that seemed like it might be mayonnaise-based.

I took the first bite and moaned unintentionally, "Oh my God."

He laughed and took another huge bite. We chewed in silence.

My grandpa always said that the sign of a good meal was the conversation left unsaid. And we were not talking. The fries were crispy, the burger was juicy, and I was dying. The beer made the meal so much better. He was fucking right, damn. It was the best meal I'd had in years.

I drank a big swig of beer and smiled, "So you're going to have to keep it quiet at the apartment when I'm studying and stuff. You realize that right, Mr. Rock Star? I maintain a very strict study schedule."

He laughed, "I'm indie, not rock, and yeah—it's cool. I won't be there much. We're on a circuit. We'll be bar hopping and playing five nights a week. Plus, I need to get to know the new band and the fans." He gave me a look, "What's up with you wanting to be a lawyer? You don't seem like the type."

I frowned, "What type?"

"Strong and mean like the ones on CSI and SVU. Those are some spicy ladies. You seem like you're scared of your own shadow. Like a small dog with a big bark."

"Fuck you."

He grabbed my hand, "Wait, that came out wrong. I meant like you're soft, like a lady. Not like you're a dog or weak. You're obviously prim and proper and raised with garden parties and the country club. I just mean that maybe you shouldn't be around hardened criminals and bad things all the time."

I scowled and dragged my hand away, "You don't know me."

His eyebrows knit together, making his eyes do the dark burning thing again, "Fair enough." He was flexing his hand.

I drank a gulp of beer, "When did you decide to take up the music scene?" We needed a new subject.

He shook his head, taking a monster bite, "I've always been in music. The band came looking for me this summer. I agreed and here I am."

I was mystified, "You came here because some dudes were putting together a band and looking for a singer... in a random band. Boston must be more expensive than Tennessee. Weren't you worried about paying rent and stuff?"

He laughed at me, "No. They were making killer money last spring when they had to fire the last lead singer. It's a huge risk for them, not me, but the old singer's a junky. What could they do? It was either break up or find a new singer. They saw me singing and asked me to join. I start this week with them. First show is tomorrow. You should come."

I glanced at the server, "How did she know who you were, if the first show is tomorrow?"

He chuckled, "I was doing alright on my own. I had a good following." The darkness left and he was sparkly again. "So, what kind of lawyer?"

I watched him for a second, like he had done to me, "Prosecutor."

He shook his head, "Why on earth would you want to do that, be surrounded by that negativity?"

An evil smile crossed my lips, "Lawyers are the people who put the bad people away. They make a difference. You can see the darkest parts of it but I see the good in it. Without lawyers, bad people wouldn't go to jail. Laws wouldn't be passed. Changes wouldn't be made."

The light left his eyes, leaving a darkness that seemed sincere, "You gonna come to the show?" It wasn't necessarily a color change in his eyes. I didn't think that was possible, but the way his brow shadowed them and his stare intensified, they seemed darker.

I took a drink, washing down the fact that he wasn't listening to me, "That's okay. I'm not really into bars."

He shrugged, "Gonna be fun." He was brushing it off, but there was a glint of something in his look. He was impossible to dislike. He was clearly a womanizing, arrogant, overly-confident asshole. And yet, I had the weirdest feeling being with him. Like I had been asked to sit with the cool kids. Girls noticed him. Guys nodded at him, like they wanted to be him, or be his friend. He brushed it off... even laughed it off, when it was just he and I. But if other people were there, I would bet he would lay it on thicker than I could imagine possible.

"Are you on meds?"

He laughed, "No, why? What the hell kind of question is that?"

I shrugged, "I don't know. I just don't get you. I'm trying to figure you out, I guess."

He cocked a grin, "You like figuring shit out, huh?" He looked around the room, "Well, when you figure me out, you let me know."

I cleared my throat, pushing aside the fact that he was an odd superstar in Boston and focused in on the important thing in our lives. "You promise you won't make me move out?"

He nodded, "I'm not an ogre, princess. I just don't need the hassle of house hunting the same week I'm starting the band and the show. I'm beginning something new here. I can't afford the risk of being stressed unnecessarily. Besides, in the meantime, it's nice to know one person who doesn't give a lick about Lochlan Barlow. We can be friends."

I scoffed, "I don't think you'll have problems meeting friends. What about the girl from earlier? The server?"

He grinned, "Met her at the place I ate lunch."

I couldn't even fight the grimace on my face, "Gross."

He laughed and finished off his beer.

The server returned and tried to ooze slut all over him. I'd seen it a million times with my brother. He was also a chaotic artist. Women threw themselves at him all the time.

I finished my burger, to his amazement, "Man, you can eat. How are you not fat?"

I nearly choked, "That was so rude."

He drank from the fresh beer, not apologizing.

"I run a lot, and I do kickboxing, and my whole family is pretty thin."

He nodded, "Well, you look good from it all."

I pointed a finger at him, "Stop that. I'm not one of those girls who fawn over guys or gives into the compliments. It's only going to make me uncomfortable and then we can't be friends."

He pointed back, "You a natural blonde?"

An exasperated sound left my lips, "You are so annoying. Do you have a filter or do you just say any old thing you want?"

He dropped his hand, "That was so rude."

I could have growled at him but the waitress was back, "You need the bill?"

I nodded, "Yes, please. Separate."

She left with a smile for Lochlan.

When she returned, he snapped the bills up quickly. I tried to grab mine but he grinned, "I want you to owe me. I mean, besides nearly blinding me earlier with bear spray." He chuckled as he got up.

I sighed, even fawned a little bit. Exasperating. He was exasperating. I caught the slightest point of the dagger tattoo on the back of his left arm as he strolled up to pay. He leaned against the counter, taking a mint. When he sucked it into his lips, I had to shake my head and refocus. Player alert. There was no way I was ever going to let myself be attracted to someone like him. Okay, I couldn't fight the attraction, but I could control the things I allowed to happen.

The server handed him a slip of paper with his change. He put a tip in her hand and winked at her. When he turned back to see if I was ready to go, my level of disgust was refilled. It might even have been overflowing.

I snorted as I walked past him, "You're despicable."

He put his hands out, "I bought you dinner. Come on. When I said I wanted you to owe me something, it wasn't hate and bitterness. I was thinking more like you make me breakfast sometime or wash my back in the shower, you know, roommate stuff."

I shook my head, muttering, "Never in this lifetime," and walked to the apartment. He got distracted along the way, waving me off and leaving with a short skirt and a bad dye job. I rolled my eyes but made myself watch the way she latched onto his arm where the tattoo was. I made a mental picture of the girl of the week for future reference.

Whenever his sparkly-blue eyes, charming smile, cocky attitude, or ridiculously-attractive body got in my way, I could always look back to that moment. I almost laughed when he checked out a redhead as he escorted the trashy blonde down the road.

Chapter Three
Costco ho

We settled into a routine. He slept from four in the morning until noon, always alone, surprisingly. I made breakfast and went for runs, trying to learn where everything was before school started, always during the day and always with my mace. The city started to get friendlier, more inviting. I spent less time worrying about where I was, and more time enjoying myself.

Tom and Leslie emailed me twice to let me know nothing new had come up.

Lochlan came with me everywhere. It started out as annoying, but after a while, I noticed he was showing me things he'd discovered. I noticed his roving eye had tamed a bit. I wanted to take credit for that. Deep down, I wanted us to be like that romance novel I'd read where the roommates fell in love. My main issue was his job. Lead singer in a random Boston band was not exactly how I figured a romantic story like that would happen. That was more like how I spent spring break…

I walked into the apartment after my run. The summers were smoking hot but also crazy humid. I wasn't used to the humidity. I bustled about, picking his shit up from the floor and coffee tables. He came into the room as I was dumping an armload of wrappers and garbage into the garbage can. I had to do it before I could stretch. I hated clutter.

"You look hot."

I flipped him the bird, "You're up early, and why can't you clean up after yourself? I asked you to please not leave shit everywhere."

I grabbed the orange juice from the fridge and drank from the carton. It was my worst habit. He didn't make a face or complain. He walked up next to me, almost touching me, taking it from my hands and drinking a huge swig. He handed it back but I shook my head. My nose was wrinkled up.

He cocked his head, "You can drink from the carton but I can't?"

I walked off my run, pacing in the kitchen, "You kiss everything you meet. You probably have Hep C."

He laughed, "Princess, I get shots and regular checkups. Thank you for the judgment though." His eyes trailed up my legs. "Those are some short shorts."

I sighed and started to stretch, throwing him another look.

He grinned, "I go to Hot Yoga sometimes; you should come. You look like you could use a stretch in the hamstrings. Why don't you bend over and let me stretch you from behind?"

I groaned and walked to my bedroom to stretch without being ogled.

He yelled after me, "Wanna go to Costco?"

I looked back, contemplating the offer, "Yeah, sure. I don't have a card though."

"I do."

Nodding, I walked into the bathroom instead of my room, "Give me ten to shower."

He laughed, "Ha, you mean twenty."

I stuck my finger out the doorframe, flipping him off again.

We left the apartment an hour later. He had an arrogant look on his face, like he knew I would be slow. The car out front was nice; it was a four door, black Audi in great shape. "This is yours?"

He gave me a look and pressed the unlock button. "The drummer, Gerry, is coming with us," he said as he climbed in. We drove a few blocks, stopping outside of a small brick building nowhere nice as ours. A thin guy with nicely-styled, dark-blonde hair and a tidy look to him walked towards us.

"Is the drummer gay?" I asked.

He laughed, "No, he's always got ladies climbing all over him."

The guy got in the back seat, "You must be Erin."

I looked back, "Hi." How did he know my name?

He put a hand out, "Gerry." His dark-blonde hair was cut like Justin Bieber's. He had on a blue and white striped tee shirt. His jeans were burgundy, and he had on the cutest loafers. He was gay. The kind of gay that made me INSTANTLY want to be his beard or his hag.

His hands were clean and manicured, and he had tiny pores. He did regular facials and manis. He wasn't totally delicate though; he was strong and handsome but in a feminine way, like a model. He gave me an appraising look, "So, how are you liking the city compared to the Midwest?"

I fought my frown, "Great. Different. I mean the humidity is murder. I have to straighten my hair everyday. That's annoying. I get frizz really fast."

He pointed at me, "Aloe Vera will solve that right now. Run it through your hair after the shower and then blow dry. It's like magic."

I frowned, "But my hair is naturally curly."

Lochlan gave me a look, "Really?" he sounded funny. I sneered at him.

Gerry laughed, "Yeah, it works like a hot damn."

I looked at Lochlan, beaming. He gave me another weird look and then looked back at Gerry, "You gay?"

Gerry laughed, "Duh? Though I will say, I haven't ever been asked so rudely."

I was about to defend Gerry when a huge smile crossed Lochlan's lips, "Dude, my brother's gay. I should tell him to come up. He always complains about Nashville and the haters."

Gerry sighed, "Fortunately, I'm from Seattle; I've never had an issue. But I know a guy who's from Texas, and his parents won't even see him."

Lochlan shook his head, "That's sick. How can you judge someone for being who they are?" He gave me a look and continued to drive.

I somehow turned out to be the bad guy in Lochlan's eyes. Had I been judging people besides him? He deserved every bit of judgment he got.

Gerry laughed, leaning forward, "If I had to be straight, I would be asking you for dinner."

I looked back at him, "I would have asked you first. I can tell you have manners. You're probably a great dancer, have incredible taste in red wines, love picking up after yourself, and bringing home fresh flowers. I bet you're even on time, all the time."

He smirked at me, "Me to a tee."

I grinned, "Me too. I bet you'd even let me order for myself."

I scowled at Lochlan who rolled his eyes, "Yeah, so I don't like red wine and other snooty shit, and I don't pick up crap in the living room. It's a living room. It's for living, princess." His grin turned into the smile that made the world stop and take notice of him, "Besides, you like it when I order for you."

I gave Gerry a knowing look, "This is what I deal with."

Lochlan snorted as he parked and we went inside. Gerry took his own cart, "I'm going to wander." He winked at me and walked off.

I poked Lochlan, "Ha, told you he's gay."

He nodded, "You called it."

I frowned, "Is your brother really gay?"

He gave me a weird look, "Yeah? Why?"

Shaking my head, I followed him to the protein powder section, "Just curious."

He glanced at the label of the huge container he was holding, "You don't think I'd be cool with a gay brother, or you just think I lie a lot?" His tone tugged at me.

I answered casually, "What?? No... I never meant that. I just thought, maybe you were being open-minded... or trying to make him feel good, what with being a rock star and... nothing," I stopped. I was starting to sound prejudice or tolerant, which I wasn't. I didn't believe in tolerance. That meant you saw the difference in you and someone else.

He stared for a second, "I love my brother, and I hope no one ever tries to make him feel accepted for who he is. That makes him different. He's not. My sister and I are straight and my brother is gay, and honestly, I think my parents love him more for it. He's the better kid for sure." The way he said it, I could hear a small amount of admiration in his voice, like his parents were amazing for being cool with whoever their kids turned out to be.

I smirked, "They probably just don't love the starving-artist path you're choosing."

He cocked a dark eyebrow, "Starving? Least I'm making money and not just costing."

I sneered and crossed my arms. He continued reading until I finally had to say it, "I'm not one of those people. It came out wrong. I don't believe in tolerance."

The cocky grin slowly crept across his face, but he kept his gaze on the nutritional information.

I shook my head, "Asshole."

He put it in the cart and pointed to the one next to it, "You want this one? It's for women trying to lose some weight. The girl on the ads is tight."

My jaw dropped. He put his hands up fast, "Joke! Don't mace me."

I sighed and hated the fact that it was in my pocket. He glanced at it, "It looks like a cock. Everyone is gonna see Gerry in his burgundy pants, and then you with the mace cock, and think we're all gay. How am I supposed to pick up girls with that going on?"

I laughed, brushing off the challenging look he was giving me, "You'd make a sexy lady."

He chuckled, pushing the cart to the dried food, "I did it once for Halloween with my brother. He wanted to actually dress up as a girl, and if I did, no one would pick on him. So I did, and let me tell you…" His grin grew, "It was bad. It was like knock-kneed, hairy, tattoo-on-the-bicep bad. I looked like Wesley Snipes in To Wong Fu. Alex, my bro, looked like John Leguizamo. He was sexy as hell and I was all muscled and gnarly looking."

I liked this side of him. I'd didn't often see him put someone above himself. In front of other people, he was so self-important but in that moment, Alex was more important.

Looking past him, I thought I saw someone I knew. I looked at the guy and tilted my head for a second. He turned around to face me, but I didn't know him. I looked back at Lochlan to say something. He was so handsome and funny. I had to give it to him. The weeks we'd spent together hadn't been at all like I'd expected them to be. Just as the sweet smile crossed my lips, I caught him bending his head, staring at the ass and tramp stamp of a girl about my age. His eyebrows rose as she bent to pick something up.

Never mind, he was scum.

It stung to watch him do it. I walked away. I needed frozen veggies and fruit anyway. Mentally, I coached myself. I was repeating to myself that it didn't matter that he wasn't into me. It was better. If he was hitting on me and being sweet, I might have been fooled by his sweet brother stories. I might have taken the bait and let him in. God knew I wanted to. I couldn't deny the attraction, regardless of the fact that ninety percent of what he said was disturbing. The other ten percent was the best, and that was all my brain focused on. Not the good brain though. Not the one in my head.

I caught up to Gerry in the book section. He flipped up one with some hot, young actor on the cover. I wagged my eyebrows at him. He laughed, "Crackers in bed would go unnoticed."

I tossed my veggies in the cart.

He gave me a look, "You okay?"

I nodded, "Yeah. Just getting stressed, you know. School starting and stuff."

I grabbed something with a sexy cover from the table and read the back of the book. Instantly intrigued, I tossed it into the cart. He gave me a look, "Why read those when you have the real thing in your house?"

My eyes almost rolled on their own, "Yeah, right."

He gave me a serious look, "He talks about you an awful lot."

"Talks shit about me and then sleeps with everything he sees, no thanks."

The grin on his lips was infectious, "Maybe he sleeps with them to make you jealous. He doesn't talk shit. He talks about smart, and clean, and organized, and Erin says this, and Erin says that. Erin doesn't like mushrooms unless they're minced really small, and Erin thinks she's so brave, but I see the way she brushes her hand against her mace. He likes you. You should give him a chance. He's sweet when he's not trying to be the lead singer." His words burned my insides with fluttering and the hopeful possibility.

I glanced over at the tramp stamp on the girl he was with and scowled, "Not going to happen, so quit. He has a better chance with you than me."

Gerry scoffed, "Please. I don't do baggage. I don't date anyone in the band anyway. I can't focus on more than one thing at a time." He pushed the cart over to where Lochlan and the girl, with the tight ass in the skinny jeans, were laughing.

I snatched my things from Lochlan's cart and shoved them into Gerry's. I passed him the cash, "I have to go to the bathroom." He gave me a look, but I ignored it. I walked away and hoped Lochlan would get a ride home with the tramp stamp girl.

I was just sliding the lock when two girls started to talk from other stalls.

"Did you see Lochlan Barlow is in here? He's with Gerry Ronson. Like, oh my God!"

"Oh my God, girl, I know. He was so hot on America's Most Talented Stars. Seriously. I voted for him every night. I couldn't believe when he got kicked off the show."

Had I been under a rock? He was on a show? That was how everyone knew him.

They continued to natter on, "He beat the crap out of some guy backstage one night."

"I don't give a shit—that makes him hotter. What were they thinking? He's smoking and unruly. I heard that he's single. I am so glad he joined Thin Ice."

"I know, right. He's been with them for like a couple weeks. We should go one night to one of the bars. My cousin Mandy went and said Lochlan kissed her after a show."

My guts were burning. I felt nauseated. He was such a pig; why did they care what he was doing? Chasing celebrities made no sense to me. They were just people. Usually sleazy people.

I flushed and walked out of the stall. I wondered if he was an actual musician, like a good one? If he was, that meant it was his first time in a band, because he was an actual singer ...who could do the show alone. He was famous, and I was mocking him constantly and calling him a starving artist. Oh God. How had I not known?

I hated nothing like I did reality TV. I hadn't watched anything since the first season of The Bachelorette. I liked crime dramas better. I washed my hands and looked up at the perplexed look on my face.

I left quickly before they saw me. I didn't even know why. I just didn't want to be the girl with the guy in the band.

When I got back up to Gerry and Lochlan, the sexy chick was gone and Lochlan had a weird look on his face. He scowled at me and pushed the cart out to the car. I looked at Gerry but his expression didn't help either. They were quiet.

Had I done something?

We drove in silence. I didn't even dare to try to make conversation; something had clearly gone wrong.

When we stopped at Gerry's apartment, Lochlan got out and helped carry everything up to the door. I climbed out to help but Lochlan had it all in his huge arms. Gerry gave me a hug but looked at Loch first, "Lochlan, the hide-away key is under the mailbox." He turned back to me, "It was lovely to meet you. I suppose we'll see you at a show then?"

I opened my mouth to say 'no,' but I couldn't. I wanted to see it. I nodded, "Yeah. When is the next one?"

He smirked like he was daring me to come, "Tomorrow night."

"Okay, good. I'll see you then." The conversation was awkward. I was awkward. I didn't know what had changed. I didn't want to know.

I got back into the car. When Lochlan got back in, he gave me a look.

"What?" I asked.

He shook his head dismissively, "You hungry?"

Not in the mood for his bizarre behavior, I looked out the window, "No, thanks."

When he parked outside of our place, I dreaded dragging

everything up the stairs but he grabbed most of it. I grabbed a couple things and ran and got the door for him. He was halfway up the second flight of stairs when a watermelon started to slip from his hands. I didn't notice until he had it pinned to the wall and wasn't walking.

He nodded at me, "Grab this."

I slid my free arm under it, cradling the huge thing in my bicep. Our bodies were pressed against each other. I froze mid-rescue when he smelled my hair.

Lifting it out safely, I quickly ran up the stairs with my now full arms.

He smelled my hair? What was that? Was he turning on the charms? Shit... Hair smelling was pretty hot. Unless he was like, 'what was that bad smell' and then smelled my head? Or if he was a crazy stalker, that wasn't hot. Shit, did my hair stink?

I placed down the bags and unlocked the door for him. He didn't even thank me. He dumped everything on the counter and started putting it all away.

I gave him a confused look, "What happened at Costco? Why were you and Gerry suddenly not talking?"

He stopped and watched me for a second. "He thinks I should ask you out and try to keep my rep a little cleaner. He thinks a nice girl like you is the answer."

I swallowed hard, "Nice girls don't like boys like you."

He stepped towards me, "I find nice girls aren't usually being honest with themselves. They're trying so hard to be normal that they forget to have fun. When you get them to loosen up, it's like striking gold."

I gulped, "I like normal. It's safe. It's predicable and easy."

He gave me a confused look, "You have one chance in life to make it something special. Why would you waste it on mediocrity? Safe and easy is for pussies. Be amazing and different. Be grateful for the uniqueness in you."

I rolled my eyes, "Thanks, Tony Robbins." I wanted to be friends with him, but mocking him was safer.

He snorted, "That's how I want to live my life. You never know when choosing safe is stopping you from being incredible." He lifted my new book, "On a lighter note, The Brothers of County Claire? Maybe you're not such a nice girl after all. Maybe you're a naughty girl." His eyes were on fire.

I reached for the book, but he lifted it. I ended up standing with my chest against his as I reached for it. He lowered it with a smug look.

I snatched it from his hands, "I like reading. Nice girls read." My stomach was aching. I wanted to be a 'naughty girl'. His motivational speech made me think about the things I was missing, like him.

He gave me a look, "How many books you reading a week? You think I haven't noticed you're here every night? All you do is hang here."

I frowned and started putting things into cupboards, "I'm getting in the habit for school. What does it matter?"

He grabbed my hand and I watched the shift. He went from joking with me for being a nice girl, to trying to take my pants off. He leaned against me, pushing me into the counter. He cocked his head, glanced down the top of my shirt, and then placed his hands on either side of me, trapping me, "My sister reads those. Calls them one-handed reads."

My cheeks flushed but I didn't back down. I leaned into him, pressing my chest right into his, "Yeah, that's what all girls call them. Nice girls just don't say it out loud. They're better than the real thing. The Brothers of County Claire don't leave their shit everywhere or have mood swings. They don't check out other girls. They get me off and get lost, and I don't need shots and regular check ups."

My Side

His eyes locked on mine, "Maybe you just haven't had the 'right' real thing."

I fluttered my lashes at him, "Oh, you mean being graced with one whole night with the lead singer of Thin Ice?" I pushed him off me and walked past him, "Thanks, but I'll pass.

He grabbed my arm, but I dropped my book and went for my mace. He looked startled, dropping his grip.

He put his hands in the air, "I wasn't going to hurt you. I would never. I thought we were messing around."

I swallowed and looked down. I bent and picked up my book. My breath got caught in my throat. I turned and ran for my bedroom. I closed the door and gripped the book to my chest with my back against the door.

I didn't want him to see it. I was strong once. I didn't need help. I had to be strong.

I curled up on my bed and started my book. I saw every face as his. He made my one-handed read better than it had ever been. Fantasy was so much better than reality.

I fell asleep as I finished the book, but the night was a hot one.

I tossed once more before flinging even the last sheet off of me. My tank top and boxers felt like a sweaty death trap. Even with the windows both open, the heat was intense. I growled, climbing out of the bed and stumbling down the hall to the kitchen. I opened the double-door fridge and let the cool air blast me. I sighed, throwing my head back. The heat was too much.

I glanced at the carton of almond milk he swore by and took it from the fridge. It was cold and damp in my hands. I held the cold carton against my chest. I lifted my tank top, tucked it under my boobs, and grabbed another carton. I held it against my stomach, flipping them both as they heated from my sweating body. I closed my eyes and moaned. "Mmmmm."

"That's a good sound." He interrupted my cooling bliss.

I jumped, putting the cartons back. My cheeks flushed, not that it mattered. They were flushed anyway.

The light of the fridge shone down on my guilty face like a spotlight.

He leaned against the counter in boxers only. I could just see his tattoos in the dimly lit room.

I turned, closing the door, "Sorry." The kitchen was nearly pitch black with the fridge closed.

He switched on the small light above the stove, "Did it feel good?"

I nodded, "I'm dying."

He walked around the counter. His heat made my skin burst into a fresh layer of sweat. He reached beside me, brushing his hairy arm against my thigh, pulling the freezer drawer out. He pulled a bag of edamame we got from Costco and passed it to me. I took it and smiled.

"How was the book?" His tone was laden with absurdity.

I laughed, "Good. Predictable. I like that." I went to put the frozen bag on my chest but he shook his head, taking it back.

He reached around behind me, "On the back of your neck." I jumped when the shocking cold hit my skin. He held it there, looming over me with his intense stare. I made a sound. I don't think either of us were sure what it was.

He looked confused as I stepped back.

"That's cold."

He nodded, "Yup." He grabbed a bag of peas and did the same thing. "So you like predictable?" he asked, as he opened the fridge and passed me a bottle like a beer but it wasn't.

"Yeah." I turned the top, taking a drink and sighing. It was a cranberry lemonade flavored wine cooler.

He grabbed a beer and drank it.

I raised an eyebrow, "You got these for me?"

He shook his head, "I like to have lady drinks on hand."

I groaned, "Ewww. I'm drinking a whore lemonade, aren't I?"

He laughed and stretched, flexing all his glistening muscles. I didn't mind the heat suddenly. If it made him look like that, it had to be good. Well, until he opened his mouth, "You're so judgmental. Don't you ever just get laid for the sake of getting laid?"

Even in the dim light, my horrified face could not be hidden.

"Okay, I guess not. Maybe you should try it, instead of just reading all the time. You're awfully stuck up, princess. I can help you relax, if you want."

I gasped, "I am not. Why? Because I don't want to give myself to everyone I meet? I have more self-respect than to let someone like you touch me."

His stare turned cold and intense. The amused look on his face was like a distant memory. He stepped into me, brushing my chest against his abs, "If I touched you, you would like it." He lowered his face close to mine, "If I wanted to kiss you, princess, I would, and you would love it and beg me for more." He lingered.

My discomfort was muted by the intense animalistic instincts rushing through my body. He grinned and backed off, "You want me as much as I want you."

I shook my head, "You're egotistical. I would never let you touch me. Not someone like you." I stepped back and around the counter.

I felt him watching me as I slapped the edamame on the counter and retreated to my stifling bedroom. I closed the door, but he was there within seconds opening it. I pressed my back against the cold wall, as he looked down on me. His body was huge and frightening in all the right ways, looming over me like that. He spoke softly, "We need the windows and doors open for the cross breeze. Trust me, you Northerners have no clue how to cool a house off. I got this."

I sipped my lemonade and relived every second of the kitchen.

The feeling of his arm hair brushing against my thigh. His sweaty, hard body standing so close to mine that my braless breasts squished against his abs. I breathed through my mouth and shook my head. He was right; I wanted him. And even worse, I loved that he wanted me.

The memories of the redheads and the trashy blonde, and the sleazy look he got on his face in Costco were hard to reach with that much blood being gone from my brain.

My attraction was undeniable. That should have been a deterrent but no, my body wanted him and my brain was even on board. Didn't I care that he slept with every girl he spoke to?

I wasn't sure that was accurate. He probably didn't even have to talk. Had he kissed me in the kitchen, I would have done it. I would have leapt into his strong arms and let him have me on the counter.

I held the condensation-covered bottle to my forehead and took deep breaths. I grabbed my phone and emailed Tom to see how the apartment hunting was going. Lochlan and I had been roommates for a couple weeks, and I was ready to do things I hadn't done in a long time, things I hadn't ever done with someone I barely knew.

Within minutes, I noticed a difference in the temperature in my room. The air felt new and clean again, instead of tasting the way I imagined he did, heady and salty.

He leaned in my doorframe, "Told you."

I sighed, "Yup. I guess being a country bumpkin is good for something."

He folded his arms, "You think you got me pegged, don't you?"

I laughed, "That display in the kitchen pegged you. You could try to not drag me into your perversions and overly fluffed ego, and I might not think so little of you."

He walked into my bedroom and sat backwards in the chair at my desk. He sipped his beer.

I had to force my eyes not to even try to peek at his boxers in the moonlight, "This is a bad idea."

He frowned, "What is?"

I pointed at him, "Me and you living together. A single guy and a single girl cannot be roommates and friends. I'm pretty sure Harvard has done studies on this."

He leaned forward, "Can't keep it in your pants, princess?"

I sipped my lemonade, "Oh, I can."

He grinned, "Wanna make a wager on it?"

My gaze narrowed, "What kind?"

"The kind where whoever gives in to the obvious attraction between us moves out."

I laughed, "Done. Deal. Sold. You want to start packing now or wait till it's light out."

He chuckled, taking the last of the beer in a huge gulp, "You underestimate me."

I shook my head, "I'm a grad student in law school. I have a 4.0 GPA and have only ever dated three guys in my life. I don't drink much, never do drugs, don't smoke, and eat clean, except when celebrities buy me lunch." I leaned towards him, drank the last of my lemonade and passed him the bottle, "I am the queen of self-control."

He swung his leg off the chair, moving fluidly to the floor and knelt in front of my bed. He grabbed my calves, dragging me down the bed so he was between my thighs. His eyes bore down on me as he licked his lips. He leaned forward like he might kiss me and whispered, "But the thing you're forgetting is that I can have any girl I want, any time I want, any place I want. You, on the other hand, will be getting arthritis in your right hand from all the daydreaming you're gonna do about me while reading your books." He winked and released me. I didn't even realize my hands were digging into his round shoulders, instead of pushing him away. He laughed and left the room, again rising in a fluid motion.

I swallowed and made the weird sound again, "Wait."

He popped back into the doorway, "Yes?"

"The deal needs to be stricter then. No sex for either of us... with anyone."

He looked down on me, "Including the Brothers of County Claire?"

I nodded.

He put a massive hand out. I hesitantly took it. My stomach ached from the thought of touching him. The air was too heavy. His body was too naked and mine was too horny.

He shook both our hands and then just stayed there like that, holding my hand.

"No sex, no masturbation, and no getting someone else to give you an orgasm?" he asked.

I frowned, "Ewww."

He laughed but it wasn't the amused one from earlier. It was tense like he might lie down on top of me any second. I hoped he would. I would get the nearly-pulsating orgasm that was sitting there about to happen from his touch. I honestly was probably about ten strokes away with my vibrator. I smiled imagining it. I would cum and he would get the boot for making the first move.

He looked like he was struggling with something and then let go of my hand. He pointed at me, "It's on."

I nodded, "Great."

"Good."

"Fine."

"Excellent."

All I could do was pray that Tom and Leslie came up with something before school started Monday. I didn't need a distraction of this size.

Chapter Four
Kiss my Brazilian butt

I was curled up in the living room with Jane Austen's Persuasion. Nothing cured my inability to control myself like Austen, except suddenly I was seeing so much more sexual tension than I ever had. I wasn't sure if it was really there, or if I was so strung out that I was putting it in the story.

"Reading again?"

I glanced up at him as he stalked into the room in body-hugging jeans and a tight tee shirt.

He sat with his legs wide, "Gerry said you're coming tonight."

I nodded, "Yup. Where am I going?"

He passed me a business card, stroking his fingers down mine as he passed it to me.

I laughed, mostly nervously. "You're an idiot."

He shrugged, "You want me." I walked into the kitchen to get something cold. I was contemplating getting some ice to stick down my panties when I felt him behind me. He stood too close when I opened the fridge. He bent his face into my nape, taking a long breath. "You smell like your run," he muttered against my skin.

I couldn't tell you what was in the fridge or if I was holding anything. I took a breath and closed my eyes, "This constitutes hitting on me."

He licked up my neck, sending shivers everywhere, "You taste like your run."

I shook my head, "You are going to lose if you touch me."

He whispered, "We never said a single thing about touching. We said keeping our pants on. No 'flesh-to-flesh contact' is what I understood it to be."

I laughed and spun, looking up into his face, "So you want to play the 'who can be sexier' game with me?"

He grinned, "Yup."

I frowned, "You're going to lose. I'm a girl."

He cocked his head, "You think women are sexier than men?"

Sarcasm filled my voice, "Uhhh, yeah. Way sexier."

He arched an eyebrow, "Bring your A game tonight." He bent, kissing my cheek softly.

I had felt his erection brushing against my ass cheek, so I did the boldest thing I could and lied to myself it was all in the pursuit of an apartment. I slid my hand down the bulge in his pants.

His jaw dropped. I stroked faster and tilted my head. He made a growling noise. I wiggled my eyebrows at him, "The sad thing is, I don't even have to try to be sexy. You guys are just so easy." I gave him the wink he was always giving me and walked past him. My heart was beating and I felt like throwing up, but I maintained my cool.

He turned and left, "You're gonna pay for that one, princess."

I desperately prayed I would as I grabbed some ice to stuff in my drawers.

I wanted to curl back up with my book. Instead, I showered and let my white-blonde hair go into its natural curls. I bounced them, inspecting each one. They were wide and round. I had coated my hair with Aloe so I prayed it would stay frizz-free. I did my makeup far heavier than normal, not that I'd worn it since I'd arrived. It had been too damned humid. I pulled on a black push-up bra and a pale-yellow tank top. My jean shorts were tight, showing my firm, runner's ass off. It curved perfectly. They were the ones I was going to toss out because they didn't fit anymore. Well, they fit tonight. I looked slutty but still not too trashy. This was as far as I went into the realm of slut wear. My clothes were always the same. Winter was sweaters and jeans and summers were shorts and tee shirts. I didn't do anything but respectable and casual. I knew that as a lawyer, I would have to use my female wiles. Thankfully I wasn't a lawyer yet. I didn't even know where my wiles were.

I gave myself a once over and slipped on some sandals. I grinned at my mace cock and put my forty dollars in the other pocket with my cell. I sent Gerry a message that I would be there in fifteen. It was only five blocks to the bar. The night was warm and alive. A few girls were walking in the same direction as me. Naturally we grouped up. One of them smiled, "Hey, you going to the Thin Ice show?"

I nodded.

She beamed, "We are, too."

I wasn't one of the popular girls in school, being a pretty girl earned me tolerance. The mean girls accepted me into the parties when they had to, but my people were the Star Trek nerds. I ran home everyday to watch it. Danny made fun of me for it until he watched Doctor Who and decided science fiction was cool.

I smiled as I walked, thinking about Danny. I pulled my phone out and messaged him. He'd hardly messaged me since I'd arrived.

He was the popular one. Being Danny's little sister afforded me far more tolerance than my looks.

When we arrived at the bar, the girl who had spoken to me waved as she went in, "Enjoy the show."

I waved back, "You too."

The bar was huge and open. The stage was actually kind of big, in comparison to the lame stage I imagined it would be. Gerry waved at me from the bar. I lit up instantly and walked over.

He plucked a curl, "I told you."

I fingered a different curl, "It's awesome. They feel so silky still."

He pointed to me and shouted at the bar tender, "She drinks all night on our tab."

I waved my hands in protest, "No, I can buy my own."

A body pressed me into the bar from behind, "She drinks on us; she likes cranberry lemonade and red wine."

The bartender looked at me expectantly. I sighed, "Red wine, please."

He spoke quickly, "Shiraz is the house."

"Perfect, thanks." I looked back at Lochlan, "You think getting me drunk will help you win?"

He winked at me, "Nice bra."

Gerry pointed at us, "You too are a ticking time bomb."

I smiled, "You will tell me if he welches on this, right?"

Gerry put his hands up, "Keep me out of it." He turned and left.

Lochlan scoffed, "Says the guy who told me we should hook up."

I pushed back, getting him off of me, and spun around. I took my glass of red wine and leaned against the bar. I noticed it right away. The eyes were on me. The people were watching the girl with Lochlan Barlow. "You're like Elvis to these people."

He ignored my comment and put his hands on the bar on either side of me, "Who told you curly hair was my weakness?"

I laughed, "Oh my God, you have to do better than that."

He bit his lip but kept my gaze, "You want me to start trying? I do owe you that after the whole kitchen thing."

I shook my head, sipping the wine. It was surprisingly good.

His eyes turned funny again, "We could just live in the apartment... together."

I knew he was messing with me, going for the low blow. Guys think that commitment is girl bait for sure. I blinked up at him, "As fuck buddies?"

He coughed and took my wine. He took a big drink and passed it back, "That's disgusting. How can you drink that?"

I looked down into the glass distastefully, "I can't now."

He gave me a deadly stare, "No, not as fuck buddies, and I told you, I don't have Hep C. Jesus. I'm more careful than that. I have never gone bare back, I will have you know."

I laughed mostly to hide my disturbed expression, "All you famous types say that, and then all of a sudden, Pamela Anderson is like OMG I have it, too. It can't be from Tommy—no, he would never."

He snorted, "You think you know so much about me."

My gaze narrowed, "I know enough, man whore."

He bent, kissing my cheek again, "You don't know shit." He pushed off the bar and walked away from me.

Every girl in the bar instantly hated me.

"Great." I walked away and leaned against the wall in a dark corner. My glass wasn't even empty, when a new glass was placed in my hand. I noticed a bouncer eyeballing me from the side of the wall where I was. I frowned at him but he maintained his stern look. His eyes darted around me. He looked like he might walk over to me, but stopped when a girl poked me in the arm. "You could have said you were dating him. We wouldn't have cared."

I looked up to see one of the girls I had walked there with. "Hey. I'm not dating him. He's my roomie. It's complicated."

The pretty brunette put a hand out, "Lise. This is Jenny and this is Monica."

I gave a subtle wave, "Hi."

The tall blonde, Monica, pointed to a table, "That's our table. Wanna come sit?"

I nodded, "Sure," and followed them over to sit.

Lise giggled, "Looked like you were dating."

I put my wine to my lips and sighed, "No. It's so much worse. He's him, ya know? He's the lead singer."

My Side

Her eyes looked sad, "That sucks. Do you really like him?"

A frown crossed my lips and turned to a pout before I could even negotiate my feelings. "No."

Her light-brown eyes glistened, "You do. I can tell. If it makes you feel better, every girl likes him. He's here with every girl." She looked around.

I followed her gaze and saw it. He really was. Every girl was waiting for that moment when the band took the stage. That made me feel dirty and my outfit didn't help.

"What kind of music is it?" I asked.

The other girls laughed, "You don't know? You never heard him sing before?"

I shook my head. How had I not even Googled him? It was because I thought it was a joke. I thought he was a joke.

The blonde raised her eyebrows, "You're in for a show."

We sat and waited. They talked and I people watched. I knew I was awkward with them. I didn't care though. I was stunned by the fact that he was someone, not just my annoying roommate.

The lights dimmed even more than they already were and the stage lights came on. The band walked out together. He searched the crowd until he came to my face at the table. He winked and gave me his one-sided grin. I didn't even know the crowd had erupted into something equaling complete chaos. All I saw was him. He seemed uneasy until he positioned the guitar in his hands. He strummed at it a few soft notes before he opened his mouth.

Then something magnificent happened.

His voice was soft, not what I expected from him. He started to move his hips, and my eyes followed. It started soft and then picked up. I came out of my Lochlan haze and noticed Gerry hitting the drums, and the other guys playing their hearts out. It was madness, but glorious. The song was exactly as he'd said, it was indie and fun. People were dancing and swaying to the song with him. His eyes were closed in the chorus as he swung the guitar onto his back and grabbed the microphone. He moved like he was against another person, with his hands sliding up and down her body.

The crowd was going nuts.

His eyes popped open. He eye-fucked every person in the crowd but me. It was like he avoided me on purpose.

I drank back my wine, watching him swinging. His voice was beautiful, raspy, and soft but able to hit the high notes. He was the whole package.

Tight tee shirt with tattoos sticking out the bottoms of his sleeves. Tight jeans with black boots and a cocky, southern swagger. He didn't have the country sound though. He was a mix between pop and indie. He was amazing. They all were.

My glass was taken and another delivered. I barely registered it.

The song ended. I swallowed. His eyes caught mine and I was frozen.

He gave me a look. The other guys started up, sweat was cresting every brow, the band's... the crowd's... mine. His mouth moved, and I could swear every word was for me.

It was the strangest feeling ever.

He ran his hands through his thick, dark hair and started to move faster in the buildup. When the chorus broke, he came alive. My heart had never pounded so hard in my chest. The server was back suddenly. She took my glass and passed me another. My head spun when I saw the glass on the tray was empty.

The next song was really upbeat. It was a dance song. His voice went high and everyone exploded on the dance floor.

He danced like I never would have imagined him capable. I knew nothing. That was clear. Shit, he was right again.

I finished my glass, watching him use the entire stage, pointing out at the crowd, working each of us. He was every woman's fantasy. He had it. He had the moves, the confidence, and the voice. The band was as devoted as he was. They pumped out the song with him.

Everyone in the crowd moved like a sea, rocking to the beat. He was the wind controlling the waves.

I truly felt like an idiot. I drank the last of my glass and knew I was done.

He had won.

The lights dimmed, making a sickening fear in my stomach that they were done, but it was worse. A chair was brought out under the single remaining light, center stage.

He drank from a glass of beer and cleared his throat, as he sat on the stool with his guitar.

"Uh… I just want to thank you all for coming out. This has been an awesome couple weeks for us here. I've been a solo act for a long time, and I just feel really welcomed into the band. So cheers to my new brothers." The crowd cheered as he drank a gulp and then held the glass up to the crowd, "Cheers to y'all out there in the crowd, because Boston has made me feel welcomed too." The crowd went wild again as he drank again.

He held his glass out a final time, "Cheers to my princess from North Dakota."

The crowd erupted. They didn't know why they were cheering. They just ate him up.

I, however, knew.

I couldn't breathe.

I couldn't feel anything but my pounding heart.

"Bastard," I whispered to myself.

He'd upped the ante, hard.

The crowd died down and he started to play.

His fingers moved so fast my blurry vision couldn't keep up. When his voice broke out over top of the guitar, everyone went nuts. The crowd started singing with him. They knew the song. I'd never heard it before. He started stomping his boot on the stage as he played and sang.

It was like I'd never seen him. The song wasn't fast, and yet, the crowd moved with him. His boot stomp and his odd shout here and there moved them. Arms went into the air as they shouted the high notes with him. It sounded like a drinking song of sorts.

The band came in behind him at the halfway point. The boot stomping got loud and the shouts took over. Gerry played a weird-looking drum with his hands.

Each member was covered in sweat and passion. I could taste it in the air.

I got up and left the bar. The boot stomp and the shouts followed me the entire way from the bar and onto the street.

My eyes blurred. I'd drunk too much wine. I needed home.

I picked up my pace. I was near home when my phone rang. I pulled it out, seeing a weird number. I answered, wondering if it was Danny.

"Hello?"

"WHERE THE HELL ARE YOU?" It was Lochlan, screaming from the bar.

I walked faster, "I drank too much. I'm going home."

"What the fuck? Don't leave." It was the second time he's said that to me.

I laughed, "I have to."

"Why?"

"Oh, Lochlan, come on. I'm out of my league." I rounded the corner to our house. I started to laugh harder at the thing I'd just confessed. I was too drunk, and I knew I should hang up, but I

My Side

couldn't stop the things I wanted to say from slipping out. I walked and shouted, "You want me to want you? Well you win. I want you. I want you right now. Maybe you should leave that show and come home and show me what I'm missing by being the nice girl. I fold. I will give myself to you, freely, and then move out. Nothing I do is ever going to top you. Nothing is ever going to compare to you." I stopped walking, realizing what I was saying. I ran my hands through my hair. I was hurt and I didn't even know why, but my words turned to a whisper. "You're the real thing. You let me believe you were some backwater-hillbilly bar singer. You're a star. You are that incredible and amazing person you want to be. I am the normal, safe girl. You are fantastical greatness and I am not." I whispered, leaning against the brick building. I caught a glimpse of a guy rounding the corner coming towards me.

He broke his awkward silence, "Erin, you're drunk. Jesus, no one puts me on my ass like you do. If I'm ever going to be great at anything I wan…"

I cut him off, "I think someone's following me."

"Princess, I can't hear you, please wait for me. Don't leave the house. Just stay there and wait for me."

I ignored him and tried to whisper louder, "I think there's someone coming." I realized I was exactly like the idiots on the crime shows. I was such a stereotype it wasn't even funny, college girl roaming the city drunk and alone. "Shit."

His voice got panicked, "Erin, what's shit? I can't hear anything else you're saying. What's going on? Why do you sound scared? I don't care that you just said that stuff. I just want to have this conversation with you. I want to see you, when I say the things I wanna say."

"Shit," I muttered again, hurrying to the apartment and ignoring him. I couldn't hang up; I needed him to be there still, so I wasn't alone. I was about to become a skin suit and the last thing I ever said was a confession to a guy about being more than me, even in my own mind.

My Side

"What's happening?" he asked, sounding angry.

My hands shook as I looked back. The man watched me. Was he really though, or was I just acting so crazy that he was staring at the display. My hands shook as I opened the door. I pulled it shut, dropping my phone.

"ERIN!"

I picked up the phone, "Hello?"

 "What are you doing?"

I swallowed, "I thought a man was following me."

He shouted again, "Where the fuck are you?"

I shouted back, "I'm home!"

"For Christ's sake, where's the guy following you? Is he in the house?"

I moaned, "There is no guy."

I could hear him getting frustrated, but I needed water and a bed.

"Princess, I swear to God, you're going to be the death of me. What the hell? Is there a guy or not?"

I groaned, "There was. I thought he was following me. He was just walking."

"Well, I'll be at the house in two minutes."

I realized suddenly that he was out of breath and the bar noise was gone.

He was coming home... After everything I had just said? My drunk mind was whirling until a light bulb came on. It was one of those drunken evil light bulbs, but it was better than dealing with the shit I'd said ten minutes before.

I muttered really low into the phone, "What? I couldn't hear you. I'm gonna hit the hay." I hung up the phone and ran the rest of the stairs to the apartment, jamming the key in the door and racing inside. I ran to my room, pulled off my shorts and shirt, and stalked out into the kitchen. I grabbed the Gatorade he'd just bought from the fridge and cracked it open.

He rushed into the apartment. He was almost heaving and covered in sweat.

I frowned, "Hey! Don't you have more show to do?"

He looked homicidal as he glanced around the house, "So… you're… fine?" He struggled to get his breath.

I looked around like what he was saying was absurd, "Yeah." I swayed a little bit, while trying to maintain my cool.

His eyes flickered on my push up bra and panties. I turned, bending over completely and grabbed the freezer drawer, placing the Gatorade at the back of the drawer. I stayed there for an extra second.

When I stood up, I could see the look in his eyes had worsened. He took a step back, putting his hand to his mouth, "Oh man. Are those Victoria's Secret's Brazilian-butt underwear?" he moaned.

I held up the piece of ice I'd discreetly pulled from the drawer and ran it over my cleavage, "Yeah? What's up with you? You're acting weird."

He ran his hands through his hair, backing up farther, "Seriously? I ran like five blocks to get here, and this was a trap? So all that, *'Lochlan, you're the best, I can't compete with you—OMG a man is following me'* was shit?" He even raised his tone to mimic my voice, but really just sounded like a cartoon character.

I laughed, shaking my head. I tossed the ice in the sink and walked up to his chest. I looked up into his eyes, "How do you boys say that?" I tapped my fingernail against my cheek, "Oh yeah, don't hate the player, hate the game?" I blinked a few times and walked by him to the bathroom.

"You… you cheated hardcore. You made me think you were in trouble. How could you do that?" He was mystified, but my lack of clothes seemed to be making him confused enough that the dark-eyed look didn't come back.

I looked back at him, "You let me believe you were some crazy, southern hick who was making an attempt at being a rock star." My words slurred a bit, "You didn't tell me you were a famous star."

He walked to me, towering over me. The furrowed brows were there instantly, "Are you fucking dense? All those people asking me for my signature? The fucking cop on the first day we met asked for it. You assumed that. What, you can't fucking Google shit? I thought it was hilarious that you didn't know who I was. In fact, I liked it. You treated me like shit and yelled at me, like people used to do."

I flinched and looked at the door, "You probably should go back to the bar, before the crowd gets mad."

His blue/black eyes bore down on me, "We closed after that song. We only played one set."

I felt the sobering feeling of the heat of him standing over my mostly-naked body. He ran a finger down my jawline, "Princess, you scared me for real. No games when it comes to that, okay? I can't handle you not being safe."

I shook my head, "I… I didn't mean to. I really thought he was following me."

His gaze narrowed, "You have to tell me what the deal is with you. Mace, paranoia, sketchy about leaving the apartment except in the morning, and only for running with your mace. What's up?"

I stepped back, "It's nothing." My back pressed against the wall by the bathroom door. He stepped closer, putting his arms on either side of me, "It's safe to tell me."

I swallowed the vomit slithering up my throat as a shudder took control of my body.

He laughed bitterly, "You're hanging on by a thread, aren't you? You're gong to barf any second? You drank too much, didn't you?"

I nodded.

He reached for the bathroom door and opened it, "Go get sick. We can talk tomorrow."

I nodded again and slipped into the bathroom.

I knelt at the toilet, realizing he'd run as fast as he could to come and make sure I was safe.

The thought lasted seconds before the wine came back with vengeance.

Chapter Five
The New Deal, AKA playing house

I woke with a start and a gasp. My head spun. I moaned, wincing at the bad feelings covering me. I was on my bed. I didn't remember much. I was still in my lacy Brazilian-butt underwear and push-up bra. I pulled off my bra and pulled on a tee shirt and some sweats. It was cool in the room. There was a note, a glass, and a small carton of something on my bedside table.

'Princess,

Drink this, take these pills, and come wake me up.

Hurry up.

L'

I shuddered, looking at the carton. It was coconut water. I popped the pills in my mouth and poured the murky-looking liquid into the glass and drank it back. It wasn't so bad. Not as coconut flavored as I imagined it would be.

I left the room to see him passed out, fully dressed, on the couch.

I tiptoed to the kitchen. Flashbacks of me in my underwear were trying to get through the barrier in my brain. I pushed them away.

I poured a glass of water.

"Morning."

I looked back at him, "Hey."

He grinned, "How are you?"

I shook my head, "Stop shouting."

He nodded, "I suspected." He came and grabbed my hand, pulling me to the front door. He grabbed my flip-flops from the organized shelf next to the door and continued to walk.

"I don't want to go. Where are we going?"

He scooped me up into his arms, "Somewhere necessary."

He carried me down the stairs like I weighed nothing. "Put me down."

He shook his head, "No, your drunk ass is gonna go too slow, and I'm starving."

I panicked a little, mostly because I had no energy, "Loch, I can't leave the house like this."

He grinned, "I like it when you accidentally call me Loch." He always ignored the things he didn't want to hear.

When we got to the car, he opened the door and placed me inside. I sat inside and got my bearings. He climbed in, grinning, "You don't drink, do you?" He passed me my shoes. I slipped them on, trying not to heave.

My throat was burning from the puking, and my head was spinning, "No. I never pass the two-glass rule."

He didn't say anything else, thank God, until we got to a small mom-and-pop establishment. I made a face but he pointed a finger, "Trust me?"

I looked at him and with all my might I tried to say 'no,' but I didn't. The nod was almost involuntary. I opened the car door and he was there, holding a hand out for me.

I recoiled, "You're being sweet to try to trick me into losing the apartment.

He shook his head, "Not today. I swear."

His blue eyes sparkled. He didn't even know he was doing it. I groaned and let him pull me from the car. I burped. He gave me a worried look. I laughed, "There's nothing left. I got it all out last night."

He placed my hand on his arm and closed the door, "Okay, but if you throw up on me, I might just let you win."

I laughed, "I'll remember that."

When we walked inside, he pulled me to a booth. It sounded like I was squeaking against rubber when I sat. I looked around, frowning, "What is this dump? Why do you always eat in seedy, shitty places? Is that guy smoking?"

He chuckled, "Trust me."

I gave him a look, "It's illegal to smoke in a restaurant. He's endangering all of our health, including the servers and cooks. It's a major lawsuit waiting to happen."

He gave me a dead, blank stare and looked back at the guy smoking, "Yo!" The man looked over. He was the size of a Honda Civic with tattoos and a huge beard. He looked like a biker, but not the hot kind. Not the kind in the novels I liked to read.

Lochlan nodded, "You wanna put that out? She's a pain in the ass about smoke, so if you don't put it out, she doesn't put out. I ain't getting any if she's mad when we leave here. Help a guy out."

The guy gave him a look and laughed. He winked a glossy eye at me and ground the smoke into the bar, "Better be extra nice to him later." He spoke with a gravelly voice. The waitress smacked him in the arm and wiped up the ashes.

My face was on fire. I looked down at my sticky, plastic menu, "I can't believe you just said that."

He snatched the plastic menu, ignoring my annoyance, "You don't need that."

I looked up, about to snap and smack him like the waitress had done to the biker with the manners.

A gum-chewing, hair-twirling brunette with her own biker sort of look to her and too much cleavage stepped in front of our booth. She snapped her gum at me. I glowered at Lochlan.

He chuckled and ordered, "We'll have two number threes and non-stop coffee. Over medium."

She winked a false eyelash at him.

I shuddered as she left, "Who wears false lashes at nine in the morning?"

He smiled sardonically, "Oh, you think we're here for small talk?" He leaned forward, "No, princess. You need to tell me what's going on."

My stomach started to hurt again, "I hate it when you order for me. I can order my own food."

He pointed, "Start talking and not about food. Unless that's why you carry mace everywhere you go."

My fingers left the table, brushing against the mace in my pocket. It was as natural as putting deodorant on.

I sighed, "It's nothing. It's just an ex-boyfriend, and he's back in North Dakota. No big deal."

His hands slid across the table, encompassing my left hand with warmth, like a cocoon, "Did he hurt you?"

I stared at the plastic table, unable to breathe, "Not... not really." I felt detached from it, "He just wouldn't leave me alone."

He lifted my chin to look into his intensely-dark blue eyes, "Are you scared he's going to come for you?"

I shook my head, "No."

His look softened, "Tell me the story."

I nodded hypnotically, still seeing him the way I had the night before. The words left my lips like I was in a trance, "I lived in the dorms at the University of North Dakota. My parents are in Grand Forks, but I wanted the full college experience. I dated a guy first semester. We'd known each other for years; we were both in track together in middle school. One month into the relationship, he proposed."

He made a face.

It made me laugh, "Right. Who does that?"

He winked, "Britney Spears's boyfriends."

A smile crossed my lips, relaxing me, "Right, but I don't have millions of dollars or her sex appeal." He opened his mouth but I put a hand up, "I wasn't fishing for a compliment." I ran my fingers through my hair, realizing how huge it actually was. "Anyway, I broke it off because he freaked me out. It was my third boyfriend who sucked. My first one, in tenth grade, cheated on me the entire time. My second one, in twelfth grade, was a drug addict and stole my mom's tennis bracelet because his parents cut him off."

He snorted. I flashed him a look. He nodded "Continue."

I sighed, "I broke up with him and his dad started phoning me. They were threatening me, saying I had to get back together with him. He was showing up at my classes. It was bad. So I recorded the calls and got a restraining order. He and his family weren't allowed on the campus anymore. I moved back home with my parents and finished my degree."

His eyes narrowed, "Now, for the part you're not telling me."

I sneered, "That's it."

He shook his head, "I can tell you're lying."

My throat was dry. Thankfully the waitress brought the coffees. I dumped cream in and swirled it. The white slowly dissolved in a twirling pattern until it blended completely.

"I need to know."

"Okay," I nodded. "He attacked me one night. It was about five months after the 'Do Not Contact' order was in place. He hit me over the head with something and pulled me down between two buildings. He was shaking me and hitting me when a girl came. She was walking by, minding her own business." This was the part of the story that felt like a demon crawling around inside of me with sharp talons. I took a breath and a sip of coffee. "She attacked him. I think I blacked out but when I came too, he was beating her. She had tried to help me, but he turned on her. I grabbed a huge rock and smashed him in the head with it. We called the police and cried, holding each other. It was insanely frightening."

His hands slipped over mine again. They trembled a bit, "Were you guys badly hurt?"

I nodded once. "Her more so than me. She ended up so bruised and beaten. I was better off than her. I visited her in the hospital. She looked so bad. I felt sick."

"If she hadn't come along..."

"Yup." The word came out strong. I knew it was my self-defense kicking in, shutting down the fear I was remembering.

"Where is he now?" The question was growled.

I pulled my hand back and drank with my left hand. My right needed to touch the mace. "Prison."

"Does he know you're here?"

I shook my head, "No." I looked up, "He's in jail for another year. This is my fresh start."

I hated the look on his face.

Our plates were dropped down in front of us. I looked at the food and laughed, "Eggs Benedict?"

My favorite food ever... Could he have guessed that?

He nodded, "It's my favorite. This place makes their own hollandaise and the home fries are dirty good."

I smiled at the surly waitress, "Thanks."

She cocked an eyebrow and left.

The first bite was amazing. My poor stomach wasn't sure though. I ate slowly, in case it was going to come back up, which resulted in him stealing my home fries.

My Side

He switched off the weird, tense look and chatted between bites, "My mom always made Eggs Benedict for Christmas, Easter, and Thanksgiving. It's the only time we were allowed to have it. My dad has cholesterol issues."

I laughed, "My dad is the opposite. He would never eat something like this. He runs marathons. That's how I picked Boston. We came here in 2008 for him to run the marathon, before the divorce."

He cocked an eyebrow, "Your parents are divorced?"

I nodded, "Thank God."

He winced, "Yikes."

"Yup." My strong 'yup' was back in full force.

"My parents are still together, but they've had a couple close calls."

I took a huge bite and moaned, "How do you find these places?"

He laughed, "Just say it—I was right, and this is the best shit you have ever eaten?"

I nodded, "You were right. This is exactly what I needed."

He laughed, "I have had a lot of hangovers in my day."

I closed my eyes, chewing and enjoying the sound of his voice and the taste in my mouth.

"Now that you're all blissful and happy, there's something I want to talk to you about."

I opened my eyes, "What?"

He drank a huge sip of coffee, "I want to stay together. Forget the bet, forget the moving out, and forget apartment hunting. Just be roomies."

His proposal burned my insides. I thought for a second and nodded, "Okay." He made me feel safe. As much as it burned me, I liked it.

"It'll be cheaper for you to share the rent, and I won't have to worry. I'll know you're safe." His voice dropped down a bit.

My eye twitched, "You would worry about me?" I tried to sound sarcastic, but it didn't happen.

He nodded, "Yup. Besides, I am in talks right now with the band, and an agent, and some serious contracts. So if I have to tour, it's better if I have someone at the house for me." He stole my strong yup, and I knew what we were both talking about. It was the end of the flirting and the fun. I felt like I could cry any second. He was asking me to be his friend. I was being friend-zoned.

I wanted that, didn't I?

I wanted to go to school and become a successful lawyer, and be independent. He was a sleazy singer. He was going to be crazy famous. We would never fit.

I wanted that, didn't I? My heart tried to negotiate, but my brain shut it down. "So we'll be roomies?" The words felt dirty and wrong, but I made myself smile.

He smiled back. His eyes tried to talk to me with emotion he wasn't letting himself say either. We liked each other. There was chemistry.

But we both felt the pitfall the other person could be.

I would be that tag-along girlfriend who would make him less sexy to the women of the world, and he would be that guy I never quite trusted and ruined my grades over. Or worse, quit school and follow him around on his tours. The idea of him with other women made me physically sick. I pointed, "Can we agree to no dates at the house? If girls and guys are roommates, it's better not to have sex going on in the house."

He nodded, "I agree completely." He put his huge hand out "To the new deal."

I gave him my hand. He shook them for both of us, while I tried not to think about the fact that his touch lit me up.

Chapter Six
Bromance

I leaned against the counter, bobbing to the beats I'd stolen from his room. He had the best headphones ever. I felt like I was at the Imagine Dragons concert. Not that I even had a clue who they were. He was opening my eyes to music, always filling my iPod that he bought for me. I didn't hear him come into the house. I picked at the strawberries on the counter and read the text from the class I'd just left. Something shifted in my peripheral. I looked up to a whipped cream-covered pie sliding across the counter at me. I pulled the headphones off. He handed me a fork.

"What's this?"

He laughed, "We've been living together for a month with no fights, no sex, no problems. It deserves pie."

I scowled, "Do you have an inner filter?"

A devious smile crossed his lips, "Nope." He took the first bite.

I dug in where he'd taken his bite.

The coconut-cream pie melted in my mouth. Even with my lips covered in whipped cream and my mouth full, I spoke, "Is that real whipped cream?"

He nodded slowly, "From this seedy little place in the industrial section. I was going to bring you there, 'cause I heard about the pie, but when I got there, I knew you wouldn't eat there."

I frowned, "I'm not a snob."

He rolled his eyes, "I know. You're a princess."

I took a second bite, "*You're* a princess."

He laughed and ate a huge bite, "Ohhhhh my God." He licked his lips, and I looked back at the pie. Some things were safer not to watch. I hadn't been to a show since the first one. That was also better not to watch. Seeing him so alive made me hot. I clearly had issues with sexy boys and self-control.

I arched an eyebrow, "So I Googled you."

He snorted, "'Bout time." I loved the sarcasm in his voice; he could really care less about the fame when it was just the two of us. It was part of the show for him.

I bit my lip and then went for it, "I saw the articles about you getting kicked off the show."

His bright-blue eyes lifted to mine but his look turned stern like his tone, "Drop it." The tone wasn't playful.

It made me smile nervously, "No."

He gave me a stern look, "You wanna talk about your ex-boyfriends some more?"

I swallowed, and the humor left me.

He pointed his fork, "This topic is like that for me."

I took another bite, "Fair enough." I ate the bite, but I couldn't do it. I didn't feel like eating anymore. I dropped my fork, "Thanks for the pie."

He grabbed my hand, "Don't be mad."

I looked up into his eyes, "Your expressions are so weird sometimes. You can darken your face; I swear it."

He laughed, "Your brother still coming?" He was always ignoring the things he didn't want to hear.

I snapped back and stopped staring at his face, "What?"

"Brother?"

I smiled and forgot about the forbidden conversations, "Yeah. Tomorrow."

"Sweet."

I shrugged, "Maybe. He's a hot mess. He's really artistic and messy, and one minute he has a job, and then he doesn't. My parents go insane with him. You guys will for sure hit it off."

I realized what I'd said when he gave me his blank stare. I laughed, "I'm on a roll today."

He shook his head, "I gotta go rehearse. Try not to get into trouble."

I stuck my tongue out at him and pulled my headphones back on.

That night, I was studying when he came in late. I looked up, smiling and focused on our friend zone, "How was the show?"

He sat down next to me on the couch, "It was great. I heard afterward that some big wig was coming to see us play. We might have competing offers." I frowned, "What? Congrat…"

He put a finger up to my lips, "Shhh. Not yet. Nothing to get excited about yet."

His finger stayed there for a minute and then ran down my jaw. He leaned forward and lightly brushed his lips against mine. He pulled back. There was something in his eyes, "Sorry."

I shook my head, "Don't be."

He arched an eyebrow, like he was questioning the fact I'd given him permission. He leaned in again, lightly brushing his lips on mine. "God damn, you are sweet," he whispered into my mouth and got up from the couch. I sat there frozen for a few minutes, still tasting the kiss that wasn't nearly awkward enough.

The next day he drove me to the airport to pick up Danny. We didn't talk about the kiss. He was fun and playful. He cranked the car stereo and sang as loud as he could. We pulled up at a light and some girls looked over at him and started screaming. He waved at them and sang louder. I tried to only hear the radio but it was impossible. It was an amazing performance for a car ride. He beamed at me from behind his sunglasses and messy hair.

I almost ran when we got to the airport. I needed to be away from him. When I looked back at him, I smiled at the fact that he was still wearing his sunglasses. His fame situation wasn't getting better. He stood, looking like Lochlan Barlow, but in sunglasses. He needed the Mitch Pitt beard and homeless apparel. Girls pointed and swooned. I nudged him, "You're not fun to take out of the house anymore."

He gave me his one-sided grin, "You've never been fun to take out of the house."

I laughed, "Ass."

Danny came walking down the ramp. He looked the same, thick and handsome but disheveled. His dark-blonde hair was cut into the same fohawk as Lochlan's. It even hung in the back, almost like a mullet. His jeans were tight and his tee shirt was wrinkled. He stopped, grinning and shaking his head. His bright-green eyes twinkled, the way they always did. He was the most joyous person I knew, "Lochlan Barlow is your roommate?"

I looked between them, "What?"

Danny put his hand out for Lochlan. They shook hands. I sighed, "Danny—Lochlan. Let's go before we get mobbed like we have one of the Beatles with us."

Danny wrapped a thick arm around me, "You have better than the Beatles, dude. Only you would fail to mention that you were shacked up with a celebrity."

I gave him a look, "There's no shacking."

Lochlan chuckled, "She didn't know who I was for like weeks."

Danny sighed, "I'm ashamed of you."

My mouth hung open, "What?"

He shook his head, "You are shamed."

I rolled my eyes, "Whatever."

Lochlan laughed and nodded at Danny, "You should come to the bar tonight. We're playing at the nice one. Our Fridays are the best bar we play."

Danny gave me a look. I agreed, dreading the words about to leave my lips, "Yeah." Shit.

They nattered at each other about music and dudes. I didn't know anything they were talking about.

I walked behind them, stunned by the instant bromance going on. Lochlan seemed more into my brother than Danny was to him. That lasted until Lochlan went to the bedroom to get something when we got home, and Danny started silent screaming and mouthing things. I didn't know what he was going on about, but I had to assume it was like a little girl seeing Justin Bieber for the first time.

I sighed and drank from the orange juice carton. When Lochlan came back around the corner with a tee shirt for him, Danny played it cool again. I snorted at the two of them. Lochlan gave me a look and walked into the kitchen. He took the carton from my hands and drank the rest. I tried not to watch him drink, or eat, or sing, so I went to the couch and read a book.

They flirted and chatted for hours. It was sort of good. I read and did my homework.

The romance novels were making my attraction for him worse, so I grabbed the newest James Rollins instead of romance. I finished it off in the tub and got out to get ready. I didn't bother straightening my hair. A bar in the humidity of early fall in Boston was a death trap for straight hair. I hadn't worn it curly since the night we'd made fools of ourselves. I looked at myself and smiled. With barely there makeup, a plain blue tee shirt and a pair of linen pants, I looked like I was trying to be casual. He wouldn't even notice me compared to the other girls in the bar.

I walked into the kitchen to find them eating Chinese food and listening to some old song. Danny pointed, "You hear the break? So classic."

I was getting annoyed. Danny had barely spoken to me. I walked

My Side

behind the island to see Lochlan filling a plate and listening to the song. He passed me the plate and a fork. I scowled, "I don't like it when you…"

He put a hand up, silencing me. Danny shushed me.

I nodded, chuckling and leaned against the counter, "Screw you both."

They ignored me. The song ended. Lochlan smiled, "You know what? You're totally right. The way he gave the pause after the break was dramatic. I felt my heartbeat pause, waiting for it."

Danny pointed, "I know, right." He gave me a look, "How was the tub?"

I flipped him off, taking a huge bite.

He leaned forward, kissing the top of my head, "I missed you."

Lochlan looked at his fat leather watch that looked like more of a cuff than a watch, "I gotta go. Come at ten."

I nodded, looking as disinterested as I could.

He flashed me a grin and walked out.

Danny waited for the door to close and then the girlfriend gushing started, "Oh man. He's so cool. You're rooming with him? He's like rich. He doesn't even need a roommate… are you fucking him and not telling me?"

I choked on my noodles, coughing. He grabbed me a drink of water and passed it to me. I coughed again, "No."

He looked confused, "Why's he rooming with you? Didn't they ever find you guys another place?"

I shook my head, "I don't know. We just agreed this was better."

He nodded, "Oh man, please don't blow this. I always wanted a rock star brother, and a brother-in-law is just as good."

A sickened expression covered my face, "Dude."

He gave me the puppy dog look, "Please."

I sneered, "You're a psycho. This isn't a third world country. You can't just give me away to the guy you like the best."

He folded his arms, "I'll call Dad."

"Go ahead."

He smirked, "He's a huge Lochlan fan."

I sighed, "Great. Please don't tell him. I don't want him to come here and embarrass me too."

He winked, "I know you'll do the right thing. When the time comes, you'll date him."

I left the kitchen, abandoning my plate, and turned on the TV. We watched a couple episodes of Law and Order SVU.

He glared at me, "You shouldn't watch this shit. You already have your paranoia." I stuck my tongue out at him and flipped through Emma, by Jane Austen.

"How do you read and watch TV?"

I muttered, "It's easier when no one talks." He biffed a throw pillow at my head. I ducked.

It was only nine thirty when he nagged me to death, and I was forced to leave the apartment. He almost ran down the stairs. He was like a kid going to see Santa. I, on the other hand, was dreading it. Lochlan didn't need to be a bigger star in my mind.

The bar was a different one than the one I'd been to. Danny showed the bouncer a card and we walked in. I looked at the line out the door and around the block.

"What's that card?"

He flashed me a grin, "Loch gave it to me. He said we would need it to get in and get a table."

I was stunned, "Loch?"

He ignored me and walked to an empty table in a circle booth. The bar was filling up as the line was slowly let in.

Gerry strolled up, grinning. I smiled, about to introduce them, but Danny was up and out of his seat within seconds, "Oh man, Gerry Ronson?"

Gerry laughed, "You must be Danny?"

Danny shook his hand, "I'm a huge fan. You're the best drummer."

Gerry shook his head, "No way. The best will always be Rick Allen from Def Leppard."

Danny put his hands out excitedly, "I know, right. One arm and he still kicked the shit out those drums."

Gerry winked at Danny and gave me a look, "How's it going?"

A slow smile crossed my lips, although it was forced, "Great."

He laughed, "Some wine?"

My eyes narrowed, "He told you?"

He laughed and sat next to me as Danny went and attacked the bass player, Mike. We'd met briefly once.

Gerry sat down next to me, "He told me about the new deal."

My stomach ached, "Yeah?" What else could I say? Lochlan had friend-zoned me after I friend-zoned him first. Then we kissed and now we were pretending that didn't happen.

We both watched as Danny mauled Lenny, the other band member. Gerry laughed, "Your brother is awesome."

I glanced at him, "He's annoying and completely smitten with Lochlan."

"Everyone is. That's why we asked him to join. He's brilliant with business and he's an amazingly-talented singer. As long as he keeps his temper in check, he'll take us to the top."

I lifted my head, "He's smart?"

Gerry laughed, "You're an asshole. Yeah, he's got his MBA in business from the University of Tennessee. He's smart. He's already got us an agent and a few tour dates for the winter months. We got a huge offer a couple days ago but he told us to turn it down. We're just waiting to see if that move pays off." His voice was filled with admiration.

"God, he's perfect." I mocked.

He laughed, "He's got a horrid temper, and an even-worse roving eye. He's not perfect. He has groupies like I've never seen. Those poor girls are all in love with him and he… well, he's not interested."

That made me sick. He was a womanizer. The worst kind of 'not perfect.' The foul temper didn't even affect me. I could have cared less about that. He had never shown it to me. I'd seen the glimmer in his eyes and that was about it.

Lochlan strolled over with a cranberry lemonade, "I told them you can't have more than three of these, or you'll be *their* problem."

I gasped, "Ass."

He took a sip and placed it in front of me, "Hey, it's not my fault you can't hold your liquor."

I scowled, "You're mean."

He shoved me over, sitting too close. I moved over, taking my drink. He grabbed it and took another sip. I snatched it back, "I don't like it when you drink…"

He turned, cutting me off, "You wanna go to Salem tomorrow? Danny was saying that he'd be interested in seeing where the Witch trials were."

I gave him an exasperated look.

He shrugged, "We don't have to go."

Danny sat down, "Mike freaking Jones. Like… oh man, I am dying right now."

Lochlan beamed at him, nudging me, "You can tell him you don't want to go to Salem. You'll break his poor heart."

Danny's lip popped out, pouting like when we were little. I looked at Lochlan, "I never said that."

Lochlan cocked his head, "You never said yes."

"Yes." I challenged him with my stare.

He cocked an eyebrow, "Yes?"

My stomach dropped, but I kept my brave face on and nodded my head, taking a drink of my lemonade.

Danny looked at Gerry, "You wanna come too?"

Gerry shrugged, "Sure."

Lochlan continued to stare at me, even when the group of girls came over with things for him to sign.

I sighed. Danny smiled like a kid in a candy store, and Gerry watched me with a smug look.

Mike came over, "Hey, Erin."

I nodded, "Hi."

He sat down next to Danny and started to drum with his fingers, "So, you liking it here?"

Mike seemed awkward. I shrugged, "Yeah. Are you from here?"

He shook his head, "No. Lenny is. I'm from Maryland. I answered an ad, like these guys. Lenny and Vic are from Boston. They had a band before, but it was a small-time gig once a week at a small bar. The band broke up, and then they decided to try again."

"How long have you guys been here?"

Gerry looked like he was thinking, "Me, four years."

Mike nodded, "Yeah, and I was just after you. So, almost four years."

Lochlan finished signing and spoke softly, "We gotta go."

Mike beamed at me, like he wanted to say something. Danny looked at him, "We're going to Salem tomorrow. Do you wanna go too?"

Mike nodded, "Yeah." He handed his phone to Danny, "Put your shit in here."

Danny took the phone and added himself to it. Mike was the opposite of the rest of them. He looked like he should be in a rock band. He had shaggy, brown hair and a handsome face with brown eyes and a scruffy, unclean look. He and Danny could be brothers. They both looked like scruffy surfers who suited the band look.

Gerry was in skinny jeans and a tight, graphic tee shirt. He had on thick, black glasses, and his hair was perfectly coiffed. He looked like a pop star. Lochlan had on his tight denim shirt, which I hated, with his sleeves rolled up so his tattoos stuck out the bottoms of the rolled cuffs. He had on tight, dark-blue jeans with big boots and his dark hair was a mess. He looked like he belonged in a mosh pit in Ireland or the unemployment line. The sexy side of the unemployment line.

He flashed his blue eyes at me, "See you after. Don't leave, okay?"

I nodded.

They all climbed out, leaving me and Danny to watch. The bar was packed. The dance floor down front was filled with waiting fans.

The bar went black, except for a white-blue light shining down on where Lochlan stood center stage.

I was holding my breath seeing him up there.

He started to sing softly. He held the microphone so close to his face that his lips caressed it when he sang. Everyone's hands went into the air, swaying with the soft lyrics coming from him. Danny jumped up, grabbing my hand and dragging me down front. I got shoved and squished, but we made it.

Lochlan held a long note, taking it higher and higher. The rest of the band exploded, as the lights lit the rest of the stage up. The song picked up and the crowd erupted. My heart burst with the shock of the dramatics.

Lochlan moved with the beat, bobbing and swaying. He moved like the song was his heartbeat. When the chorus hit again, he held the microphone out and let the crowd scream the lyrics with him. He bobbed to the song with his arm stretched out. As the chorus ended, he kicked his boot with the beat of the drum and leaned back, taking the song slow again. The lights faded again as he took it all way down. He closed his eyes, caressing his lips against the microphone.

His arms flew into the air as the light came back on and the band kicked back in. The song was incredible. My arms were in the air, and I was swaying with him. I was screaming like all the other fans.

The song ended with the lights going down again.

We stood in breathless silence, waiting for it to hit again. The lights came on in the back, showcasing Gerry lightly tapping on the cymbals. Lochlan started to sing from somewhere in the dark.

His voice made every hair on my body stand on end. I couldn't even name the sounds I heard. The band exploded again with the lights. Flashes of lights matched the movements of the band.

The crowd frothed. Elbows hit my back. The crowd swallowed me up, but I didn't care. All I saw was him. He was so alive. He was everything I wanted to be.

The flow of their music was perfect, never letting us get comfortable. We were on edge, waiting for him to rock us, or woo us, or make us hold our breath.

I moved with the crowd, moving with him. He was the puppet master.

The show ended with the best song of the night. He let the savage crowd sing most of the song as he moved with the beat.

The lights went out, and the crowd went insane. The lights came back on and they were gone. The stage was empty. Bouncers pushed us back a bit.

I made my way back to my table. It was roped off but as I approached, a server took the rope away. Danny slid into the booth, "That was fucking nuts. Did you hear the dramatic pauses? That's what he and I were talking about."

I smiled, high from it. "That's cool. They're so good." A server brought us a lemonade and a beer. He smiled at her, "Thanks."

She eye-fucked him. I didn't even care. I searched the crowd for the band, but they never came back. I finished my lemonade, feeling the high of them and the buzz of the booze.

"I'm going to the bathroom," I shouted at Danny. He was mid-conversation with the server and waved me off. I needed to tell him about our no-sex house.

I walked down the dark hall to the bathroom. Girls were in a huge lineup. I stood at the back of it for a second, but a door opened at the end of the hall. Gerry walked out, getting mauled by the girls. He pointed at me, "Hey! Help?"

I laughed, watching them attack. Had they never noticed? Seriously, he was on our team. The line thinned out, and I smiled at him, "No way, you're on your own, but thanks for clearing a path to the bathroom."

He gave me a look. I budged ahead and slipped into the bathroom. I finished and washed my hands. Gerry must have still been in the hallway. The bathroom was dead. I looked at myself, wincing. I was a hot mess. My curly hair was huge, and my face was red and sweaty. Whatever.

I made my way back to the table, but Danny nodded at me and pointed at the stage. In the dark corner, I saw Lochlan. He waved at me, trying not to get attention from anyone. I walked over that way.

"We have to leave through the back. It's too nuts now," he shouted at me.

I laughed and looked around, "I'll meet you at the house."

He shook his head, "No way, princess." He put a hand out. I heard girls shouting behind me, over top of the DJ music. I looked back as they rushed us. I grabbed his hand and let him pull me up. He dragged me to the back of the stage and through an open black, metal door. He closed it, pressing his back against it. Hands started banging on it within seconds.

I looked up into his eyes, "They're like a zombie movie."

He nodded.

We were alone in the dark hallway.

The pounding of the crazed fans matched my beating heart.

My mouth hung open like I wanted to say something, but I couldn't.

The thing I wanted to say would have broken our deal.

"Stop looking at me like that," he pleaded.

I shook my head, "I'm not looking at you like anything."

He pushed me against the wall behind me, pressing my back against it, "You are. I saw you in the crowd."

I shook my head, "You're magnificent." The words were a whisper.

He struggled with something, and I could see it in his eyes when he lost the fight. He lowered his face, pressing his lips against mine.

It was like the moment when the lights came on, on the stage. It was explosions of sound and light.

His soft lips against mine were overwhelming. His hands ran down my body, tracing my bare arms gently. I shuddered but let it happen.

Then, like it was a second explosion of lights and sounds, I joined in. I wrapped my arms around him, pulling him down toward me. He moaned into my mouth as his tongue caressed mine. His hands cupped my ass, lifting me up into his arms. He smelled like sweat and tasted like beer.

I wrapped my legs around his waist as he held me to the wall. His body pressed against mine was exactly like I'd fantasized. His lips were softer than I'd imagined. He kissed like he'd majored in it.

He pulled back, letting me stand on my own and backed up away from me. "Oh shit. Sorry."

I shook my head, "It's okay."

We didn't speak. We breathed and tried to comprehend what was happening.

We had really crossed the line this time. I didn't want to stop, but he had shut it off. I could see it.

"That was a mistake. I'm sorry." His words burned, but at least they had the decency to kill the savage lust tearing through me.

I nodded, "I agree." I opened the door again, letting the screaming fans in, "See you at the house."

He didn't hear me. He didn't stand a chance.

Chapter Seven
Awkward as ass

Danny poked me again with his fork, "Stop scowling. You look moody as shit."

I gave him the death stare. He knew it meant fuck off.

Gerry handed me a Danish. I tore a bite out and drank some coffee.

"Just tell him you like him, too."

I looked at Gerry with a confused look, "What?"

He looked over at Mike and Lochlan signing the breasts of the girls on the street outside the café.

"Who, Mike?" I asked cheekily.

He kicked me, "You're being difficult."

I gave him a look similar to the one Danny had gotten, before he walked off to see the breasts. "He is signing the tits of a chick on the side of the road in Salem. That isn't boyfriend material."

Gerry snickered, "It's all part of the show. You and I both know that's not him."

I nodded, "If you like him so much, you ask him out."

He gave me a heartbroken look, "Honey, I would, but he doesn't swing that way."

It dawned on me then that Gerry wanted to live vicariously through me. He liked Lochlan. I looked at Lochlan and nodded. What wasn't there to like?

Gerry nudged me, his face turning serious, "You know he's the big ticket item musicians like us need. The spark in him is huge; he could light the whole world on fire with it."

I smiled, "I know."

He leaned forward, "You could consider dating him and keeping him calm. I have noticed you keep him calm and relaxed. People like him are prone to emotional outbursts and addictions. They're larger than life and their personalities are bigger than their bodies."

I frowned, "You want me to consider dating him to help Thin Ice out?"

He shrugged, "We both know you like him, and if he loses it like he did before, he could ruin his whole career. Divas don't get to have tantrums in the beginning. They have to earn their right to be a crazy artist."

I didn't say anything else. If I dated him, it wouldn't be for that reason.

Gerry got up and left my side, and Mike took the chance to come over and sit beside me, "So, are you and Lochlan dating?"

I laughed, "Not a chance. We're roommates."

"You seeing anyone?"

I shook my head, "No. I'm busy with school."

"Wanna go on a date?"

I shook my head, "Thank you, but no."

He grinned, "You have to eat, right?"

"Yeah?" It was starting to get awkward.

He shrugged, "We could just go have a meal?"

I looked at his lips as he spoke and nodded, "I guess." It was a petty whorish thing to do to stare at the thing I couldn't have, and say 'sure' to someone I didn't really want. I instantly shook my head, "Actually, no."

He looked confused, "Which is it?"

"I would go for a meal with you, but only as friends. I don't want to be the girl who broke up Thin Ice because I dated the bass player and lived with the lead singer. Then the bass player and I broke up and the lead singer took my side. Or worse, took your side and I ended up homeless. You know what I'm saying?"

He nodded, looking a bit down, "Yeah, I guess. I can ask him if you want and see if he thinks it's awkward for us to eat a meal together. We can go as friends."

I agreed, "Okay. If he doesn't think it's awkward, I'd love to go for dinner, even as a group." I knew Lochlan would say no. It would be easier to let Mike down with Lochlan telling him 'no way,' than for me to do it.

His face lit up. He stood and walked over to Lochlan as the group of girls left. The two of them talked. I tried not to watch as Lochlan's cheeks flushed and his eyes flicked to me. Mike put his hands in the air defensively. Gerry gave me an evil look. I gave it right back to him. Danny started laughing. Whatever was happening in the powwow of doom, I assumed was bad.

Lochlan stalked over, "Not funny."

I scowled, "It was nice of him to ask me out for dinner. I told him it would be awkward, since I'm your roommate. It could end badly."

I could see he was fighting his anger. "What about last night?"

I took a bite of my Danish, "You said it was a mistake. I agreed. Did something else happen I wasn't aware of?"

He sat in the seat, "Why are you playing these games with me?"

"Me? Games with *you*?"

He nodded, taking my Danish and having a bite. I snatched it back and got up. I walked away from the group of them and headed to a magic store in an old building down the road. I had spotted it when we had been doing our tour. The door tinkled from the bell attached to it as I entered. An old lady in a cool old-fashioned dress with long, gray hair smiled at me. I was about to say hello when Lochlan entered after me.

I sneered at him and looked back at her.

She pointed at my pastry, "You can't have food in here."

I opened my mouth to ask for a garbage can, but Lochlan grabbed my hand and lifted the pastry to his face. He ate it from my fingers. I made the weird noise I seemed to make with him.

He licked my fingers, which I enjoyed more than I was willing to tell him. I contemplated the mace in my pocket, but he pulled me down a crowded aisle. The smell of herbs and candles were everywhere.

He looked down on me, running his hands down my cheeks, "You can't date anyone, ever."

I laughed, "What? Are you high? What was in that Danish?"

His eyes didn't have any humor in them as he stroked his thumb across my bottom lip. He replaced it with his lips, sucking my lip into his mouth. We both tasted like pastry. The kiss was slow and intense.

"I want you to date me," he whispered into my mouth.

I shook my head, "But we live together. You were right. Think how intense that would be? Roommates dating is too much."

He swallowed, "I want you."

I bit my lip for fear I would return what he'd said, or up the ante and say something so much worse, "You said kissing me was a mistake."

He shook his head, "I meant kissing you behind the stage with groupies everywhere, like we're hiding in a corner, was a mistake. I won't ever treat you like you're just some girl." He kissed me again, "Go out to dinner with me."

I laughed, pulling back, "No. Goddamn, Loch. You're good at this."

His eyes were filled with something not good, "You said 'yes' to Mike?"

"I said 'yes' to him as a friend, firstly and secondly, I knew you'd say no to him and get me out of dinner. I didn't want to hurt his feelings so I let you do it. I'm sorry for that."

He lowered his face over me, forming himself around me almost, "I got mad because there's something here that I can't shake. I need to see if it's what I think it is."

I closed my eyes and forced the images of the other girls, and the signing of the breasts, and the flocks of women out of my head. I swallowed, "You're not what I want."

He lifted my face sharply. I opened my eyes to see a look I'd never seen before, "Bullshit." He was vibrating and holding my face. I looked around at the small store, and the old saying bull in a china shop started to become a possibility.

I panicked as he gripped harder, like he was stuck that way, or just barely holding himself together. I lifted my hands up to stroke his, "Hey, calm down." I looked into his eyes, "It isn't you. It's what you do. You, I want more than anything. I want you to steal my food, and snuggle me on the couch, or window shop for dresses like we did last week. Lead singer with girls crawling all over him and totally famous, I don't want that. I don't want people watching me or thinking bad things about me because they want you."

His vibrating hand stayed on my jaw, still gripping too tight.

I tapped his fingers, "Loch, you're scaring me a little bit—talk. Say something," I whispered calmly. I trusted him. I didn't trust the look in his eyes. I had pushed him too far.

He took a couple deep breaths and planted his lips on mine again, "You have to give me a chance. You're assuming I'm going to be that bad rock star boyfriend and I swear I won't." The dark look was gone when he stood back up.

I took my first real breath, still whispering and searching his eyes for the thing I'd seen, "Your face gets so dark sometimes."

He tried to smile but it was like it was broken, "I'm sorry."

I gripped his fingers, "Lochlan, you were like frozen."

His eyes pinched, "I know. I'm sorry. I had to go to anger management after the show. They told me to slow everything down and take breaths."

I swallowed, changing the subject, "If I say yes and you break my heart, we can't live together anymore. We won't see each other anymore. We'll lose the thing we have."

He nodded, "I know."

I maintained my stare into his eyes, "What do you want more: to be near me always, or with me and gamble it all away? "

Without any hesitation or thought on the subject he spoke, "With you, anyway I can have you. You know me, baby, I'm always going to say yes to the incredible."

I nodded, "Okay. We can go out to dinner."

A slow smile crossed his face, "I'll make you dinner at the house."

My smile matched his, "Danny?"

"I'll ask Gerry to take him to do something." He bent his face close to mine again, "I'm sorry I got mad when Mike asked you to dinner."

I shook my head, "No. I shouldn't have even entertained the thought of dinner with Mike. It was mean. I was mad at you for the whole kiss last night."

He leaned his forehead against mine, "Promise me you'll use your words next time."

I laughed, "Pot calling the kettle black. You're an asshole."

He nodded his face against mine, "I know." He took my hand and pulled me to the door. We walked down the road, holding hands. He glanced over at me, "Why a magic store?"

I looked back at it, "I wanted to ask for a spell to get over you."

He gave me a sly smile, "You that hooked on me?"

Refusing to answer, I bit my lip. He wrapped his arm around me,

"You know you are."

I looked up at him, "Every girl in Boston is."

His eyes sparkled, even under the dull, gray sky, "You need to look into my eyes and see the person I'm looking at. There won't ever be anyone but you in there. When you see me at the show or signing autographs, that's not me. This right now, with you, is me." He stopped, pulling me into his embrace, "It's always been me with you."

He was right. When I looked into his blue eyes, I could see myself.

I pulled him down, pressing my lips against his.

We left Salem, both holding onto the intense feelings of the possibilities of what was coming. Gerry left us at the apartment, and he and Danny took the car. Lochlan walked to the small store near us to get groceries, and I went upstairs to get cleaned up for dinner. Technically, not for dinner.

I pulled on the only pretty outfit in my closet and looked at myself. White eyelet skirt and pale-pink tank top. My hair was a curly mess but he liked it. Weirdo.

He liked me the way I was naturally, even if I didn't.

My stomach was in knots. I fidgeted and walked around my room, pacing and playing out how the evening was going to go. He would come back and make me dinner. We would have a glass of wine and laugh.

I had to shake my head and rearrange a few things.

He was going to make me hot dogs or Kraft Mac and Cheese and we'd drink beer.

Whatever.

We'd eat and have a drink. Maybe we'd kiss, and then somehow, end up in his bed. The images of the other girl in there killed that, "My bed," I muttered, tapping my fingers against my lips.

I heard the door to the apartment, making my head snap towards my door. I didn't move. I didn't know how to be cool about having sex with him. He was experienced in a way I wasn't, not to mention, we were roommates. If we didn't work, we would have to contend with it. Mostly, it was his sexuality that scared me. I'd had sex, but it was only with the three guys I'd dated, and they were all nineteen or younger. They weren't amazing. They all were fairly average and new to sex, like me. I'd dated guys like me. Nerdy, book guys who hung in coffeehouses. Guys like Gerry.

This was uncharted territory. He had tattoos in places I hadn't even touched on other people. I'd had sex in the dark with my eyes closed.

He'd already made me feel like I was burning up from the inside out, which was more than any of the other three had ever done. I chewed my lip.

I had a horrid feeling that we were making a mistake. The idea of losing him hurt more than not having him. I reached for the door and turned the lock. I dropped to my knees and leaned my forehead against the door.

He called me. I didn't answer. I felt sick.

I heard his footsteps on the hardwood floors and closed my eyes. He turned the locked handle on the door.

"Erin?"

I stopped breathing.

"You okay?"

I shook my head, "I don't feel good."

He turned the lock harder, aggressively, "Let me in."

I placed my hands on the door, "Can we reschedule? My stomach is hurting."

"No. I know why it's hurting." There was a thump on the floor, and suddenly his voice was next to mine through the hollow door, "Mine's hurting too."

I whispered, "What if we fuck this up?"

He was quiet for a second, "I don't know. I can't think that far ahead. I just want you. I'll always want you."

"What if that's all it is?"

"Princess, remember when I told you that I could have any girl I wanted?"

I wrinkled my nose.

"Don't make that face. You know you remember that night."

I laughed. He couldn't see me but he knew. I whispered, "I remember."

He sighed, "I wasn't joking. Being Lochlan Barlow is awesome, but it's not who I am. With you, I'm just Loch. I like that part of me. I like who you make me."

My eyes watered, "I'm normal and plain, and you're the light that could brighten the whole sky. You're too big, and I know we're going to fuck it up, and I can't take not being with you, even as friends." I was grateful for the door. I could never say any of that to his face.

"Princess, you're extraordinary to me. You're the amazing and the fantastic. I look at you and I think 'home.' It's bigger than anything in the world. No record deal, mountain climbed, no creation made, can compare to the feeling I have when I'm with you. Nothing I ever accomplish will be as great as getting you to be my girl."

I reached up and clicked the lock. He pushed the door and me back. He swept me into his arms, holding me to his chest, "I'm as scared of you as you are of me."

I shook my head against his scruffy face, "No."

He looked at me, "Yeah." He put me down slowly, sliding me down his body.

I ran my hands up his torso, dragging his tee shirt with it, running my hands along his taut, warm skin. He pulled the shirt up over his head, dropping it on the floor between us. I traced his tattoos with the tips of my nails, appreciating each one. His left shoulder had a huge triangle that covered the whole round of shoulder and went up his neck a tiny bit. His chest had two sentences I didn't recognize. His arms had daggers and skulls and weird artwork. He looked savage without a shirt on. His body was ripped and inked and he had a nipple piercing I never noticed before. It blended into the ink over his chest. I pointed, "Is that new?"

"No."

It was a small black barbell through the nipple. I grimaced, "It must have hurt." I flicked it with my fingertip. He sucked in, "Not any more."

I smiled and looked up at him while my hands went to his leather belt with metal studs all over it. I undid it, maintaining his stare.

He looked like he was ready to pounce but I shook my head. I wanted to see him.

I pulled the belt from his pants, struggling with the studs. I dropped it to the floor and dipped my fingers into the front of his pants. He jerked, like he wasn't ready for it. Taking his button in my fingers, I grinned as I undid it and pulled the zipper down.

His breaths were slow and controlled. He was holding himself back. I had a bad feeling that when he let go of the control, it would be like unleashing a wild animal.

The blue in his eyes was almost black. I frowned, "You okay?"

He bit his lip and nodded.

I dropped to my knees, dragging his jeans to the floor. His legs were thick and strong. I unlaced his boots slowly, knowing how close my face was in relation to his groin. His tight, white underwear had a wide band with Calvin across them. I looked up at his thick erection, outlined behind the white cotton. I wanted to pull it out, but I assumed that would be too much for him. He was already wound tight.

I pulled off one boot and then the other.

His jeans were hard to take off, but when I got them off, I sat back and looked at him. The black socks were wrecking the picture. I lifted his feet one at a time and pulled them off. Then I sat back and took a mental picture. I wanted this to be the way I always remembered him.

My gaze travelled his body slowly. When I reached his face, I nodded, "Okay, but it has to be slow."

He leapt, sweeping me into his arms in a fluid motion. He laid me on the bed on my back, tugging at my shirt. He pulled it up, but stopped when it reached my eyes. It became a blindfold that trapped my arms above my head. His lips brushed against mine, like a butterfly kiss. He planted them everywhere. He dragged my bra up my body, doing the same as my shirt. I was helpless and blind. His mouth hovered over my left nipple. I shivered when I felt the heat of his breath there. He lowered, taking the whole nipple into his mouth. I moaned, arching my back but his hand still held my arms above my head and my shirt over my eyes. He sucked slowly, swirling his tongue and flicking. He kissed the mound of my breast and made a path of hot, wet kisses to my mouth. He sucked my lip and finally thrust his tongue in my mouth, releasing my hands. I struggled to get the shirt off.

His hands were finding other places to explore, running up and down my inner thigh, tracing softly on the cotton of my underwear. He slipped them to the side, running a finger up the center of my lower lips.

I sucked in a sharp inhale and held it, as his finger made its way into me. He moved slowly, stroking my abdomen and sliding his finger in and out of me. He sat up, watching me as he methodically moved his finger. He pulled his finger from me and ripped my underwear down all the way. They were still looped around one foot, when he spread my legs as far as they would go. He looked down on me. I closed my eyes. I couldn't watch him see me spread apart. He bent his face, kissing my inner thigh. My stomach was in knots still. I waited in agony until he licked the entire length of my slit. Then I contracted, gripping the blankets.

He murmured into the kisses and sucked, "You taste good. I knew you would."

I shook my head, "Shhhh. No talking."

He chuckled, licking again, but this time he pushed his finger inside of me. The licking and sucking, combined with the thrusting, and I felt my body break into a flush.

"Cum for me, princess," he murmured. As if because he commanded it, I did. I covered my hands over my face, knowing he'd just watched me orgasm in a bright bedroom. I couldn't focus on it though. My whole body was contracting and twitching.

He kissed the inside of my leg and sat up. I could feel his eyes bearing down on me. He bent forward, kissing me, and I could taste myself on his lips. I wasn't sure how I felt about it, but it was there.

"Open your eyes, princess."

I shook my head, clutching my hands to my eyes.

He kisses my cheek, "Please." He pried my hands from my face.

I opened them, discovering a look in his eyes I'd only ever seen when he was on stage. It was the passion, and anger, and pain, and bliss, and joy he felt when he was singing. That dark look was there. He maintained my stare when he pushed himself inside of me. It hurt for a second. It had been a long time since my last partner, and he was much larger than any of them. But he pushed in slowly, letting me get used to him. He thrust once and bent his face. "You feel as good as I knew you would," he whispered into my neck.

His body moved against mine in a rhythmic way. I found myself pushing back, grinding and rotating against him. His hands caressed, worshiping almost, as his lips placed kisses everywhere. It was slow, and not at all what I was expecting. His self-control was insane, considering he'd looked like he was going to maul me when I was undressing him.

I'd never had an orgasm with actual sex before, beyond my

vibrator, so when the build up started, I felt my eyes widen. He increased the speed, "Look into my eyes when you cum."

My breaths shortened and became the sound he always made me make. He gripped my ass, lifting me up and pumped harder. "You look at me when you cum. I want you to remember this moment."

I reached above me, grabbing the rails that made up the headboard. I used them to get the angle I needed. I didn't even know I needed it until my body started to lift and clutch. He gave me his cocky one-sided smile when he felt it. I tried to keep looking at him, but my body was on fire. I focused on the blue of his eyes and how black they had gotten. I could see the demons swirling around inside of the blacks of his eyes. My body clenched and convulsed and my eyes closed with the intense look on his face burned into my memory. It was the same one he got when he sang.

I got to have him the way I wanted him.

I cried out, wrapping my legs around him, forcing him to freeze for a second. Every muscle tensed to the point that my calf started to cramp up. I flexed my foot and straightened my leg, "My calf... cramping."

He pressed on my foot until it went away.

I opened my eyes and looked at him, "What the fuck?" I asked breathlessly.

He laughed, "I'm not done showing you how I feel, but I need to put a condom on."

I shook my head, "I'm on the pill." I always was, just in case. 'Course this was the first time I was letting 'just in case' happen.

He didn't need anything beyond that. He lifted me up higher and thrust into me like the animal I knew he would be. It wasn't slow anymore. He gripped my thighs so hard I was sure to bruise. I was covering my mouth to muffle the screams leaving my lips, when his body tensed and I felt him finish inside of me. He jerked and collapsed on me, squishing me, but in a good way.

Everything changed in that moment.

He kissed my arm, my breast, my chest, my throat and then my cheek.

Everything changed, and I prayed it wouldn't be awkward as ass.

Chapter Eight
The record deal

We didn't leave the bed for twenty hours, probably scared of what was waiting in the real world. We slept, had sex again, and talked. He cut up a plate of fruit and cheese, and brought a packet of crackers when the hunger was too much. We ate in my bed, which made me laugh. I wasn't kicking him out of bed for cracker crumbs. I was changing my sheets though.

He looked at his huge cuff watch, "I have to go. You coming?"

I wanted to be supportive, but I shook my head, "I think it's better if I don't come."

He looked hurt.

I kissed his stubble-covered cheek, "I want to be there, but I don't want to watch you sign girls' boobs and arms and stomachs."

He laughed, "Fair enough. I sign paper too, ya know? Maybe like one in twenty girls asks for a body signing, and they ask the other guys too."

I shook it off and pointed at the huge pile of books in the corner, "I don't want to talk about it, and I have homework anyway."

He kissed the tip of my nose. I watched him get out of bed. He had a nice ass. It was the kind that you wanted to bite. "How is your body so fit?"

He looked down on himself, "You enjoying the view?"

A smile crossed my lips, "Yup."

He shrugged, "I lift weights a few times a week, and I run. I don't know. I do a show every night; that's a lot of calories."

I winked, "But you eat a ton. You know it's going to catch up with you. You'll be three hundred pounds by the time you're forty."

He dropped to his knees in front of me, "You better still love me then, if I am."

It was an awkward moment for both of us.

I felt myself closing off, but he was the antidote to my natural wall building. He pointed, "Stop that. I just meant if I get fat, you better still want to be with me."

I laughed and fought the awkwardness, "If you want me to want you in twenty years, then you better still look like David Beckham."

He blushed, "You think I look like Beck?"

I shrugged, "Kinda. The tats, the hair, intense eyes, and the muscled body, but not crazy thick. You're still lean. You're handsome like him. Yeah, if I had to say anyone, I would say him."

I watched him look bashful for the first time ever and jumped out of bed, "Yeah, I'm coming." I pulled on a tee shirt and some cargo pants.

"You sure?"

I looked at him, studied him and nodded, "Positive. You can't go alone. Those bitches will eat you alive."

He scoffed, "Stay here if you're going to be mad at yourself for not finishing your homework."

I rolled my eyes, "I'll lay here and wonder what you're doing."

"I don't want that. I want you to be able to do your thing and me do mine, and neither of us worry what the other person is doing."

I took a breath and looked at the stack of books, "No, you're right. You go. I'll wait here."

He kissed me once and it was enough. He was right. Acting like a psycho wasn't going to make dating him easier.

Of course it lasted about an hour. Then I couldn't take it any longer. My eyes wouldn't focus on the book I wasn't reading, and I had already watched three performances of his singing on YouTube.

I ran out the door, barely even paying attention to anything, except of course, my mace. I wasn't ready to let that go. All women in a city alone needed mace. It was like a religion for me.

I sprinted down the stairs and up the block to the bar. The Sunday night performance was the least popular one. They had talked about cutting it. But when I got around the block, I gasped at the line.

"Shit."

I walked up to the door to where the bouncer was. He gave me a look. I pointed and whispered, "I'm Erin Benson… I'm… uhhh, friends with Lochlan. We're…uhhh…"

He was about to laugh in my face when Mike walked out front and handed him something, "Hey, Erin."

I smiled, relieved, "Hey, Mike." The line went crazy seeing him. He blushed and waved to everyone.

He looked at the bouncer, "She's with Lochlan." He lifted the rope back for me. The line started to grumble.

"Hey, she's fucking the lead singer!" he shouted at them.

I ran inside, hiding my face. Mike grabbed my arm, "Hey, I just wanted to tell you I'm sorry. I didn't know about you and him. I'm a blind idiot… clearly."

I shook my head, "No. I assumed it was never going to be anything with him."

He scoffed, "Yeah, no kidding." He stopped laughing and looked down, "Sorry."

A grin crossed my lips, "It's fine. I've lived with him for like almost two months. I've figured out what he's like."

"He's like that for them. When we're alone and it's just us guys, he's normal."

I nodded, "I know."

"We start up in five." He smiled and walked to the back of the bar.

I found my brother sitting at a table with a blonde. She gave me a look. I almost smacked him, but he looked up before I could, "Hey. This is Gabby, Gabby, this is my sister—Erin."

She smiled at me through the glare in her eyes. I felt warmth behind me as a kiss was planted on my head. I should have known he was there; Gabby suddenly had a lost puppy look on her face and was adjusting her shirt.

I looked up. He smiled and bent, kissing my cheek, "You came." He placed a lemonade in front of me.

I grinned and turned, meeting his lips with mine, "I needed my fix."

He murmured alongside my mouth, "Uh oh. Someone is becoming a groupie."

I rolled my eyes, "Whatever. Don't make a big deal about it."

He whispered into my ear, "I missed you anyway. I have some news I want to share with you. Come backstage after the show." I pressed my face into his kiss and felt him slip something in my pocket next to my mace.

"I see you have your cock with you."

I grinned, "Always."

He looked away from me to sign a girl's stomach. She giggled and clawed at his hand. She jumped up and down. He laughed and shook his head. Her friends came running over, all getting his autograph on their chests and stomachs. I looked away. I hated the petty jealousy burning through me.

He waved at Danny, "See you after, man." Danny nodded at him, still playing it cool even though he had probably just peed his pants. He walked away without saying goodbye to me. Girls mauled him the entire way to the back of the stage. I turned around and drank my lemonade.

The girl was all doe-eyed now, "You're dating Lochlan?"

I shrugged, "I don't know. Sort of."

Danny smiled at me, "They're roommates."

She winked, "Friends with benefits?"

A frown replaced my indifferent look, "No. I don't do benefits." I turned and looked at the front of the stage. People were milling around the front. Some of them were looking at me and pointing. I sighed and walked to the front of the stage.

The lights went down, making the bar black as night. My heart started to pound in anticipation. I could tell by the breath of the people next to me that they felt the same. Lights came on, but instead of shining on the stage, they focused on the fans in the crowd as the song started. The band played in the dark and Lochlan sang softly. I could barely make out his silhouette.

All of the light was on the fans. The crowd filled with hands lifted into the air. They were illuminated with pale-blue lights and swaying with the song.

When more lights came on, I didn't watch him. I watched the crowd. The faces of the people were filled with the same emotions, like they were living through him or for him. They felt something deep from the intensity of his words. Seeing their faces, I knew he was giving them his soul and they were taking it... loving every second of it.

The exchange was reciprocated; he got a high off of them too. Their devotion and reverence was ever-present as they hung on every word he sang with all his heart and soul. Every set of lips sang the words with him. Some of them cried with joy, or sorrow, or whatever the puppet master told them to feel. They moved with him, like him.

I didn't have to watch him. I could watch them and know what he was doing.

The lights on the stage all flicked on, just as he unleashed the beast, singing loudly into the microphone with fiery anger. Just as it hit, the band crashed with him. They came to life in the crescendo and mellowed for the break.

He bent towards the crowd, rocking with them. Each band member was the same. Their individual instruments worked the fans. They caressed the instruments the way Lochlan's lips did the microphone and his eyes did the crowd.

His sex/singing face was the most mesmerizing thing to watch. He had me under his spell from the minute the show started to the end. He maintained the emotions and the passion from the start to finish. Watching him sing was like making love to him, truly. Every sin and seduction committed was brought to life by the motion of his body, whether he was singing or fucking. The caress of his lips and the fiery beast in his eyes were there for both.

I hated that every screaming woman was getting the same experience I got. His passions were raw and exposed for everyone to enjoy.

I blushed when he said goodnight and the girl next to me threw her underwear on the stage, screaming about wanting to suck his...

I turned and walked to the backstage entrance.

I held up the thing from my pocket. The bouncer opened the door for me.

The guys were all standing around, wiping off and getting drinks. A woman with long blonde hair, tight black pants and a red halter-top was rubbing Lochlan's arm. She squeezed and gushed, and he let her. I frowned as she hugged each of the other guys, but went back to Lochlan. She was excited about something. I watched as he gave her the one-sided smile and winked at her.

"Oh God," I muttered, backing up. He was that rock star boyfriend. I wrinkled my nose. I hated seeing him like that, touching other women.

I backed out into the hall. The bouncer gave me a weak smile, "Rock stars."

I winced when Gerry turned to see me watching. His eyes instantly flicked to the woman linking her arm into Lochlan's. She pressed her chest into his arm and planted a bright-red kiss on his cheek. He blushed, looking down.

Why had he done it, if he knew I was coming backstage? Did he want me to see it or had he just forgotten? Why was he letting fans touch him like that?

Gerry's mouth parted, like he wanted to say something but he didn't. He didn't even point out that I was there.

This was always going to be my reality. He wanted me to be the real world for him, and I wanted him to be the fantasy, but only for me.

Panic was filling me. I wanted to bail but I was stuck. I wanted to go back and be his flirty friend but I couldn't. I was going to lose him if I couldn't be with him. Seeing her maul him, I knew I couldn't. My back hit the wall, and my heart hit the ground and broke into a thousand pieces, scattering across the floor. I left it there, broken and destroyed, and turned to run from the bar. My feet burned from the run to the apartment, but I didn't slow down. I quickly packed my bags as fast as I could. I wanted to cry but my broken heart was still at the bar, sitting on the cold, black floor. The tears wouldn't come.

I dragged the bags down the stairs and up the road. It was brutal, carrying it all the way to Gerry's. It was a five-minute ride but an hour walk with the heavy bags.

I started to sniffle as I felt under the mailbox for the hide-away key I remembered from the Costco trip.

Self-pity started making attempts at my heartless chest but I shook my head, "You fucking watched him do it at Costco. Fucking fuck." I smacked myself in the forehead and opened the door, shoving my crap inside. I knew better than to let it be more than a friendship. Now I would lose him forever.

I slammed the door and collapsed on the floor on my knees. I bent forward on the tiles and sobbed. Eventually I lay down, pressing my face to the cold floor. Had he done anything really wrong or was it just too much? I'd been exposed to him and my pride was lost, not shamed but gone forever. He'd seen me spread wide open in every way possible, but it wasn't enough to make him act like he was mine. I closed my eyes and no matter how hard I tried to make the mental picture I'd taken of him in his underwear play in my head, all I got was the red kiss on his cheek. Another trashy blonde with bleached hair and a round ass.

Gerry found me there, passed out. He lifted me off the floor and helped me to the couch. I sobbed inaudible things into his soft dress shirt. He let me. We didn't need to talk. He knew.

After a while he spoke. "It isn't what you think it is," he whispered.

I shook my head, "It doesn't matter. It won't ever change, and I knew that. I knew what he was the minute I met him. He's charming and alive, in a way that most people aren't. I'm not. I know I'm not. There will always be some other girl pressing herself into him, and he has to let them in order to be the success he wants to be. I hate that it's me or his dream, and I'm honest-to-God wanting to ask him to pick. It's me that's ruining us, not him. I'm the problem. I can't do this. My first boyfriend cheated on me, and I swore I would never date another man whore again. 'Course that was in eleventh grade. I sort of assumed guys matured."

He lifted my chin and wiped my tears with a tissue, "Never assume guys mature. Erin, he loves you. I can see it. He would never cheat on you."

I shook my head, "It doesn't matter. I can't be comfortable with it. She kissed him and mauled him, and he sat there and took it. Even though he asked me to come to the backstage. He knew I was coming. He knew I would see that. He had to risk that."

He shook his head, "He got distracted. It's a major record deal.

My Side

She works for the record company. This is huge. Major. We'll be doing tours and playing the Grammys and concerts worldwide. It's what we wanted. This is our dream coming true. He got caught up in it."

I knew then that Gerry would never be on my side. I didn't want him there anyway. He was part of the band. He wanted to be on the ride with Lochlan, in more than one way. He wanted to sit at the cool kids table the way I had. Lochlan made him feel alive with the way he saw what he wanted and went after it. I'd liked it when the thing he wanted had been me. 'Course that was yesterday. I gave it to him, and like with every other girl, he was done. I almost slapped myself. Was that a fair thing to think about him? Was he really like that? Did I believe it or was I hurt-talking? I shook my petty, self-pitying head and smiled weakly at Gerry, "Congratulations. I'm sorry. I am happy for you, Ger." I had to be happy for Gerry. His dream had just come true. It was huge, and I was being whiny. Was it better that I saw the whininess or worse that I wasn't stopping myself?

He shook his head, "I can't be happy and see you like this."

I shrugged, "I just need a day. I'll be fine. I never let it go that far."

He gave me a dubious look. I smiled weakly, "Truly, I only let myself fall yesterday. I just didn't know how far the fall was with him."

He shook his head, "Take all the time you need. The spare room is ready for you. Danny slept there last night, but tonight he went home with some blonde."

I made a face, "You guys are so nasty. You'll fuck anything."

He scoffed, "That's bitterness talking and it's not attractive, Erin. And don't lump me in that group."

I gave him a cocky look, "Being gay doesn't make you less of a man in a band."

He stuck his tongue out at me. I walked down the hall to the bedroom. I didn't make it all the way when the pounding started.

"ERIN!" Lochlan screamed into the doorframe. His demons had him. He rattled the handle. Gerry answered the door, "Loch, you're going to get me evicted. Stop."

"ERIN!"

Gerry's soft tone changed, "Enough."

Lochlan sounded desperate, "Dude, just let me in."

"I don't think that's a good idea. She's upset."

I leaned my face against the wall and closed my eyes.

He sounded like he was about to switch and let the beast out completely, "Ger, man, don't get involved. Just let me see her. I just want to explain. I swear. I'm cool." He sounded like a junky.

Gerry softened, "Come back tomorrow when you're cooled off for real. Okay?"

He raged, "NO!"

I jumped at the fury in his voice and quickly walked around the corner before he hurt Gerry and then hated himself for it. His look was dark and crazed. His anger melted when he saw me, "It's not what you think. The bouncer told me what you saw. It's not what you think."

I nodded, "I know."

He swallowed, like he was trying to understand, "What do you mean?"

I blinked the tears out of my eyes, so I could see again, "I know. Congratulations on the deal."

He looked flabbergasted, "Who fucking cares about it? I want to explain to you. Don't leave."

I crossed my arms, "Go home, Loch."

He grabbed my bags off the floor and gave me his black stare, "You come home, or I won't be responsible for the things I do. I'll end up trashing the fucking place and then we're both homeless.

Jesus." He walked out with my stuff. Gerry gave me a look. It was exactly what he'd talked about. Lochlan was so close to his goal, and he would shoot himself in the foot again.

I followed him but stopped beside Gerry, "I'm sorry I brought this here."

He shook his head, "I don't know if you should go."

I gave him a weak smile, "He won't hurt me. Not like that. Besides, it's better for the band if he calms down."

When I got on the street, he was there. He was holding my bags, "You can't do this and not talk to me. This is about me, too." The veins in his arms were jacked, like he'd just worked out. They made his tattoos more ominous.

I nodded, "I was just mad. I'm sorry." I felt myself shutting him off. I would help him calm down, but my heart was gone. He didn't see it on the floor of the bar. He probably stepped on it and didn't realize.

He gave me a pleading look. I could see in the street light that the blue in his eyes was lightening again as his brow lifted. His anger was calming and the beast was leaving. "I would have stopped her, but she was in the middle of offering us a contract. I told you. It's part of the act."

"I get it."

He looked torn, "I see you not getting it. This isn't fair, Erin. You need to give me a fucking break here. I just won the God-damned lottery for musicians. You're making this about you. You never see my side."

I shook my head as the pain started to surface, "What if some guy came up to me and started grinding against me, rubbing his cock on me?"

He looked crazed instantly, "Did that happen? That fucking bar is a pit. I don't want you coming there anymore. We won't be playing the bars much longer anyway."

My Side

I shook my head, taking patient breaths, "Hypothetically." My tone was showing the signs of my anger.

"Hypothetically, I'd break his arms and then mace him with your little friend there." He said it so matter of fact that I had to shake my head at him.

I pointed at him, "You winked and gave her the smile you always give me. You let her press her tits all over you and kiss you. So should I go mace her?"

He sighed, "You drive me insane. I told you—it's the act. Why can't you be happy for me instead of jealous and insecure?"

I lost it. The snapping sound in my brain was so loud, I figured he must have heard it too. I was breathing like fire would come out of my mouth any second, "Fine. I was thinking about getting a job. I'll apply to Hooters and a few strip joints and we'll see how you feel when I give strangers lap dances." It was petty and only making him worse, but I was angry. I couldn't stop myself. He'd called me out on my being insecure.

He laughed, dropping the bags. He took a huge step towards me, cupping my face in his hands, "Look into my eyes, princess. There's no one there but you. You're jealous of yourself. There's no one else in my eyes." He pressed his lips against mine, but all it did was seal the fate of our day-old relationship. The kiss felt like a goodbye. He felt it too. He tried to force it to be something it wasn't.

"It can't work, Loch," I whispered into his lips.

He stepped back, "Just don't leave. I won't touch you. Please, just don't leave."

I nodded, "Okay." It was like winning the lottery. He wanted to be friends again… maybe. Maybe we would just torture each other. Either way, I didn't want to be the reason he blew the whole record deal for everyone else. He was gripping to me because of the stress of everything in his life. He was so close to success, and the last time he blew, it was with a moment just like this one. I nodded against him, "I won't leave." Even if he had called me jealous and insecure. I had no argument for that. The proof was there.

We walked to his car. He threw everything in the back seat and drove with no words. When we got back to the apartment, I covered my mouth, looking at the mess he'd already made.

He stood beside me, overshadowing me and spoke flatly, "I panicked. I thought that guy from North Dakota came for you. I thought I'd left you vulnerable and you wouldn't answer your phone. So yeah, I got mad," he muttered. "I went back to the club to find out who had seen you last. Jimmy, the bouncer, told me what happened."

My insides burned, looking at the mess everywhere. "I'm so sorry."

He shook his head, "I'm sorry. I shouldn't have said all that shit to you. I'm making you insecure." He carried my stuff to the bedroom and walked back out as I closed the front door and locked it. He looked rough, "I'll quit."

I laughed on the verge of tears, "Quit what? Quit being you?"

He shook his head and knelt in front of me. I was only slightly taller than him with him on his knees, "Quit the band."

I ran my hand down his cheek, "You can't quit being you. That's you up there on the stage, winking at the ladies and having fun. You're alive up there. It's me that's taking something amazing and rare and ruining it. It's like dating a God. I'm bringing you down to my level, with my problems and flaws, and ruining you."

He ignored me as usual and changed the subject, "Can we give it time?"

I sighed, "Loch, we had sex and we live together. Time for what? We fucked up, just like I said we would."

His eyes glistened, "Slow it down. Take it back to the flirty place we were yesterday."

I shook my head, "No."

"Can we be friends?"

I kissed his forehead, "Of course."

"Same deal as before?"

"Yup."

He looked a bit relieved. He took a breath, "I want to take it all back. I want to take it back."

I sighed, "Me too."

Chapter Nine
Cold feet

Classes dragged on. I always wanted to text him. Even worse, I wanted him to text me, but he'd done the friendship thing perfectly. He hadn't overstepped his boundaries once. He was worse than before.

We laughed and joked, and he ordered and plated my food. It was blissfully normal in the fakest way imaginable, and I seemed like the only one who saw how awkward it was.

All I could do was wonder if he was fucking other girls when he wasn't at home, or if the reason he didn't meet my eyes with his was guilt. He signed boobs and kissed cheeks whenever we left the house. He posed for pictures. I got to the point that I never left the house, except for class and groceries.

He acted like it was normal that all we did was hang out in the apartment, watching entire series on Netflix.

I knew it wasn't.

I left class and headed for the Starbucks near the house. Gerry was meeting me. He was worried about me. I was too. I wasn't any happier with him being Lochlan Barlow and single than I was when he was my Loch.

I walked, noticing the bite in the air. The end of October was cold compared to the muggy warmth of September. I wrapped my sweater around me tighter and walked quickly.

"Erin!"

I looked back to see one of my professors. I waved, "Hey, Dean." He insisted we called him by his first name. He was the cool teacher.

He jogged over, smiling. He was good looking and only about thirty-five, at the most, so he was the typical hot prof.

"I meant to talk to you about the civil rights paper you handed in." He breathed heavily as he reached me. His charming smile faded into a serious look. He cocked a dark eyebrow and ran his hand through his short chestnut hair, "It wasn't your best work."

I winced, "Sorry." I didn't have time to worry about it; my torts homework was also due.

He shook his head and pulled it from his briefcase, "Here, I'm giving you a second chance."

I gave him a confused look, "What?"

He nodded and started walking the way I was going, "Yeah. I know you're good for at least an A, if not an A plus. This was shit. I gave you a C."

I laughed, giving him a wounded look, "Don't sugarcoat it."

He shook his head, "Hey, you're not an undergrad. I'm not going to babysit you."

I looked down, "I know."

He gave me a sideways look, "I heard Lochlan Barlow broke up with you. I sort of assumed that it was directly related."

I gasped, "What?"

He blushed, "Sorry. I'm not trying to pry."

"Where did you hear that?"

He pressed his lips together, "A blog that follows the band. They said that he was seen with other girls and that you weren't in the picture anymore." I almost threw up.

I got control of my near gagging and frowned, "They knew my name?" He nodded, giving me a grim look.

I sighed, "You're a fan?"

He laughed, "I'm not that old."

"My dad's a fan and he's nearly sixty; it isn't about age."

Dean shrugged, "He's an amazing singer. The drummer is very skilled. They're just one of those honest bands that has natural talent. I saw them live in the bars a few times and it was life changing. Very raw and moving. They love what they do."

My throat burned.

He hit my arm, "Forgive me. I'm sure it hurts to talk about it."

I nodded, "Something like that." I let it be that Lochlan broke up with me. I let that be the truth, because what did it matter for my career?

"Where are you headed?"

I pointed up the street, "Starbucks."

He smiled, "Me too. I'll walk with you."

A smile crossed my lips, "Okay."

"So did you watch the footage last night on the case going on in Los Angeles with the mom who murdered her kids?"

I nodded, "Yeah. They're really trying for that insanity plea."

He scoffed, "She isn't insane. She's selfish. You can see people's sins in their eyes. Watch hers; they don't dart like a crazy woman's would. She's sane. She has remorse and demons in there now. Guilt is impossible to hide in the eyes. If you choose defense as your career, you have to make sure you inspect the eyes of every potential client. They say that eyes are the window to the soul, and when it comes to passionate emotions like hate, love, guilt, and sorrow, that's true."

I knew that to be true. I'd seen the demons release the beast in

Lochlan. His demons swirled in his eyes.

Dean got the door for me. He walked to the counter, "What should I get you?"

I shook my head, "You don't have to buy my coffee."

He smiled, "Of course, I do. I just bored you to tears with my eye speech. Now tell me, so I don't order the wrong thing."

My chest burned instantly. Lochlan always ordered for me against my will. I opened my mouth to say caramel macchiato, but all that was there was, "Soy vanilla latte, please." It was the drink Lochlan always got us both—regardless of the fact that I didn't like soy milk much. I got us a table and sat down. I made sure I got one with a few chairs. I knew Gerry would be there any minute.

Dean carried over my drink and sat down. He took off his sweater, and I noticed how attractive he really was. His body was tight and fit. He was tanned and athletic looking. I smiled and imagined what it would be like to date someone like him. He was my kind of perfect.

"So did I tell the class the joke my grandmother emailed me this morning?" He sipped from his drink.

I shook my head, lifting my cup to sip.

He laughed before he told the joke, making me laugh. It made the sexy mature man seem cute and adorable.

He calmed himself, "Okay, why do male attorneys usually wear tight shirt collars and ties?" He snickered. I shrugged. He fought his laugh, "It keeps their foreskins from creeping up and covering their faces."

I laughed out loud. Hearing him say foreskins was weird.

Dean was almost crying.

"Your grandma?" I asked.

He nodded, wiping the tears in his eyes. He sighed, "She's a crazy old bitch."

I laughed harder but Dean stopped. He looked up, red-faced instantly. I turned to see Lochlan hovering above me with a savage look in his eyes. I smiled, "Hi."

His eyes never left mine. I hadn't seen this face since we'd left Gerry's that night. It made me nervous to see the beast so close to the surface in a coffee shop. I pointed, "This is my professor, Dean Hamilton. Dean this is my friend, Lochlan Barlow."

Dean stood, putting a hand out. He looked like he might cry.

Lochlan didn't take his eyes off of me. I looked behind him to Gerry at the till. He grabbed the drinks and hurried over. I pointed to him, "And this is the drummer of Thin Ice, Gerry Ronson. Gerry, this is my professor, Dean Hamilton."

Gerry put the two coffees down and shook his hand quickly, "Lovely to meet you."

I grabbed Lochlan's hand and squeezed, "Can I talk to you outside?" I smiled at Dean and Gerry, "Excuse us."

Gerry nodded, understanding the awkwardness, and put a hand on Dean's arm, "So, a professor, huh?"

I dragged Lochlan out the door, pulling him to an alley. It was a quiet spot. It didn't matter where we went, he was Lochlan Barlow. People were taking our picture and watching us. I shoved him behind a dumpster and paced for a second.

When I looked at him, he looked frozen over but he spoke softly, containing his rage, "What was that? I thought we weren't dating other people."

I tilted my head, "You haven't kissed a single girl or fucked one stranger?"

His eyes twitched with the guilt Dean had been talking about. I nodded, "I figured as much." I was shaking inside but I remained calm on the outside, "That was my teacher. I have bent over backwards to ensure that you stay calm. I do everything I can to not make a scene for you and your reputation. You can't give me the same courtesy?"

He loomed over me, "Are you fucking him?"

An astonished look stormed across my face, "Are you hearing me?"

He stepped towards me, forcing me to back up. My back pressed against the brick building. He bent down low to me, "Are you fucking him?"

My lip trembled. I nodded out of spite and hatred of the way he made me feel, "Yup."

The switch was fast. His face went dark. His hands balled up. I shoved him back, like an idiot, and turned to walk away. He grabbed my arm, spinning me, "Why? Why him and not me? He's your teacher, for Christ's sake." He was shaking. He was homicidal. He wasn't fun to toy with. He was too crazy.

I sighed, seeing the poor choice I was making, "He's gay, you idiot. I just said it to piss you off so you know how it feels to be jealous and insecure. I know what you've been at since... before... me and you. The funny part, though, is that now you know how it feels. Granted, he's gay so it's not like I'm going to get any, but at least you know how this feels. And that makes me petty and horrid and happy." I covered my face with my hands, shaking my head.

"I saw the way he looked at me when he met me. He looked nervous."

I flailed my arms, shouting for all the spectators, "YOU ASSHOLE, HE THINKS YOU'RE HOT! LIKE A SUPERSTAR! HE LIKES YOU, NOT ME! HE FOLLOWS THOSE STALKER BLOGS ABOUT YOU! HE WAS TELLING ME ABOUT WHAT'S ON THERE, SO FUCK YOU!"

My chest was rising and falling rapidly. I bit my lip and tried to get control of myself. I was a hot mess. He made me crazy and out of control. I looked at him with daggers and pointed at the café, "I guarantee he's getting Gerry's digits right now. He's a huge fan." I covered my trembling mouth with my hands and took deep breaths into my palms.

His body wrapped around mine. I hated his touch. I shoved him off of me and stalked down the alley. A guy snapped a picture of my tear-stained face as I turned away from the coffee shop and walked home.

I was on the couch eating from the Ben and Jerry's tub when he got home.

Danny had mated for life with the blonde Gabby bitch and wasn't there to be a buffer for me. I knew we would be talking about it, no matter what. I was ready for him.

He looked adorable carrying my pretty, pink Coach school bag that I'd left at the coffee shop, but I didn't acknowledge him. He walked over to the couch to see what I'd done.

He dropped the bag on the couch, my side of the couch. He started to laugh, "Are you fucking kidding me?"

I ignored him until he took a step for me. I put my hand out, "This is my side. You stay on your side. All your shit is there anyway." And it was. His jeans and pop cans and water bottles and food wrappers were all shoved to one side of the room. My side was immaculate. The divider was a thick, black line painted onto the wall and floor. Duct tape made the line on the couch.

He stared me down, "You're making me crazy. I was a fun guy before I met you. I rarely lost my tempter or worried what girls thought or did. I had sex, I drank, I sang, and I liked my life. You are killing me and making me insane. I'm doing things my anger management coach would have a heart attack about."

I shrugged, "Then I guess we'll be nuts together. No one is getting out of this fucking apartment sane." I didn't care. Not anymore. He'd fucked other chicks, I knew it. I could practically smell them on him.

He crossed the line. I jumped off the couch, holding my mace at him, "I told you I won't leave. I'll stay here like your fucking prisoner, but you stay on your God-damned side. Your stuff is on that side of the room and mine is on this one."

He stepped into me, calling my bluff, "Mace me. I don't give a shit. The only fucking thing I care about in this God-damned room is on your side."

He sat on the couch and pulled me down with him and sat me on his lap. I struggled, but he just held me and whispered, "I'm sorry."

I shook my head, "I don't care. I don't fucking care."

"I apologized to him. Dean seems really cool. I'm sorry. I saw him looking all professional and clean cut, like you. And you were laughing so hard, and I assumed the worst. He deserves someone like you. He's professional and smart and I'm not."

I looked at him, "I know you have your MBA, so don't play dumb Little Drummer Boy with me. Besides, you've been fucking other people, so you can't care if I have coffee with my teacher. I'll do what I want and who I want."

His eyes flickered again, "Firstly, I will give you points for being witty, but I'm the singer not the drummer. Secondly, I haven't had sex since you and me."

I saw myself in his eyes and my heart believed him. I freed one of my arms and scoffed, "I see the guilt."

He sighed, "I was drunk and a girl kissed me. I stopped it. I'm sorry. Someone posted it to a blog, and I assumed you saw it. I felt like shit." He looked down.

I lifted his face, staring into his eyes with burning hate, "You said you wanted me. If you wanted me, you wouldn't kiss other people."

His eyes stayed true and strong, "I want you. I'll always want you." I looked at my face in the darkness of his pupils and swallowed the venomous things I wanted to say. His eyebrows pulled together, "I am fucking trying, princess. I am, I swear. I've been trying so hard to show you… to deserve you. I swear it." He closed his eyes and leaned his forehead against mine, "Do you really feel like a prisoner?"

I shook my head, "No. Sometimes it's a little bit like Beauty and the Beast with you though. You get so crazy, and I don't know what to do."

He looked up and gave me his smug smile. I pointed a finger in his face, "You call me the beast and you're dead."

He laughed hard, pulling me into him. He smelled my hair. I did the same on his neck. We snuggled for a minute, but I couldn't take it. I pressed play for my show. I needed there to be someone else in the room.

He took the carton from my hand and we snuggled on the couch, watching Downton Abbey while he ate the rest of my ice cream. "This show is insane," he muttered, taking a huge bite.

I pointed at the screen, "You missed some hot stuff about ten minutes before you got home. Little bit of back-door romance."

He gave me a look, "Anal sex? They show that on the BBC?"

I laughed, "No, like clandestine love affairs. Like sneaking around."

I laughed harder when he took a bite and shrugged, "Whatever. In the South, backdoor means taking it in ass."

I plugged my ears, "Ewwwww."

He grinned and sparkled, and became the guy I couldn't resist, even if he was saying dirty shit.

We fell back into the comfortable relationship we liked. I wouldn't let him remove the paint or the tape, even if he refused to stay on his side. Against all the odds, we became the people we were before. The ones who lived together without sex and drama. He was texting me more. It made me happy, too happy. We were headed down the same flirty road as before. I knew the sex was inevitable. He was being sweet and staying in the apartment with me.

The only saving grace was that he was traveling a lot with the band. They had left for Detroit the day before for a concert. It was his first televised concert since the show he had gotten kicked off of. I looked at my phone to see if he'd messaged me or not. The girl in the chair next to me nudged me, "You and Lochlan Barlow still dating?"

I gave her a confused look, "No."

She leaned over to another girl and whispered my answer. I looked at the girl and smiled. It was Lise from the bar. She gave me a wave. I smiled at her. How had I not noticed her in my class?

My head was up my ass for sure.

After class we walked out together, "So, no more bad-boy singers, huh?"

I shook my head, "No. We shouldn't have ever crossed the roommate boundaries. It was stupid." I didn't mention, we were currently about to take the same crash course as before.

She winced, "Yikes."

"Whatever, so have you been in this class the entire time?" How had I not seen her?

She laughed, "No. I switched out of the one on Fridays. It's the same class and I begged and pleaded so they let me. I had to get a job and I work Fridays, Saturdays, and Sundays now."

"Awesome, where?"

She gleamed, "The bar where Thin Ice plays on Fridays. I can make five hundred in tips those three days."

My jaw dropped, "No way."

She nodded, "You want a job? I know Brian is looking."

I nodded, "Hell, yeah. I don't have anything after eleven on Fridays, I'm free from lunch on."

She pulled her cell out, "Call this number, ask for Brian, and tell him you're my friend."

I looked at the number and punched it into my phone, "Thanks, Lise."

She shrugged, "Us hot law majors gotta stick together. The rest of them look like trolls."

I laughed with her, but hated that she included me in her mean-girl mentality.

Brian was stoked that I was able to start Friday. He actually used that word.

I sat on the couch, doing homework and watching another episode of Downton Abbey when Danny came in. He gave me a look, "You're not watching the performance?"

I looked at the clock and shrugged, "It's recording." I had been avoiding it. He did bad things to my self-control without the singing. Adding it was like putting gas on a fire.

He grabbed the remote and changed it to the show. It was obviously cool in the streets where the stage was. I could see Gerry's breath when the cameras went to him.

My skin shivered, hearing Lochlan's voice. When the camera landed on him, my heart skipped a few beats. I couldn't breathe. He was rocking it, as always. He held the microphone in his left hand and hopped with his right hand in the air. He kicked with the drums and bent down towards the crowd. He pointed at someone up front, winking and grinning.

I felt sick but I couldn't look away. He was my own personal train wreck.

He finished the song and shouted into the microphone, "We want to thank y'all for having us. Big shout out to Boston and the amazing folks there for helping us get to where we are. And I personally want to shout out to North Dakota, the state that holds my heart! Goodnight, Detroit!"

The crowd erupted.

"He says that North Dakota thing every night now," Danny muttered.

I nodded, "Great."

Lochlan waved and walked off the stage. The camera zoomed in on him. The broadcasters were talking, but I just watched as he pulled his phone out.

'*You having a good night?*' I instantly, got the text I watched him send.

I smiled when I saw it.

'*Yup!*'

A different band walked onto the stage and the crowd started back up again.

'*I have some good news!*'

I smiled, '*What?*'

'*Gonna call. That cool?*'

'*Yup.*'

I answered on the first ring, "Hey."

He laughed, "I can hear the show in the phone—you're watching it?"

I took a deep breath, like hearing his voice made that possible.

"Erin?"

I opened my eyes, smiling, "Yep. You guys were amazing, as always."

It got quiet where he was suddenly, "We got invited to do a couple of the night shows in New York City in November, just before Thanksgiving."

My jaw dropped, "Oh my God. Congratulations."

"Thank you. Can I see you Friday night? Like we could hang out, like before? Maybe go to dinner?"

I ran my hands through my hair, "I can't. I have to work."

His voice sounded panicked, "You got a job?"

"Yeah. My friend Lise got me one at that bar you guys always play on Fridays. I start there this Friday."

He didn't talk. I pulled the phone from my face, checking for signal. "Hello?"

He sounded pissed, "You can't work there. Brian is a pig and tries to sleep with every chick that works there. He's famous for his job interview."

I scowled, "I already have the job. I don't need an interview. And you work there, don't you? What do you care?"

His tone didn't improve, "You can't work there."

I sighed, "Okay, well, we can talk about it when you get home on Friday." I hated that I was the on thin ice with him for the sake of Thin Ice. If I rocked the boat, he'd trash a hotel room or beat someone up. God only knew.

"I'll be home tonight."

I sighed, "You have shit to do. Stop being a pain in the ass. How's this? I won't work a shift until you speak to Brian and assure him I am to be left to work and not hit on."

He paused again. "Deal."

Another deal.

"I am looking out for you."

I licked my lips, "I know." I knew he thought he was, but it felt more like being controlled, and I didn't want any of that.

"I miss you, princess."

I nodded, even though he couldn't see me, "I know. I miss you too, beast."

He laughed but it was bitter and sad, "I want to take it back. I want it to be like it was."

I sighed, "I know. Me too." Guess I wasn't the only one noticing the awkwardness.

I heard a bunch of people in the background yelling at him. He closed a door and whispered, "Do you think it feels like we can't go back because we're supposed to go forward? Not like move on, but be with each other?"

I wanted to shout yes, but I held my breath until I could keep it calm; it was my heart on the line, not his. "No. I think if we ever went forward, it would be under a different situation. Right now, I'm pretty sure my GPA is taking a hard hit and you have to focus on the band. They need you and you need them."

He sighed, "I know. It's not good for business to have a mopey lead singer. I know how this works."

"Is Gerry hounding you?"

He was silent for a minute, "Did you talk about me to Gerry? About how I would let the band down?"

I didn't want to say no, because that wasn't entirely true and I would never lie. "I've never told anyone you would let the band down. I don't believe that's a possibility. You're a hard worker and a star. I believe in you."

"You do?" he sounded surprised.

Tears filled my eyes and I didn't even know why, "Yeah. Of course, I do."

"I gotta go."

I was about to say bye when I heard the phone beep, like I'd lost the call. I stared at the blank phone and then went to bed. Sleep was better than constantly thinking about him. But my sleep betrayed me. I dreamt about him.

I was mid-dream when something cold was touching me, waking me up. I spun, almost leaping out of bed for my mace, but I realized it was Lochlan. His cologne and smell was in the air around me.

"What are you doing? Are you really here?"

He gave me a kiss on the cheek, "If this isn't okay, I'll go sleep with Danny in my bed."

I pointed at the door, "It's not okay."

He brushed his lips against mine, every so slightly touching his tongue to my top lip, "You'll get over it."

I laughed, "Why are you home?" He always ignored the parts he didn't want to hear.

He rolled me on my side, facing away from him and spooned me. "I told you I would see you tonight."

He kissed my neck and pulled me into him so hard, I was sure we would become one person.

"What's changed?" I asked into the silent dark.

"I can't live without you. I won't. I'm yours, body and soul, and I'm done pretending we can be friends."

I blink a tear down my cheek, "Fair enough."

He took a deep breath of air from my neck, "Last night I had this dream. I was on stage, and I had a horrid feeling that you weren't watching me sing. I woke up and the hotel room smelled... like sterile or something." He took another long sniff of my hair, "I realized that it doesn't feel like I'm inhaling all the way, unless you're part of the air I'm breathing."

I turned to face him, pressing my tear-stained face against his. My tears mixed with our kiss but I didn't ever care. "I just want you," I whispered.

He dragged my shorts down and then his. I pulled my tank top off. My warmth and his cold mixed, like my tears and our kiss. We slid against each other, caressing, but I was impatient. I climbed under him, forcing him between my legs. He kissed my throat as he pushed himself into me.

"You're already wet."

I nodded, "I was dreaming about you when you woke me up." He pushed into me hard, forcing a gasp from my lips. He filled me up, his light, his craziness, his body, everything. Even his demons made me feel whole, like they needed me. I wrapped my legs around his waist and let him make me feel complete. The touching and thrusting was slow and methodical. Every movement served a purpose.

"I love you, princess, with my whole heart," he murmured into my ear as he bit my lobe.

I gripped his shoulders, pulling him onto me… into me farther, "Bite it harder."

He moaned into my nape, "Why?" his words were breathy as his body thrust in and out of me.

I clung to him, "I want to make sure I'm awake. I think I'm still dreaming." He had not just said that he loved me. I ignored the words and let everything be the dream I'd been having.

I felt him shake his head, "If it's a dream, I don't want to wake up either." I agreed silently. I wanted the 'us' that was okay in the apartment. I wanted the fantasy. The reality was that I would screw it up again.

Chapter Ten
Unspectacularly wrong

I woke to the smell of bacon. I smiled and climbed out of bed. His sweats and tee shirt were on the floor. I pulled them on and stumbled out of the room. My stomach was still in knots. I didn't know what it meant, what we were. It felt too big to try to sort out. He'd said he loved me. I didn't want to think about that. I liked that he'd flown home to see me. That was all I was going to focus on, that and the bacon.

But it was Danny frying the bacon when I got to the kitchen. He gave me a grin, "Someone went a little nutty with the cleaning this morning."

I glanced at Lochlan cleaning the paint off the floor. He looked pissed. I rushed over, "I said no, it stays."

He laughed bitterly, ignoring me, "Princess, remind me never to piss you off again. Seriously, this is some crazy, repressed anger. If you got it out more like I do, with daily flip outs, you wouldn't go so crazy."

I gave him a look and turned back to the kitchen, "Fine, clean it up, ass. Your daily flip outs aren't any better, trust me." I sat at the barstool and picked a piece of bacon off the plate, where it was sitting on paper towel.

He chuckled behind me, "At least when you do lose it, it's a respectable effort."

I snorted and chewed my bacon.

Danny gave me a look, "Dad called."

I frowned, "Okay."

"He wants us both home for Thanksgiving or they're coming here, together."

I shuddered, "Yikes." Our parents together were a nightmare of epic proportions. I sighed and drummed my greasy fingers on the counter, "So home for Thanksgiving and Christmas?" I wasn't sure I could do it. I hated flying, and I didn't like it when they did the holidays as a family. It was awful. Two flights in two months would definitely be overdoing it for me.

He cocked an eyebrow, "You bringing him to meet the folks?" He grinned like he knew it would be a disaster.

I glanced back at Lochlan picking the duct tape off the couch, and smiled when he cussed and picked at tape bits. His eyes darted to mine. I shook my head, "I don't think so." Lochlan pointed at me, "Me and you aren't done with the conversation that needs to happen about all this shit."

I sneered and looked back at Danny, "He's crazy. Bringing him home is going to be a disaster. No."

Danny shrugged, "Too bad. I already asked him."

I closed my eyes, as if holding them shut would hold back my annoyance, "You did what?"

He laughed, speaking loudly and winking at Lochlan, "Yup. He's already booked the flights. He's going to New York for the Tuesday and Wednesday before, and then meeting us in Grand Forks on Wednesday night. He booked our flights, too."

I swallowed hard, glancing back at Lochlan, "You sure you want to come for Thanksgiving? You have so much going on that week."

He frowned, "You don't want me to?"

I shrugged, "It's kind of a big deal, meeting someone's family. Thanksgiving is a gong show at our house. I just think that you and me need to go slower than that." Like never leave the apartment.

He looked hurt, "How is it you can say shit like that, and I'm the asshole in this relationship?"

I didn't even like hearing him say relationship. It felt too big, too soon. I sighed and looked back at Danny with the death stare. He pointed at me, "Keep your shirt on, Er. He has a point. He's sweet to you, and you're always an asshole to him."

"Thank you, Danny," he shouted from the paint stain.

I got up from the bar and walked back to my bedroom. We had gone from separate sides to snuggling and sex, and now he was coming for Thanksgiving. I wanted that, this. I wanted it, right?

The door opened and he leaned against the frame of the door, "If you don't want me to come, I won't."

I thought for a second, "I don't want you to come. I want to see where we are before we add other people."

He shrugged, "I'm coming."

I rubbed my face, laughing, "Why are you so difficult?"

He knelt at the edge of the bed, "You want me. You want to be with me, but it's like you only want it here, in the apartment. Why?"

I held my hands over my face, "I'm scared of you out there." I pulled my hands away and looked at him, "I'm scared to watch you be that guy. I don't want to share him with the world. I just want him to be mine." His face was stoic so I continued, "I know it's a selfish shit thing to say, but when I was a little girl and I was daydreaming about the life I would have, this wasn't it. Some girls dream about famous guys and fancy things. I dreamt about my own condo in Manhattan, fancy shoes and things I bought myself, a successful career as a lawyer at a firm in New York, and a BMW. I always wanted a BMW."

His look darkened, "I'll buy you a fucking BMW tomorrow. But you can't choose how things are going to work out. You have to roll with the punches and try to take life in stride."

I cocked an eyebrow, "Says the guy who beat the shit out of the competition who was winning on the show, and got kicked off for it."

The demons won the battle of dark and light in his eyes. He leaned into me, "You don't know shit." He got up and left. I bit my lip, panicking and unsure of what to say or do. I'd pushed him too far. The slamming of the front door made my eyes widen.

"Shit." I grabbed my phone and dialed Gerry.

"Hey, girlie."

I shouted into the phone, "I PISSED HIM OFF—BAD. HE JUST LEFT."

He sighed, "God dammit. Erin, we're two weeks from the fucking Late Night and After Hours shows. Two weeks."

I got up from the bed and slipped on my flip-flops and grabbed my wallet, "I'm not his fucking babysitter. I'm his... I'm a..."

"Just stop fucking with him. Jesus Christ. You're his girlfriend or you're gone. That's it. It's you making him bat-shit crazy. He used to be normal."

I screamed into the phone, "FUCK YOU, GERRY! IT'S MORE COMPLEX THAN THAT!" I hung up the phone and ran from the apartment. His car was gone. I ran as fast as I could, until I saw a cab. I flagged him and climbed in when he stopped. I heaved, "Dirty, trucker-stop restaurants." I gulped air.

He gave me a confused look. I pointed, "The greasy-spoon truck stops in the industrial parks. Now, please."

He gave me a crazy look. We dove for an hour, hitting them all. He was nowhere to be found and the trip cost me two hundred dollars. I didn't know where else to look for him. I drummed my fingers against the window as he left me back at my place.

"Thanks, Jim," I said and climbed out.

He waved, "Good luck, Erin. I hope you find him." I closed the door and stepped up to the door of the house.

Jim shouted through the open window, "Did you consider checking

My Side

the buzz website? They track celebrity sightings. I seen there was something about that girl from Star Wars, like a week ago. She was having coffee and they were taking pictures."

I tilted my head, "Duhhh, of course." I ripped my phone out and Googled. I clicked on a site and instantly my stomach dropped as I saw the photos. There were hundreds of sightings. Lochlan kissing girls, signing body parts, getting group shots, and being goofy with hoards of girls. I lowered my phone, "Nope. Thanks anyway." I didn't want to find him. I dialed the number I hadn't dialed in ages.

"T&N, Tom here."

I put the key into the door and walked inside, "Hey, Tom. It's Erin Benson. I'm wondering if anything ever came up."

"Hey, Erin. Yeah, but Lochlan called and canceled the hunt. He even gave me five grand to not answer your emails even if you begged for an apartment." How did he have so much money? Why didn't he buy nicer clothes, instead of bribing landlords?

"Yeah, well he's insane." I nodded as I climbed the stairs, "I need one. Just a one bedroom, furnished. I don't care where. I'd like closer to the school, but I'd take anything."

"I promised him, I wouldn't. I'm sorry, Erin."

"Yup." My strong yup was back. I hung up and walked into the apartment. I went directly to my room. I didn't care about any of it. I turned the lock and lay down with my books. I needed to study. I needed to succeed in my career, the same way he did.

I looked at my watch and grunted, "Shit." I had a class. I ran with my books, just barely making it. We had a guest speaker. A lady with shiny hair and a hard face. Dean watched me from the side of the room as she spoke, "Good afternoon. My name is Donna King. I work for the district attorney's office. I have been a prosecutor for fifteen years." She took a sip of her water, "Much like many of you, I always wanted this. I find lawyers are like doctors; they wanted it from an early age and never looked back. The time management, dedication, overtime, and workaholic tendencies are much the same in both groups." She walked over to a board, "Statistically speaking, we work longer and harder hours than surgeons. We dedicate ourselves to the job, to the point that most of us never marry or have kids." Her eyes flicked to Dean. He smiled brightly. The class laughed but there was a tension in all of us. She was bringing up the flaw in the job that would become the flaw in us.

"I won't ever have kids, but I look at the kids I've saved from the streets or domestic violence, and I see that as an important role. Could I have kids and do this job? Absolutely, but it takes a special kind of partner. You need to be supported by a person with regular hours and an understanding heart."

She lost me there. Everything I was feeling and thinking got worse. The thick black line on the floor was still there in my mind. On one side, it would be about me and on the other, it would be about him.

I sat and spaced out until she finished. I clapped along with everyone else but I was sick. I fled the classroom before Dean could corner me. Gerry had, no doubt, told him of the bad thing I'd done.

I walked home slowly to do my homework.

Of course, I ended up looking up more sightings. Just putting his name into the Internet yielded a million responses. Him shopping with Danny at the mall. Him drinking a soda with a dark-haired girl, giving her a smile I would sell my soul for. There wasn't a single picture where he was doing anything wrong. Everything he was doing was normal, celebrity shit. It was me. He wasn't the problem. He was just chasing his dream, and I was willing to crush it to make him mine. I hated the person I was becoming with him.

There was something wrong with me. I was becoming something like my ex-stalker with Lochlan. I understood Mitch's need to control me and have me be with him. It was an addiction. I had used Lochlan's love and guilt as a weapon. I'd manipulated him. I didn't recognize myself. I packed my bags. I needed to get away before he got home, hating himself for whatever he'd done when he was angry.

I packed everything and slipped out the door to the living room. Danny was gone too. I dragged my bags out the door and down the hall. I didn't ever know where I was going. The closest hotel was the Sheraton. It was going to have to be my new house for a couple days until I could find something else.

I flagged a cab and jumped in as he loaded my bags. He drove fast, maybe sensing the crazy inside of me. I paid him and dragged my bags to the door.

The bellhop grabbed my stuff and carried it inside. I got my room and followed my bags to the elevator. It was like every step I took, little pieces of me dropped off onto the shiny floor. By the time I got into the elevator, I was completely numb and totally hollow.

I was making a mistake. I knew that. I was taking the wrong turn at the fork in the road. I was choosing the unspectacular and protecting my heart. I would regret it for the rest of my life. I knew that. The problem with picking the safe road was that your mind instantly wanted you to see all the things you'd missed on the other road.

His smile flashed in my mind as I held myself and fell asleep, telling myself I was doing it for him, when really I was picking me. Unspectacular me.

Chapter Eleven
Good Night North Dakota

I had everything mapped out for the project. I nodded when I saw how I had reasoned it all. I was back on top. My torts were done. My project was completed. I had my debate on swamplands polished and memorized.

Granted, I had to turn off my phone, forbid any calls to come through to my room, ignore my own brother, and not watch any sort of media to do it. I sat back and smiled, crossing my arms over the robe and sighed. It was a blissful sort of peace being away from him.

The pounding on the door took all of that away.

"Erin, it's Gerry. Hurry up." I looked at my project and then at the door. The panic in his voice claimed me. I ran for the door, opening it.

He looked rough, "You're okay?"

I nodded, confused and scared, "Is he?"

He nodded, "Yeah. God bless your brother. He took him home to North Dakota. We canceled the shows for the week."

My jaw dropped, "He did what?"

He nodded, "He is a saint. I fucking swear it." He came in and closed the door.

I swallowed, "Oh my God. He took him home?"

Gerry scowled, "Be grateful. He was a wreck. He was so mad at you I thought he was going to destroy the house. He came to my place. I think he expected you to come there. Anyway, Danny came and was wonderful. He's an amazing guy. Half our success is Danny. He keeps Lochlan cool and makes it about the music, ya know?"

I shook my head, "What are you talking about?"

He ate some of the chocolate from the wrapper on the counter, "I'm talking about your brother? Have you been doing drugs or drinking?"

I covered my eyes with my hands, "My Lochlan is in my hometown?" I shook my head, "Lochlan, he's at my house?"

He laughed, "I have a flight booked for you to go see him, don't worry. I know *I'm* not bloody well missing it."

I crouched to the floor, hugging myself, "Oh my God. He's in Grand Forks, with Danny. Do you know what this means?"

He shook his head. I swallowed my stomach acids, "He's meeting my parents and winning them over, and when I break up with him, I'm going to be the monster. No one can be mad at Loch. No one." I slapped my forehead, "Oh fuck, Danny. You asshole."

I pulled off my robe and pulled on my clothes. Gerry blushed and turned around. I sneered, "Oh please, we're on the same team."

He snorted and started shoving my clothes into my bags.

"I have to turn in this project before we go."

His cheeks blushed a deeper red, "I can get Dean to pick it up from my place; he has a key. He might even still be there."

I laughed bitterly, "Of course he does. God, tell me he is as sexy under the clothes?"

He gave me a sly smile, "Girl, whew." He fanned himself. I nodded, "I knew it. I could tell."

He gushed, "He's so sweet, and he wears those professor sweaters with the elbow patches. Oh my God. He lifts weights and runs and plays tennis. He is so fit. His friends are amazing and fun. They're foodies, and they love wine and music. They think he's the lucky one. He does, too. He thinks he's lucky to be with me." He sounded so mystified, I loved it.

I nodded, "He is the lucky one."

His eyes glistened, "I'm so sorry for screaming at you."

I shook my head and leapt into his arms, "I needed it."

He hugged me, "You and Dean are the same. You're so clean cut and straight-laced, and you don't see how amazing you are."

"He can't live without you, Erin. He can't. No one can live the star life all the time. They need the other half." I wanted to choke him. I wanted my job to be as important, but we both knew the truth of it.

We raced from the room, to the car, and then to Gerry's to drop my stuff off. Dean was still there. The only time I wasn't having a stroke was when Dean kissed Gerry goodbye. My heart melted when he ran his hand along his jaw and pulled him in. He took my bags and my report, and gave me a wave.

Gerry got back into the car, giving me a sideways glance, "Shut up."

I gushed, "Oh my God, you guys are so cute."

He put a hand up, "I don't want to jinx this one, okay? So stop!."

I zipped my lips and beamed. He rolled his eyes.

When we got to the airport, we ran as fast as we could to catch our fight. Even the ride on the plane didn't stop me from obsessing. We hit turbulence, and I barely batted an eyelash at it. I didn't do my usual paper-bag thing or anything.

Nothing was going to get in the way of my desperate fears. One side was a broken heart, and the other was a barren wasteland where I lived, trapped because I never stayed with him. I never let him love me or gave him a chance.

We had barely landed and I was on my feet. I wanted to pull the emergency hatch and run down the tarmac.

We finally deplaned, which resulted in me running as fast as I could through the airport. Gerry was wheezing behind me when we got to the taxi stand. He paced with his hands on his hips, and finally after a second, he pointed, "Loch's right there. Whew… Erin, I'm naturally thin. I don't really do the whole running thing."

I ignored his sweaty sniveling. My eyes followed his pointed finger.

My Side

Lochlan was surrounded by a group of girls. He didn't see me. He hadn't made it into the airport to get me. He was swamped.

He passed the paper back to the girl jumping up and down and lifted his eyes. He stopped doing what he was doing and pushed his way through them. They followed, but he ignored them. He walked as fast as he could to me, scooping me up in his arms. "Sorry, I got held up."

I shook my head, "I don't want to do this here."

He grinned at me, "Stop making everything so hard." He kissed my cheek and put me down. He grabbed my hand and patted Gerry on the shoulder, "Hey man. Thanks for getting her to come here." My stomach sunk. I'd been played. Fuck, my brother I expected—but Gerry? I gave him an evil look, but he was swamped by screaming girls. He waded through them, finally making it to where we were. We ran to my dad's truck. Lochlan jumped in, locking the doors as we got in.

He grinned at me, "You okay?"

I frowned, "I don't know."

He laughed and patted my leg, "You'll get used to this." He drove off like a bat out of hell. I was squished between him and Gerry. Gerry gave me a grin. I shook my head, "I can't believe I just got played."

Lochlan laughed, "You were acting so crazy, so angry and weird. We figured this was better than you driving me insane, and me murdering someone for the sake of doing it. I figured you'd be better at home, more normal for us both."

I sighed, "I have classes, and I start work tomorrow."

He shook his head, "No, you don't. I phoned Brian and told him that if a single bar in Boston even thought about hiring you, we would break the contract."

My right eye twitched, "Are you insane? Did you seriously just make a decision for me, without asking me?" I shook my head, "You know I keep feeling bad for how crazy I've been, but it's not me. It's you. You're making me crazy. You think you were the only normal one before we met?"

He wrapped an arm around my shoulders. I froze until we got back to my parents'. I didn't want Gerry to be any more uncomfortable.

I looked at Loch as he turned onto the road to home. He knew the way to my dad's house?

Danny was out in the yard raking leaves. That, at least, warmed my heart. He waved at me, but I hopped out of the truck and went straight to the back of the house. Our dad kept the house from when we were kids. He worked as a lawyer in the city, but the commute never bothered him. He loved the feel of the country that the expensive golf course we lived on provided. We each had full-acre yards and fancy houses. Mom loved the cleanliness of the city. She liked tidy lines and pavement. When they divorced, she moved Downton into a condo. It was nice and clean. She ran a very successful real estate firm. Dad did all the legal work for it... still.

I went right for the swing set and sat on the big swing. Lochlan followed me. He went behind me and gave me a big push. He spoke just loud enough that the others couldn't hear from the front yard, "Everyone knows you're my girl. I can't have you out in the public, especially in a bar like that. I have to keep you safe from all that. I don't want you in the act with me. I want you to be the home I have in the real world."

My eyes started to water, "Loch, this started so normally and it's snowballed too fast. You're not the guy I thought you were. I didn't know you were about to skyrocket to fame when I met you."

"I was already there when you met me. I'm still the guy you love, Erin." He rarely said my name. He grabbed the swing, stopping me and walked around the front. He knelt in the leaves, "That's right. I know you love me. You don't say it, but I know it. I was singing and I watched you fall in love with me. The difference between you and the fans is that you know the person I am.

You've seen it all."

I gulped.

He shook his head, "Don't be scared. I won't ever be Lochlan Barlow with you. I'll just always be your Loch."

I couldn't see him clearly through the tears; I grabbed either side of his scruffy face. He kissed my palm, "I need you. I need you with me to be the success I want to be. You are the music for me."

My lip trembled, "I'm sorry I said that about the show and you getting kicked off."

His face came closer. He kissed my cheek, "Stop pushing me away. I'm not going anywhere. And stop running away."

I sniffled and nodded. He wrapped my legs around his waist and pulled me into his arms. He lifted me and carried me to the back of the house. He pinned me against the siding, "I love you."

I nodded, leaning in for the kiss. His lips didn't brush softly, like I expected them to. They laid claim. He kissed me like he was starving for it.

Dad called from the window above us as I was sliding my hands down the back of Loch's shirt, probably choking him but I didn't care. I wanted to touch his skin.

"Erin, get in this house."

I looked up smiling, "Hey, Daddy." He slammed he window shut.

Chapter Twelve
Cougar hunting

Mom scooped the fruit salad into bowls with the ice cream, "James, why do you insist on keeping these ugly bowls? Look at them. This one has a chip in it." She shook her head and passed out the dessert.

He gave her a grin, "One of the benefits of being divorced, Jane, is that I don't have to give a shit about those silly things. Hell, I might not even do the dishes tonight."

She gave him a look and sat with her dessert.

He beamed. I frowned, and Danny ignored it the best he could.

Mom gave Gerry a sly smile. "So Gerry, you're the drummer?" I almost threw up.

He smiled sweetly, "I am, Mrs. Benson."

She twirled her long, brown hair, "Jane, please. That must be quite the workout then, hmmm?"

Danny winked at him, "He has strong hands." Gerry blushed and tried to swallow his bite. Lochlan fought his laugh, pretending to be chewing, when I knew he was long done. No one chewed fruit and ice cream that long.

I needed it to end. I leaned forward to my mom, "Gerry's dating my professor."

She giggled like a fucking schoolgirl, "Oh, you like older women, Gerry?"

I gagged. Danny coughed on his fruit. Loch smacked him on the back, fully laughing, "Erin's prof is a man, Mrs. Benson."

Her face flushed, "Oh, wow. Good for you."

I cringed and gave Gerry a look. He laughed, "Thanks, he's quite the score, I will admit."

My dad gave me a quizzical look. I shook my head, "So, I guess we won't be coming for Thanksgiving since we're here this week."

Danny looked like he might cry, "Mom and Dad are coming to Boston." I could kill him. He started this. He had to bring Lochlan here to lure me from my hiding place. Fucking fuck. I took a deep breath, downed my entire glass of wine and looked at my father with desperation.

Dad lifted his eyebrows, "You know I love that city. And we really want to see Thin Ice live in a small and intimate setting, before they only play places like Madison Square Gardens and The Fargodome."

Gerry gave me a look, "Oh my God, I love Fargo. I knew your accent sounded familiar."

I sighed, "I don't have an accent."

He laughed, "Oh man, Fargo is in North Dakota?" He smacked his head, "Wait, what was that line they always said?" His eyes opened wide, "The heck do ya mean?" He looked like he might pounce on Danny, "Say it."

Danny snorted and did it perfectly, "The heckdoya mean?" He grinned and spooned the last of the ice cream into his mouth.

I covered my eyes. Dad instantly did it, "The heckdoya mean?"

I nodded and glanced at Lochlan. He smiled wide, "So many things explained in one meal." I swatted him. He caught my hand and kissed it.

My mom turned it on thick, seeing Dad and Danny getting attention, "Oh, jeez."

Gerry clapped and butt-hopped in his seat.

But they continued, "Ohhhhkayyyy."

I was dying. My face was burning my hands.

"Errrrin, don't be shyyyy. Doooo it for your friends. Ohhhh jeeeeez, don't be embarrassed."

"Yahhhhhh."

I got up from the table and walked to the kitchen with my bowl.

"Ohhhhh sure, leave the table."

I dumped it in the sink and leaned against the counter.

His warmth surrounded me, "It's funny."

I looked around to face Loch, "Not in Boston. Not when the press show up and want to interview them."

He nodded, "I'm getting the impression that you fussing about my meeting them at Thanksgiving had nothing to with me."

I swallowed and whispered, "I feel bad. They're my family, but it's a train wreck. She's hitting on younger men all the time, and he's trying to be the younger men."

He took my hands in his, "Princess, they live on a golf course. Tthey have fancy stuff and look very respectable. If I saw them on the street, I would assume they had a lot of money. This house is very expensive and impressive. Trust me, when you come meet my parents, you'll see some shit that you're not prepared for too. Yours are doing the whole mid-life thing…" His face darkened, "Mine are not."

My stomach burned. He wanted me to meet them. It was too soon. I couldn't even imagine what they would be like. He was so full of charisma. A whole house full of people who were amazing. I imagined them all playing instruments and having sing-alongs. I had to shut it down before I made it into something too big. I shut my brain down and nodded. I could do that. I could meet his family. I could do it all. It felt right to do it. I looked up and smiled, "Let's tell my parents no to Christmas and go see your family."

He gave me a stunned look, "Really?"

I nodded.

His face lit up. He cupped my face and kissed me until I was dizzy.

We all sat in the living room with Irish coffees when my mom left. Loch got his guitar and sang for us. It was like a private show. Gerry's foot never stopped keeping the beat, and eventually he grabbed a couple wooden spoons and drummed, using the mantle and a glass of water. It was awesome.

Dad seemed to really like them. He was in awe. I think his mid-life crisis made him want to be friends with them. Lochlan's voice was amazing and soft in such a small space. The gravelly sound was more present. I loved him. He finished the song, and I tried to see past the stars in my eyes. I was exhausted.

"I'm going to bed. You coming?" I ask, putting my cup in the kitchen.

He glanced at my father and shook his head, "No. I'll sleep in a guest room."

My dad's eyes opened wide, "Son, don't be crazy. We're liberals. I know you're committed to my daughter, and you already live together."

Lochlan chuckled and suddenly his Tennessee got so thick he sounded like an episode of Duck Dynasty. "Sir, I don't live with her like that; she won't agree to it. I won't disrespect your house that way." He looked at me, "Or your daughter."

I rolled my eyes, "Whatever. Night."

I climbed the stairs to my room. It was supposed to be the attic of the house, but when Daddy had it built, he made them convert it into a huge loft. It was all mine. Danny got the basement, and I got the attic. I looked around the room, smiling. My marching-band pictures were still on the mirror. I dragged a finger across the dust.

In the last five years, it slowly got dustier and less sparkly. Mom was clean and tidy, and slightly crazy with her OCD. Dad was busy. Busy meant frozen pizza, cleaning lady once a week, and TV as a companion. Grade twelve had been a hard year with them divorcing, but it had made things better. I couldn't deny it.

Mom relaxed, controlling the space she had, and Dad enjoyed sitting with his one hand tucked in his belt and a beer in the other. She wasn't nagging him and it pleased them both.

I pulled on pajamas and climbed into my bed. The cool air made me miss Boston. I liked our apartment. I liked it being the two of us, well, and Danny. But he was more of a pet.

I pulled the covers up, switched off my light, and closed my eyes. When I heard his footsteps, I smiled.

"You're a loser."

He made a sound I didn't recognize. I opened my eyes to see a glint of something in the moonlight. It shone bright—sparkled.

I frowned, "What's that?"

He whispered, "Be mine."

I closed my eyes, "What are you doing? Are you proposing? 'Cause I already told you how that makes me feel."

He climbed onto the bed next to me, "No. I would, but your ex-boyfriend already stole the thunder on the one-month proposal. This is my idea of a guarantee. I know you won't marry me, but wear this and be mine."

The ring was huge. I shook my head, "I can't accept something like that from you. Are those diamonds? Is this your first time having money?"

He laughed, "Sometimes you're such a bad person. They're white sapphire so you don't say something shitty, like I can't accept that from you, and is this your first time having money."

I laughed softly. I looked up at his face, "I am yours. I don't need jewelry to prove the point."

He flicked the light on and pulled the ring out of the Tiffany's box. He took my hand and slid it on my ring finger, but of my right hand. I looked at it and smiled. The band was a music note that wrapped around my finger. It was amazing and stunning. I looked up, "Okay." I did love white sapphires.

His blue eyes lit up. He lay beside me, not kissing me.

"Why won't you sleep with me?"

He looked over at me, "I don't like to do things my mom would be ashamed of."

I cocked an eyebrow, "Liar."

He made a condescending face, "I mean, the stuff I would actually tell her. I'm sure she has no desire to know about the random acts of…. anyway. If she ever asked me if I disrespected you…" He gave me a sincere look, "I don't lie to my mom. She's a saint."

I smiled and kissed his nose, "You're so weird." I was already touching the ring, rolling it back and forth. How did he know my size? How did he know I would say all of that? How did he know me so well? I thought about the things I would have guessed about him; there weren't many things I was sure of. Of course, I was predicable and he was chaotic, but that didn't help me. "I think you're being dramatic. We've had sex and neither of us is innocent in anything." I held my hand up, "And you gave me a ring."

He kissed my cheek, "I have a serious question to ask you."

I waited as a smile played with his lips.

"Is there seriously something called the Fargodome?"

I laughed and smacked him, "You suck. Stop with the Fargo hate. That movie won a lot of awards. It was well done, and yeah, so we talk funny if we relax our hold on the accent."

He rolled on his side, "Just say it. Say oh jeez, or yeah, or the heck do you mean, or okay. Say it."

I cocked an eyebrow, "What's in it for me?"

His look melted my heart, "I gave you my heart, a ring, my loyalty, and I think you even have my soul. What more do you want?"

I licked my lips.

He nodded, "Fine. I'll make it worth your while."

Thinking about it for a second, I nodded and put my hand out. He shook it and kissed it softly.

I cleared my throat and gave him an evil look. He grinned. I sighed and spit the whole thing out at once, "Ohhhh Jeez, Marge. You okaayyy? Ohhh yaaaaaaa, me tooooo. What theheckdoya mean?"

He laughed hard, silent but hard. He shook his head, "Brilliant. I never knew you had it in you."

"Me either," I rolled my eyes and turned the light off, "My payment, sir."

He flicked the light on, "I want to see you."

I made the sound I made around him, "No lights." I closed my eyes but he bit my arm. I gasped, "Ow."

He gave me a look, "You watch what I do or no deal."

I pleaded with my eyes, "No. That wasn't part of it."

He got a wicked grin, "My way or no way." I had already humiliated myself in front of him, so how was this different? I nodded before he got some crazy notion about leaving.

He pulled down my boxers, kissing my calf and massaging my leg, as he made his way up to my thigh. I sucked in when he kissed to the top of my thigh. He ran his tongue across to my slit, licking the whole way up. I clutched the sheets, forcing myself to look down on it. It was hot, seeing the passionate look in his eyes, but it was much hotter seeing his tongue flicking into me.

He sat back and kissed my other leg. He took his time, kissing and licking until his tongue was back between my legs.

He got a devilish look on his face as he inserted his finger into me. "You want this, princess?"

I was having a hard time taking a full breath. I nodded. He was slowly dragging his finger in and out of me. It was so slow, I tried to push against him, to fuck his finger myself. He shook his head, "What should I do next?"

I felt the horror on my face. He dragged the finger slowly, agonizingly slowly. "You tell me what to do, or I stop."

"Faster," I managed to get out.

He tilted his head, "Faster how? One finger or two?" He inserted a second finger. I moaned, "Two."

His smug smile lifted, "You want me to fuck you like this?" His fingers thrust faster. I gasped, but then he changed his movement, "Or do you want me to massage the G spot?"

My eyes started to droop, "G spot."

He ran his free hand up my torso, lifting my shirt and freeing my breasts. He slid down beside me and started to suckle, also slowly. He bit my nipple lightly, tugging it. Watching him wasn't uncomfortable anymore; it was beautiful. His perfect lips wrapped around my nipple, kissing and sucking, making me hot. He smiled, "What's making you so wet? The watching or the feeling?"

I bit my lip. He stopped everything and looked up at me, expectantly. I growled, "All of it."

"You like watching?"

I nodded. It was a white lie. I didn't like it, but it turned me on.

He shook his head, "I can't hear you."

I gulped, "I like watching." My words were weak, desperate.

He sat up again, sticking a hand under me, tilting my angle by grabbing a handful of my ass. He thrust his fingers fast again, but maintained the motion he was doing. My eyes shut, there was no opening them. He fucked me, until I lost control and came for him. He rubbed his thumb over my clit as the pressure released. I clamped around him, twitching and trying desperately to not cry out. My ragged breath was interrupted by his lips.

He slid his tongue into my mouth, pulling his fingers out as my orgasm ended. He kissed me, taking my breath from me. His lips played with mine, toying with me with nibbles and bites.

I whispered into the side of his face as he kissed my cheeks, "I want you to fuck me, Loch."

He shook his head.

I opened my eyes, "I want you inside of me." I pleaded with my eyes.

He gave me a look, "No. This is non-negotiable."

I pushed him on his back and climbed onto his cock. I moved slightly, pushing my wetness against his rough jeans. He clenched his jaw, "Fuck off, Erin."

I grinned at him and said it before I lost my nerve, "I'm going to fuck you, then."

He laughed, something like the bad guy in a movie would. It was dark and sinister. I slid his shirt up the way he had mine, so only his mouth was showing. His nose and eyes were covered by the shirt up over his head. I leaned forward and sucked his bottom lip, biting it. I raked my nails down his inked chest and dropped my mouth onto his nipple barbell. I flicked it with my tongue as my hands went for his belt. Undoing his pants was hard, being on top of him and holding him down. He was trying to struggle with his shirt, "Jokes over. This is exactly what I want but, come on, not here. I promised your Dad, baby."

I hopped off of him, grabbed a couple scarves from the rack on the wall and leapt back onto him, just as he was pulling his shirt down and giving me an evil look. I shoved his head back, wrapping a scarf around his wrist.

"Oh, you wanna play this game, do you?" a darker smile crossed his lips. He tried to pull me off with the other hand, but I pushed his arms down with my legs. My bare pussy was close to his face. I wasn't sure how I felt about that. Well, I was sure, but I wasn't letting myself think about it, or what I wanted to do about it.

I wound the scarf to the bedpost and grabbed the other one. I dragged his hand and tied it to the other post. He wasn't fighting me anymore. His breathing was messy and his heartbeat was wild.

I sat back and looked at him, my prisoner. I smiled at myself, but then I didn't know what to do next.

I wriggled my lips and looked back at the massive erection he was sporting. I got up and pulled his jeans and socks off. I dragged the boxers down and looked at him. Running my hands up his thighs, I dug in hard. He was soft with me, maybe too soft. I wasn't going to be. I raked my nails up his inner thigh and grabbed at his skin. He sucked air.

I kissed his thigh, next to his balls. I didn't have any dirty talking, so I had to work harder than he had. His singing and dirty talking was half the orgasm for me.

I sucked one of his balls into my mouth. He gasped again, making me grin. I kissed next to his cock, sliding my tongue along the shaft. He was writhing, "Put it in your mouth."

As if by instinct, I tugged his barbell. He moaned. I shushed him with a giggle. I kissed his belly right where the top of his cock was. He tried pushing to make it go in my mouth, but I moved again. I dragged my tongue down the other side of his cock.

I'd watched porn. I had something of an idea on what to do. I'd given a blow job before, but not to someone like him. I sat between his legs and grabbed his erection. It was strong and thick. I bent forward and licked the top. He bucked. I grabbed his barbell again, "Sit still, dammit."

He grinned, "Suck it."

I laughed. I liked the tone in his voice and the words he said. I bent forward and put the head in my mouth. I licked my tongue all around, getting it wet. He was moaning and thrusting on his own by the time I got it in my mouth. I could swallow back half of it. I wasn't a porn star, just a porn Googler. I licked up and down the shift and put my mouth on it again, lowering as far as I could go. I stroked the part I couldn't fit in my mouth. He was getting into a rhythm and I could feel his cock starting to tense in a funny way. I stopped instantly. He tried to push it at me, "Erin, you're killing me. Come on. Finish me off, baby."

I sat there with my hands on his thighs and an evil idea in my mind. Who knew I was such a deviant. I crawled up his body and sat on his cock. His breathing stopped. He struggled with the scarves and blindfolds, "Don't you do that."

I rotated my hips, sliding my wet slit up and down his hard cock. He shook his head, "I gave my word."

I leaned forward and lifted his cock, "Fuck your word. You gave yourself to me. So your word only matters to me." I lifted his cock back and slid myself down the shaft. I moaned as he filled all the space there was, and even made some room. I lifted and sat back down.

His mouth was completely slack, as if frozen in shock. I could have clapped my hands, giddy with the control I had over him. He was big and strong, and yet, there he lay, under my thumb.

I rode him, slowly like he had me. I lifted right to the head and sunk back down. My breathing was starting to go nuts. I moaned and rotated my hips. I sat forward sticking a nipple into his mouth. He sucked and I fucked. He sped up the flicking and sucking, and somehow it made me move quicker. I was about to orgasm a second time, but I stopped myself. I sat there, pulsating on his shaft. I made a hard decision. I slid up him slowly and let his erection lie back on his belly, covered in me.

He shook his head and tried to get out of the scarves. I leaned forward and kissed his lips, "Your word is intact, sir."

He snapped at me, "I'm going to fuck you so hard."

I grinned against his face, "I don't think you will." I ran my fingers along his chest, tracing his tattoos and laughing softly.

He flexed and ripped one of the scarves a bit. I saw how red his hand was from the blood pooling in it and wanted to help him get it off, but I didn't. I sat back on top of his erection, resting it between my wet lips and giggling, as he struggled with it all. The shirt made moving his arms difficult, and the scarves were not easy to tear. In a hard tug he got one hand free. He pulled the shirt off his head; his eyes were black as night. He ripped the second scarf to shreds and growled. My heart was racing. I wrapped my arms around his neck, kissing him with all my might. He sat up, grabbed my hips and positioned me for reentry. He thrust in, grabbing my hips and forcing me to ride him.

His thrusts were rough and angry. The sex was angry. I leaned back and he pushed me on my back. He shoved back inside of me, plunging deep and hard. He nestled his face into my neck and moaned into my hair when he came. He instantly took my hand and shoved it down between my legs, "Finish yourself off with me inside of you."

I nodded. I was wild with the near orgasm. I started, fast and intense. I didn't need a build up. I didn't have to rub long when I clamped down on his hardness. As I came, he gave me a few thrusts. I closed my eyes and smiled. "You're sleeping here, too."

He nestled into my neck, "Yes, ma'am."

I almost came again when he said it.

We laid there a minute, wrapped in each other and completely disgusting. He kissed the side of my head, "I knew it. I fucking knew it."

I gave him a confused look, "What?"

He laughed, "You almost sat on my face, which by the way, don't hesitate next time. I love it. You tied me up, pulled my barbell, teased me into oblivion and forced me to fuck you."

I shook my head, "I don't want to talk about it."

He laughed, "You are not a nice girl, and I just want it noted for the record, Your Honor, that I said it from the beginning. Not a nice girl but a naughty girl."

I laughed and blushed, "Let's take a shower, and I can tell you all the things you didn't do quite as well as the Brothers of County Claire." I grabbed his hand and tugged him to my ensuite.

"I'd let those brothers fuck you, just to see it done better than that. That was some hot sex."

I looked at him doubtfully.

He wavered, "Okay, I'd kill anyone who talked to you, but you get the point. Those lame-ass Claire brothers ain't got shit on me." He looked at my bathroom, "Seriously?"

I started the shower, "What?"

"Your own full bathroom?"

I smiled, "Hey, I'm the princess, remember?"

He snorted, "I knew that about you too, the minute I saw you screaming and waving that mace at me."

Chapter Thirteen
Night Life

The bar was packed. I scowled at Danny, "I wanted to go to Stormy's Sledsters."

He rolled his eyes, "Big D's is more fun."

"What's a sledster?" Lochlan leaned in and whispered in my ear.

I laughed and gave him an amused look, "Winter sports are big around here. We get a lot of snowmobile enthusiasts. We call them slutters, instead of sledders but you get the general idea. They take their rings off, and they're single for the weekend."

He laughed, "It's like Vegas for guys who like winter sports. You got college girls and horny men with cash."

I nodded, "Yeah, but less like Vegas than you'd imagine."

He snorted, "I can see that."

The bar was nice, for Grand Forks. I'd been to Big D's in Fargo and it was the same. We sat in the booth and ate Danny's fries. He scowled at me.

I pulled my hand back before he stabbed it.

Gerry gave me a worried look, "So, should I be scared? It feels a little like Deliverance country here."

I winced and gave Danny a look. Danny shrugged, "Probably."

Gerry didn't look amused. I laughed, "You're like the only gay guy here. You're golden."

The bartender walked over with a picture, "You have to sign this for me, please. I almost had a stroke from the other side of the bar when I saw it was you guys."

I pointed, "Told you they would know who you were."

Lochlan sighed and signed it, sliding it over to Gerry. "Look man, we're just trying to have an uneventful night out."

He winked, "Mums the word. I won't say shit. Thanks guys. I'm a huge fan. I drove all the way to Boston to see you perform, twice." He was glowing.

Gerry smiled at him, "Thanks man. We appreciate the support."

The bartender looked like he might hug them, but he turned and took the picture of the band back to the bar. He tacked it to the wall. I laughed and nodded. They never noticed he was doing it.

Danny tapped his fingers against the wooden table, "So I was thinking that maybe, if we run a couple charity concerts to start you off with the humble U2 vibe, people would have that impression of you. It might help get them past Loch getting kicked off the show. You know, the bad boys of rock and roll are kind of over. Girls think it's sexy when the lead singer has a puppy and hugs his grandma, ya know?"

I was lost. Danny never said nearly intelligent stuff like that.

Lochlan grinned at Gerry, "We have a gay drummer who is totally comfortable with his sexuality. We're fine."

Gerry laughed, "Asshole. I'm not being the poster child for gay musicians; Elton John has that covered."

Danny gave them both a serious look, "I'm serious. You all need to decide which direction you want that to go. Me and Lenny and Vic were talking about it. I want to maintain this positive type of public perception."

I pointed, "Are you working for them?"

Danny beamed, "Yeah." He said it like it was obvious, like I should have known it.

I looked at Lochlan. He shrugged, "He was right about the dramatic pauses. The intensity of the show was upped. The lights on the crowd only—he has good ideas."

Gerry nudged him in the booth, "And he's cute."

Danny blushed, "Anyway, you want AIDS or kids in Africa, Romanian orphans, or what?"

Lochlan sighed, "Why didn't Vic and Lenny decide? They started Thin Ice."

Gerry looked confused, too.

Danny drummed his fingers against the table, "Lenny has kids and a wife. He wants to take a serious backseat in all this. He never started the band and was never comfortable with a leadership role. That was Harris' job, and they don't want it."

Gerry nodded, "It is typically something the front man would control."

"What about Vic?"

Gerry looked at Lochlan and shook his head, "He never wanted this. He liked it being a small Boston band. He's starting a company and leaving the band. He's going to tell you all when we get back. He emailed me yesterday. It's too big."

Lochlan looked upset, "Is it me?"

Gerry shook his head, "No way, man. You've been the best thing that ever happened to Thin Ice. Me and Mike want this to be big. We hunted you for a reason. If we have to just hire a keyboard and guitar, then so be it. Drums, singer, bass, and one guitar are the most important anyway."

Lochlan looked stressed. My buzz was killed. I sipped my glass of red and looked around the bar. A girl waved at me from across the dance floor. I smiled and pushed Lochlan, "Let me out."

He looked confused but climbed out. I kissed his cheek, "Be back in a minute." The shoptalk was boring, and somehow I felt like I might be to blame. Lochlan had been moody since he met me. I pushed it to the back of my mind and ran to the girl across the bar. "Serena, hey."

She had been my roommate for the months I was at the dorms. She was an 'it girl,' popular and slightly mean. She had been in love with my brother, thank God. It earned me a place in her world. I never had to worry about being bullied or tortured. I was Serena's friend.

I wrapped my arms around her. She seemed thinner than before.

"How are you?" she smiled.

I shrugged, "Good. Law school in Boston. How are things with you?"

She looked around the bar, "Same old. I'm a project manager for a construction company." I assumed it was her dad's, but I didn't say that.

"That's great."

She tilted her head, "I've never seen you let your hair go curly like that. You always did the sleek look."

I grabbed a curl, "Oh yeah." I sounded like I was from North Dakota. I cleared my throat, "My boyfriend likes it curly."

She glanced at the table of good-looking guys I'd just left, "Is that you boyfriend?"

I nodded, "Yeah."

"He looks like that guy from that America's Most Talented Stars."

I laughed, "Yeah."

"So he tells you how to wear your hair?" It was a shitty thing to say and my face made her backpedal, "I mean it's just weird. You were always so strong and never cared what people thought. You were independent and free. I always thought that was so cool." She used the term like that part of me was long gone.

I nodded, "I still am."

Her pretty face got serious, "How's Danny?" I was grateful for the change in subject.

I wanted to say awesome, he'd just landed his dream job, and was happy like he'd never been. Instead I shrugged, "You know Danny."

Her eyes got lost in thought for a second, "That I do." She snapped out of it and became the blonde, tanned, queen of the mean, "So law school. That always was the dream, wasn't it?" Her tone was patronizing.

I ignored it, "Yes, it was. I'm pretty excited."

She smiled, "I'm really happy for you."

"Thanks. I'm happy for you, too."

Her glossy lips stayed frozen in her fake smile, "It's great we're both doing so well." I caught her gaze travel to the table again, "Say hi to Danny for me."

"I will. Anyway, I have to go the bathroom. It's good to see you."

She smiled, "Yeah, you too." I hugged her again and walked away, "See you around."

She waved. A pop song started to play really loudly. It had hit eleven, the magic dancing hour. The lights dimmed as the dance floor started to get crowded. I walked to the bathroom, weaving through the crowd.

The bathroom was nearly empty. I washed my hands and looked at myself. I looked different. I felt different. The way I'd gushed about law school felt fake, like what I wanted to gush about was Lochlan. I wanted her to know I was dating him. It was for petty reasons. The other girls left in a pack. I'd never had a pack. I'd never had female friendships that I'd actually maintained.

I walked out of the ladies' washroom, stopped cold by the stare bearing down on me.

I slipped my hand in my pocket. It wasn't there. He was there but it wasn't.

My throat closed. I backed into the washroom, choosing the wrong place to flee. He didn't chase me. He walked slowly, methodically, as if he'd imagined this moment a thousand times. He closed the door, slipping the lock into place. I was back against the far side of the wall. My breath was stuck; my scream was behind it.

His brown eyes looked crazier than I remembered them being. He pointed at me, "I missed you."

Tears fell from my eyes, "Mitch, please."

He laughed, "You going to hold out that piece of paper you got to stop me from seeing you?"

I shook my head as the tears streamed down my face, "No. I swear. I'll leave and never come back. I promise."

His face grew angry, like it had before, "Why would I want you to leave? We're just getting reunited." How was he out already? Why had no one told me?

My back was pressed against the wall. With my eyes closed, I could see my mace on the bedside table, where I'd left it.

I jumped into a stall, slamming the door and locking it. My hands shook as hard as the door that he pounded the shit out of. I dialed Lochlan's cell. It rang and rang, but went to voicemail. The door bent. I could see the screws were getting ripped out. I screamed, "HELP ME!"

"HOW COULD YOU, ERIN? HOW COULD YOU FUCK HIM? YOU THINK I DIDN'T SEE YOUR SLUT FACE ALL OVER THE BLOG SITES? YOU LET HIM SHAME YOU, LIKE A WHORE!"

I closed my eyes and redialed. It went to voicemail again. I spoke into the phone, "I'm in the bathroom. Help me." I hung up and texted, 'I'm in the bathroom, he's here.'

I was dialing 9-1-1 when he kicked the door in completely, knocking me onto the toilet. I slid the phone along the floor, as he grabbed my arm and dragged me out over the broken door. He slammed me into the counter. I screamed but he hit me hard. I was scratching and flailing, but his hands were everywhere. He held my arms to the floor and sat on my stomach.

"You and me are meant to be together, Erin. I love you. I always loved you."

I shook my head, "Please, stop."

He screamed, "I LOVE YOU! YOU UNGRATEFUL BITCH!"

I nodded, "I know. I love you too. Let's just go out to the car. I don't want to be in the bathroom anymore. Please." I pleaded through the tears, "I love you too."

He didn't buy it but, he looked like he wanted to. He snorted, "Not yet, you d on't, but you will." He ripped at my shirt. I screamed again, "HELP ME! I'M AT BIG D'S, HELP ME!" I screamed in case I was connected to 9-1-1.

I heard a bang and screaming. The lock turned and the door flung open. There was a series of flashes and movements. I saw the tattooed arm around Mitch's throat. Mitch was ripped off me and tossed. I jumped up, leaping into Lochlan's arms, wrapping myself around him, getting between him and Mitch. I whispered, "Don't baby, don't hurt him. He's not worth it."

I made sure my face was pressed into his neck so he couldn't see the blood I could taste in my mouth. I looked at Danny, "GET HIM THE FUCK OUT OF HERE!"

Danny ignored me and grabbed Mitch. He punched him and kicked him. "YOU FUCKING TOUCH HER, I'LL KILL YOU! I'LL KILL YOU, YOU SON OF A BITCH!" Mitch was lifting a foot off the ground with every boot. Danny grabbed him and started to punch him again. I screamed, "STOP!" I pushed Lochlan out into the hallway. Gerry grabbed Lochlan by the arm, dragging him back. I pulled Danny off Mitch as the bouncers made their way in. One grabbed Danny and tossed him. I pressed myself against Danny, pinning him as best I could to the wall. He was vibrating and massive. I wouldn't stand much of a chance holding him back.

"He's not worth it. Think of the press."

Danny shouted, "You get him the fuck outta my face or I'll finish this shit! You fucking come near my sister again and I'll ki…" I slapped my hand over his mouth.

I turned to the bouncer who winced when he looked at my swollen face, "I'm going to take them all out the back and wait for the police there. Take him out the front and tell some cops to come to the back. Don't tell anyone else we went that way."

He nodded, pinning Mitch to the floor. He was screaming at me but I didn't hear him. All I saw was the psycho in the hallway being pinned by four bouncers and Gerry. He was winning against the other five men.

I walked slowly to him. I grabbed his face and focused his black eyes on mine, "Hey!"

He saw my face and jerked with rage, but I squeezed hard, "Stop. Think about the band, and the press, and the fact that if you kill him, I'll miss you while you're in jail. I need you to stay with me. Don't leave me."

He was shaking with savage fury, but he stopped fighting the bouncers.

I looked at the corn-fed guy next to me, "Take him out back—fast." They dragged him down the hall. I followed, dragging Danny with me. Gerry wrapped an arm around me, "You okay?"

I shook my head, "Nope, but let's worry about that later."

We stood out in the cool night air. It felt like it would snow any second. Lochlan was wrapped around me, completely. The bouncers stayed with us, guarding the back door.

"I need to kill him."

I nodded, "I know."

He lifted my face but I pushed it down into his chest again, "Just wait, babe. The ambulance will come and clean me up, and you'll be better. Don't look."

Gerry grabbed Danny's arm and dragged him over to Lochlan. "You both need to stay calm. Erin is okay, and douche-bag psycho

My Side

is with the bouncers. The cops will be here any second. Let's stay calm. This is probably going to hit the press if anyone finds out who we are." He grabbed Danny's crazed-looking face, "You have to give the statement, do you understand? If you want to be the manager, you have to talk to the press if they come."

I was confused, "There isn't really, like, press here. It's North Dakota."

He gave me a look. I got that he was using it as means to calm them down.

A police car came around the corner, all lit up. The pair of them got out and ran towards us.

I sighed with relief when I saw them. We gave our statements. Of course they'd heard of the case a few years before, with Mitch and me. Lochlan didn't even want to let me go to give my statement, but they needed pictures of my face, arms, and shirt.

Dad's truck pulled in behind the cop car. He came running over. I started to cry when I saw him. He wrapped around me, "Shhhh. Baby girl, that boy is going away for a long time." He stroked my head and helped me to the ambulance.

The young cop gave me a weak smile, "If it makes you feel any better, he got his ass handed to him by the bouncers. You know how men are in Grand Forks about women getting hit."

I frowned, "It doesn't make me feel better. He's a sick man; you need to put him in an institution."

My dad shook his head, "He's not getting the cushy insanity plea. Fuck that. He's serving maximum time in a maximum facility. I'll make sure—I know the judge."

The cop winked at my dad, "We'll make sure he resists arrest." He turned and left. I felt sick. I looked at my dad, "That's illegal." Did I honestly care about my attacker being beaten? I knew the answer. I did care.

His eyes were frightening, "The justice system doesn't always touch the right spot. Sometimes you need to be outside of the system a little to make sure someone pays."

I was confused; my father always seemed so just. He was an honest lawyer with a strict conscience.

His look softened, "When you have kids and they get hurt, God forbid it, you'll know how this feels. I would break every law in the world to make you safe."

I nestled into his chest and tried to forget the way Mitch's eyes had looked.

Chapter Fourteen
Remember me

The flight home was uncomfortable. I was stressed about flying but so exhausted, I couldn't give it the effort it wanted. Every time I fell asleep I relived the scene in the bathroom. So I stayed awake and listened as the flight attendants basically offered everything from crackers to a blow job. Lochlan was in the worst mood ever. I was wearing a pound of makeup and sunglasses to hide the fading black eye. I leaned over to Lochlan, "You know, being with you all and wearing these glasses, I look like a junky groupie."

He gave me a fake smile.

I sighed, "Can you calm down, please? You aren't the one who got beat up, so you have no right to be this shitty about it."

He looked sick. It was wearing thin on me. I sighed, laid my seat back, and ignored the world.

When we got home he had to run off and deal with the band business. I was forbidden to leave the apartment, and he'd called three times already to check on me.

I pulled my laptop out and started to check out my emails and random stuff. I had notifications about being tagged in pictures. I clicked the link. My hand shot to my face. Serena and the mean girls had tagged me in about ten photos. Each one was Lochlan and Gerry and the girls. I leaned forward, zooming in to see that as Lochlan was signing Serena's breasts, his phone was lit up. I could see the word PRINCESS on it from the angle the shot was taken.

My stomach sunk. He was signing boobs, and I was being assaulted. It made me think about the thing Mitch had said about my pictures with Lochlan on the net.

I Googled Lochlan Barlow and clicked images. I sat there in the weak moment and scrolled down, one after another of him signing, kissing, and rocking the crowd.

I knew they existed, I knew how it was. I had no right to be angry. I wanted to stop looking, but it was impossible. I Googled Lochlan Barlow Girlfriend. The images filled the screen. Me, with no makeup, out for a sweaty run. The blogger actually had the decency to add that "Must be able to suck a watermelon through a garden hose to land a hottie bad boy like Lochlan" and then pasted perfect pictures of him everywhere else. He was posing and dressed nicely.

Air got harder to breathe all the way into my chest, as the pictures got worse. Me eating in my bathing suit at the pool at my parents' country club when I was fifteen; me eating a whole sub in a window of a deli; me screaming at Loch in an alley; my stomach hanging out a little bit as we left a restaurant with a caption that said "Lochlan trapped by pregnancy". I gagged. There were few pictures that looked nice. Mostly they were hideous. I Googled my name, Erin Benson. But every page that came up was Lochlan Barlow's girlfriend, Erin Benson.

I got up and pulled on my sweats. I tied my hair back in a ponytail and threw on my runners, transferring my mace from my jeans to my sweats, and left the apartment.

My feet hit the pavement with fury. I wasn't an ugly girl. I was a normal girl. My long, silky blonde hair was my best feature. My pale skin that never tanned and my short stature were not my best features. At the wrong angle my nose could look big and my lips were a bit too fat for my small face. But there wasn't anything so hideous as the cameras suggested, was there? Was I that horrid girl in the alley, screaming at him and raging like a jealous bitch? Was I not worthy of him?

I shook my head and ran harder along the Charles River Reservation. It was my favorite five-mile run; I always ran to a park along the way and turned around. But this time I paced, catching my breath. The air was cold and the day was ending. I sat on a bench overlooking the water.

I was vanishing. A montage of images floated through my mind. I was vanishing. I wasn't Erin Benson, law student and soon-to-be lawyer. I was Loch's girl, what was her name again? Who knows, but she treats him like shit and eats too much...

I saw the irrational thoughts for what they were. But the petty bitch inside of me, who hated the self-conscious, little sniveler I could be, took over. She pointed out that I wasn't a weak little bitch. I needed to see myself the way Serena had in school. I had fought back when Mitch attacked me. I had called Dad for help. I was out for a run, against Loch's orders, and not even letting Mitch take my sense of security from me again. I knew he was locked up tight. My security came from inside of me. I was strong and no asshole, crazy guy was going to take that from me. But neither was a bad-boy lead singer. It was me who controlled my universe.

I grabbed at my curly hair and hated the fact that I'd become his fucking doormat. My first instincts about him had been right. He served me up, ordered my drinks, but drank from them, like he was letting me know he owned them. He owned me. He was charming and beautiful, and I didn't believe I deserved a boy like that, not a normal girl like me.

Was he really so perfect though? His behavior was possessive and psychotic. He was a playboy and I was buying into it all. I was convincing myself that I was lucky to have him, because he was magical at something. Like the pied piper, he could lead all women to their ruination.

In my mind, my strength and courage were nothing, compared to the star he was becoming.

A horrid resolve and a terrible attitude started to form in my mind. I got up and walked home, not a new person but an old one. When I got to the apartment, they weren't back. I took the time to grab all his things and move them out of my room. I needed my space back. I needed a backbone. The reflection of the huge ring on my finger in the mirror made me stop. I ran my finger over it and pulled it off. I placed it on my bedside table, and pulled on a cute black skirt and a white blouse. I did my makeup, straightened my hair, and walked down to the bar. The bouncer gave me a funny look, "We don't open for a couple hours,"

I flashed him a sweet smile, "I'm here to see Brian about a job."

He got a sly smile and let me in past the closed door, "Head to the office upstairs."

I climbed the stairs, disturbed a little bit by how dingy it was with the lights on and no Lochlan to liven the place up. I took a deep breath and knocked on the door that said office.

A greasy-looking, forty-year-old man answered. He gave me a once over and grinned, "You looking for a job?"

I nodded, "I am."

"Come on in." He looked like a hungry wolf.

I shuddered, hating him instantly. Loch had been right; the guy was a pig. I almost bolted for the door, but $500 for two days of work was too good to pass up.

I sat in the leather chair across from his desk. He sat on the corner of the desk, hovering over me casually. His dark hair was smoothed back and his face was worn, making him look older than he was. He had beady eyes and a crooked grin.

"What's you name?"

I cleared my throat, "Erin Benson."

He smiled until the name hit him, "Fuck, Lochlan's girl?"

I shook my head, "I'm not his. I'm a human being. He has no control over me." I ran a hand through my silky hair.

He snorted, "Yeah, right. Look, I'm not pissing him off. He's famous and has a temper like a mother fucker. So take your cute butt back to his place. There is no job for you here."

I stood up and leaned into his face, "You don't think that having the infamous Lochlan Barlow's girlfriend working here will bring in the business? It'll guarantee he's here more; that's good for business. Not to mention, I used to help out at my parents' country club at Christmas time for extra money, so I actually know how to serve. I'd be useful, unlike half of your staff, and I would bring Thin Ice in on their own time."

He sighed, "You're going to get me in fucking trouble."

I shrugged, "Think of the ride you could have for the time I work here. I'll do Friday and Saturday nights, and you won't lay a hand on me or Lise."

He looked confused, "Lise?"

My gaze narrowed, "Brown hair, beautiful, law student."

He nodded slowly, "Right, her."

I stuck a finger in his face, "You touch her, and I use my claim to fame as Loch's girl for bad things. Slanderous things."

He chuckled, "Man, I had you pegged differently. Guess the whole law school thing should have clued me in." He nodded and stuck a hand out, "Deal." I shook his hand. "Start tonight then?"

I grinned, "Of course."

He pointed at my black eye, "That might be a problem."

I shook my head, "I'll get the other girls to patch me up. It'll be dark in here soon anyway."

I walked out of the office and down the stairs.

Lise screamed when she saw me, "Ahhhh, you came."

I hugged her and smiled, "I did. I start tonight."

"What happened to your eye and your lip?" She looked horrified.

I sighed, "Ran into an ex-stalker in North Dakota. He attacked me. It's in the papers."

She laughed, "I'm sorry. Oh my God, that's awful. I just remembered I saw that fat picture of you and you were all fat. The media hates you."

I rolled my eyes, "Laugh it up."

She gushed, "Well, you working here should be fun for them to take pics."

I never thought about that. Was that what Loch was talking about, keeping me out of the public eye?

She pulled her makeup out and fixed my eyes, "Thin Ice plays tonight. You ready for some serious cash and the sorest feet ever?"

I laughed, "I am."

My phone rang. I pulled it out and sighed, "I'll just go get ready."

She nodded.

I answered, "Hey."

He sounded panicked, "Don't leave. I should have told you and I'm sorry. I'll be sorry for the rest of my life. I had no idea you needed me. I couldn't hear the phone."

I frowned, "What are you talking about?"

"You moved all my shit back in my room, and I saw your laptop. Just please don't leave. I know I keep fucking up."

I laughed, "I'm not leaving."

He was silent for a second, "You're not?"

I laughed, "No. I just need to buckle down, and I don't need you to distract me constantly."

"Erin, I know you're mad about the pictures."

I laughed again, "Yeah, not cool. Sucks to be me, I guess. Another cost of dating you." That was off side and bitter.

"Where are you?"

"Work. I'll see you guys when you get here."

He shouted instantly, "I told you no. Brian is a seedy fuck."

I looked at my black eye in the bathroom mirror, "I know. I got that from him."

"Did he touch you?"

I sighed, "No. He's scared of me. I threatened him with a lawsuit if he touched me. I also told him that I was comfortable misusing my obvious stardom from dating you. I told him I would slander his bar in every corner of the world. He's being a good scum bag for now."

"I'll be there in five to get you. Just wait outside."

I noticed the fierce look in my eyes and wished he was there to see it, "Nope. You even try to get me fired, or make me quit, and we are done. I like my hair straight and smooth. I like to pick my meal. I like to serve myself and I like my own drink, not a shared one."

"Is this about the money? I can buy you anything you want or need. I have money, princess. I always have."

I sighed, "I also hate the way you choose not to hear the things I say that you don't like. This is our first real couple's fight, Loch. I want to be the girl I was, not the girl you're making me. I want to be with you on my terms, not yours. It's all about you. I'm living through you—your career, your friends, your success, your name. My fucking name doesn't even Google anymore. I Googled me, and it comes up as Lochlan's girl, Erin Benson. Apparently, I'm ugly, pregnant, and manipulating you. People think I'm an evil whore who can suck-start a truck. I'm not me anymore. I'm yours, and that's not cool for me. I'm stronger than that. At least, I used to be."

He sounded pissed, "We'll talk about this after we leave the bar together." He hung up on me. I worried for a while that he would come and drag me out. He didn't. He showed for his stage setup, ignoring me.

I served drinks, dodged groping hands, and smiled until I was blue in the face. Lise was the most fun person to work with ever. She danced and drank shots, and made me have some. She stuffed money down my underwear, making customers think it was okay. I thought the money flowed amazingly until the show started, then it got busy. I saw the blank stares in their eyes, the seduction of each person, the pleasure of senses being driven wild. I saw it all. He lit the fire on the stage with his voice, making love to each of us. I caught myself staring with them. I had to fight the urge to get caught up in him. It was his best show yet. His passion was explosive. I shuddered, imagining him between my thighs with that kind of power, and made the noise he always made me make.

He finished the set and shouted into the crowd, "Good night and thank you for coming." He didn't say the North Dakota thing. Fear crept around inside of me. He didn't want me strong. He wanted me malleable. He was done with me if I was taking a stand against him and being my own person. He wanted a weak girl to be his.

My heart snapped as fears became facts, without any evidence really.

I was serving drinks to a group of young college boys, when I felt a sweaty face pressed into my nape. My eyes widened but then I smiled. He kissed me and pointed at the bar, "I'll be over there." He grinned, "Why don't you get me a beer."

I laughed and nodded.

The guys at the table were either in awe or suddenly interested in me. I left them and grabbed him a beer. He smiled at me, "I'm sorry for the media shit, and the old-roommate Facebook pictures, and the fact that I wasn't there when you needed me. I won't ever actually forgive myself for that. Danny told me that chick was kind of a snotty bitch, and that she'd tagged him and you in the pictures. I panicked when he got the notifications, and then I got home, and you were gone and my stuff was moved."

I shook my head, "I'm sorry I blamed you for the fact that I was becoming your groupie and not your girlfriend. It's my fault, not yours."

He took my finger and slid the ring back on. I laughed, "I didn't want to lose it."

He shook his head, "You're making me lose it, I swear." He pulled me in, kissing my cheek, "I never saw you as a groupie. I see your strength and your beauty. I always just see you." I looked into his eyes and saw it too. I was still in there, even with the shiny hair.

Chapter Fifteen

What happens in New York...

He was pacing the living room with whoever he was on the phone with. I was trying to study but he kept lifting his arms in the air, showing off the new tattoo he'd gotten on his lower abdomen. It dipped into his pants and made me want to touch it.

I sighed, walked into my room, closed the door and continued reading.

He came in a few minutes later, "Can we do my parent's at Thanksgiving and have your parents here for Christmas?"

I frowned, "What?"

He was leaving in two days for New York and the tickets were booked. He looked worried. I got off the bed, pulling his face down to mine and kissed him hard. "Yeah, of course. I'll take care of switching the flights and shit."

He sighed, "Okay, here." He handed me his credit card.

I kissed him, "Stop stressing, baby. You got this. New York is going to be amazing."

He looked stormy, "I want you there."

I shook my head, "No."

He didn't return my kiss when I pressed my lips into his. I stroked his cheek, "Easy, beast, you can't push me around anymore."

He struggled to look angry, but his lips curled into his sexy grin, "You sure about that?"

I bit my lip and nodded, "Yup." He shoved me lightly. I fell back onto the bed. He stood over me and pulled his shirt off, "I think I just did though."

I laughed as he dropped to his knees. I wrapped my legs around his waist and tried to sit up. He shoved me back down and lifted my shirt. He placed soft kisses on my belly button, as he undid my jeans. The door opened, "Hey, Er..." Danny stopped mid-sentence, "Oh fuck. I'll never un-see that." He turned and walked out.

I laughed. Lochlan shook his head and kicked the door shut, "Knock, Danny."

Danny shouted from the hallway, "No, I'm good out here. Just wanted to mention that we gotta go."

Lochlan made a face. I sat up but he pushed me back down, "I need five minutes."

Danny groaned, "Gross dude, that's my sister."

Lochlan grinned and ripped my pants off. He sucked his middle finger and slid it inside of me. I sat up on my elbows, the way he liked, and gasped, watching his finger move in and out of me. He flipped my shirt and bra up, releasing my breasts. He ran his hands over my body and rolled one of my nipples lightly. It made me tighten everywhere with the sensation. The base of his finger glistened. I was panting when he pulled it out, but I never expected him to flip me over. He licked up my back, kissing and biting lightly while grinding his erection on my ass cheeks. He stood behind me, lifting me up and arching my hips back. He inserted himself slowly. I'd never had him this way. He spread my legs more and pulled my ass back. Luckily, my face was in the covers when the weird sound he always made me make left my lips like tiny mewls. He bucked hard, making a loud moan replace the soft noises. He stopped and reached for his phone. He fiddled with it for a second, and then Sail by AWOLNATION started to play loudly to cover our noises. He moved slowly with the song at first, sliding in and out of me, massaging my ass cheeks. He reached his hand around, stroking my clit, but still thrusting leisurely. I buried my face into my bed but he jerked me back up.

The song ended and started again. He stopped rubbing my clit and increased his pace. He pumped hard, his balls replaced his finger, slapping against my clit. His body spanked against mine, and the vibration brought my climax fast.

I struggled for breath as I came, standing and bent over. I gripped his cock, forcing his orgasm. He fucked hard as he filled me up. I couldn't stand any longer. I fell forward, bringing him with me. He lay beside me and kissed my nose, "I'll see you in three days."

I smiled, "I'll miss you."

He laughed, "Just stay off the Internet and trust me, okay?"

I nodded. He kissed me and climbed off the bed. I lay there, waiting for him to leave so that I could let pathetic, whiny Erin have her minute.

I didn't go on the Internet, but I did watch the live show. He was sexier on TV. It was frightening. It was his place. He deserved it, needed it, and earned every glorious second of it. Seeing him there, he wasn't mine. He was a sexy guy who was rocking a stage and making everyone dance and shout, and wave their hands in the air.

I saw it then, there were really two Lochlans. The one on the stage was there for everyone. He was fun, crazy, and inspiring to watch. It was amazing to see someone take their dream and make it fly with such skill and charm. He made you want to find your dream, be a success, live for the moment, and he made it look easy. His swagger and grace were beyond controllable.

They were singing their bar song; it was the one that got the drinks flowing and the crowd feeling brotherly. It made me feel that way. Very indie and free. It was the song that had the most Tennessee in it. It was a Lochlan original.

He kicked his foot to the drum and held the microphone out for the crowd to sing. The entire show burst into song. They knew every word. The smile on his face could have fed me the rest of my life. Gerry and Mike were beaming. Even Lenny, the homebody, was grinning from ear to ear over the keyboard. They had borrowed a guitar player from another local band. They tried to poach him but he had stayed loyal to his band. Bostonians were the most loyal people.

The camera fell on Lochlan as he finished the song with his head back, a peaceful look on his face. The crowd erupted as the host walked over, clapping. "Man, you guys are hot!"

Lochlan smiled. I saw him wink into the crowd. It made my stomach hurt, but I pushed it away.

"I heard you guys in Boston not too long ago. Amazing show. Ladies and gentlemen, thank Thin Ice for coming and playing for us. Their album will be available..." he looked at Lochlan, who laughed, "Soon."

"There you have it... soon. Stay tuned. We have the entire cast of The Dreamers up after this." He waved and the screen went to commercial.

My phone didn't ring. No texts came through. I stared at it for a while, and then decided it wasn't too lame to message him.

'Awesome show, baby. I loved it.'

He never messaged me back. I could see it had delivered, but there was no message back.

I forced myself to study and not look on the net, or think about why he hadn't texted me.

I woke to messages, weird ones like 'hey, sorry there is just so much to do, I'll call later' and 'hey, princess, we're exhausted from the sets and rehearsal. Talk later.'

I shrugged it off until my late-morning class with Dean.

He waved me over after class, "Did Gerry or Lochlan send you the pics from the people they've met?"

I shook my head, clutching my books and forbidding myself to think the worst.

He pulled out his phone and held them up. There were pictures of everyone; it was crazy chaos. The band was in front of restaurants, at bars, and I couldn't believe the famous faces gracing Dean's phone. Lochlan letting famous female singers lick his face and kiss him. The group of them were smiling brightly and hanging themselves off dozens of different people for pictures.

Dean noticed my face and pulled the phone back, "He's such a joker."

I nodded blankly. I was secretly hyperventilating. I smiled weakly, "I better go. I'm leaving in two hours for Nashville." I could feel the glossy tears starting to form.

He swallowed, "I'm sorry. I assumed you didn't care about the fun drunk he was, or you wouldn't date someone like him." Oh my God... he was drunk for the pictures. God only knows what he did.

I laughed awkwardly, "Oh, I am. He's crazy. I'm just tired."

He hadn't done anything wrong. I needed to remind myself that he was acting the part. He was hugging famous people and doing things mere mortals would never have the opportunity to do.

The walk home gave me the chance to ponder if I was doing what abused women did? Was I justifying him? I needed to see inside of his eyes. I needed to know if I was still there.

I packed my things and caught my flight to Nashville. It wasn't nearly as bad, probably because I had been flying so much. His family lived in a small town just on the outskirts of Nashville called Mt. Juliet. I knew nothing about them beyond that.

When I got to the Nashville airport, I pulled my carry-on to the waiting area. I smiled when I saw a handsome dark-haired guy in a lime-green tee shirt and tight jeans holding a black jean jacket. I walked right up to him, "You have to be Alex."

He smiled, and it was insane. They were identical, but Alex was better looking. He had spiky, dark hair, styled perfectly, and the brightest smile. He flashed it at me and I almost fainted. He was a thinner and cleaner Lochlan. And way better dressed.

"Erin!" he squealed and attacked; his emotions were everywhere, like they had exploded from a box.

I hugged back, "It's nice to meet you."

He pulled back, "Oh my God, you are delicious. Look at you; no wonder he loves you."

My stomach burned. I'd hardly spoken to him since he'd left for New York. It was weird.

I cleared my throat, "Thanks for coming to get me."

He rolled his eyes, "It's a twenty minute drive. It's not a liver."

I laughed. He looped his arm in mine, "Mom and Dad and Lissie are going to go nuts. They have been dying to meet the unstoppable Lochlan Barlow's beautiful girlfriend who he never shuts up about."

I glanced at him, "I can't wait to meet them too."

He shook his head, "It's crazy that you guys just met. It feels like he's known you forever."

I nodded, fighting the frown on my face, "I know. It was August 12th at 4 in the afternoon. I maced him and some fake-breasted female. Got them both handcuffed by the police and we've been inseparable ever since."

He winced, "Longest three and half months of your life?"

I shook my head, "It's felt like I've crammed everything humanly possible into the time." I almost stopped myself from talking, but he was easier to be around than any one person I'd ever met. I gave him a soft smile, "But I wouldn't trade the time. It's been fun. Bizarre and fun."

He laughed and led me to a car in the short-term parking. It was beautiful, a red BMW M6. I knew the car because it was on the 2013 calendar hanging in our kitchen. My hands trembled when I touched it, dragging my fingers along it.

"It's so beautiful." It was my dream car. The one I would have bought for myself if I were rich.

My Side

He flashed me the smile and tossed me the keys. I instantly went in two directions at once, "I can't." One side of me wanted to but the other really didn't.

He nodded, "Yeah, you can. It's paid for and insured. I just watched you cargasm. You can drive." He climbed into the passenger side, after sticking my bag in the trunk. I sat in the driver's seat, taking mental pictures of every angle. It was stunning. Not too showy but sleek and sexy. It had the European flare and class, but the red paint gave it the American bad-ass feeling I loved about the car. I stroked the steering wheel and put the key in. The engine gave a slight roar and then purred. I looked at him, "Oh my."

He laughed, "Oh my, indeed."

"You look so much like him."

He frowned, "We're identical twins."

My jaw dropped open, "Oh."

He frowned, "He never said that?"

I shook my head, "Must have slipped his mind."

He pushed on his sunglasses, "Yes well, a great many things slip his mind. Small details don't fit with all that personality."

I laughed and pointed, "Oh, we are going to get along great."

He chuckled. I put the car in reverse and started the trek to his parents' house. It was much less than twenty minutes in an M6. I barely had time to make the turns he told me to take. When I pulled into the new subdivision, I was stunned. The houses were new and pretty. It was a small, clean area with plumbing and underground electricity. It was a beautiful family neighborhood. I was confused, "I imagined it more like a farm."

He gave me a look, "Turn here."

I looked at the street name, "Erin Lane?"

He laughed, "Yes ma'am." He definitely sounded more Southern than Lochlan did. "This one."

I pulled in slowly. The house was a new rancher with beige siding and burgundy trim. "My mom would love it here. She likes new."

He nodded, "Dad bought it a couple years ago. It's easier with mom to be in a rancher. We had a huge house before, but she can't get around like before."

I started to feel like I was completely in the dark. I swallowed, "Is she okay?"

He frowned, "Wow, did he talk about us at all?"

I nodded, "He did, but it was like Alex does this and that, and when we were little Lissie hated this, and when we went to Disney, Alex cried because they made him put on a prince outfit instead of a princess."

His cheeks flared, "Of course, he remembered that one." He sighed, "You will discover he's bad with the people he loves. He kind of gets distracted." My heart hurt instantly but then he smiled, "But you'll never meet a person who loves anyone as much as he does. Lochlan is the best person I've ever met. Our mother had a massive stroke a while ago. She has been pretty much cared for by our father. It was intense."

"I'm so sorry." I wanted to cry but I couldn't. Who cries as they meet their boyfriend's family?

He shook his head, "It's fine. She is fine and we are fine. Don't make a big deal about it, okay? She hates that."

I nodded, "I'm going to kill your brother. Are they still getting in tonight after the show?"

He shook his head, "They fly in at five in morning. I have to go get them. They had to change it when they found out they were playing two songs and the show is longer than they expected."

I smiled and muttered, "Figures." He had just stranded me with his family for the next few hours, alone. I was at least grateful that Alex was amazing.

"Oh, we don't bite, not hard anyway."

My smile increased.

"So Loch said you're in law," he said as he grabbed my bag and we walked up to the door. The front porch was beautiful.

"I am, and you're a dentist?"

He rolled his eyes, "Pediatric dental surgeon."

I laughed, "Those are the same thing in Loch's mind, apparently."

He chuckled, "Loch doesn't have room for the small stuff." He opened the door. A kind-looking man with dark hair, bright-blue eyes and red cheeks greeted me with a smile, "You must be Erin." He hugged me. I didn't expect any of it. He was chubby and tall. His face was a huskier version of Alex and Loch's.

Lissie walked in with light-red hair and the same bright-blue eyes. She joined in on the hug. She was tall, thin, and very pretty. Her skin was ruddy and freckled. I assumed Lissie looked like their mother.

Alex pulled me into the living room. A woman with short, strawberry-blonde hair and a slack look on her tired face moved her eyes to see me.

"Mom, this is Erin. Loch's Erin."

She didn't move. I was about to lose it. He never warned me or prepared me at all. I dropped to my knees immediately, taking her hand, "It's lovely to meet you."

Her eyes filled with tears. She gripped my hand with little strength.

Her eyes darted about the room.

Alex leaned forward, "He'll be here tonight. It's okay. He's coming."

I was near to tears. Lissie came and sat beside me, thankfully talking, "So he told us the mace story. I don't think I've ever loved anyone before I met them. But you, I loved you."

My Side

I started to laugh, "It was a bad day."

Alex laughed with her, "No, it was our best day. Anything that humbles the super hero in the family is good." He winked at Mom. Her eyes shone with delight and pride.

Their dad came in with a tray of sweet tea. He passed me one, "Hope you like your tea sweetened."

I nodded and drank a small sip. He sat next to his wife with a spoon in her glass, "I made yours the way you like it, love."

He spoon-fed her tiny sips, not taking any of his. Lissie and Alex acted like it was normal, so I tried not to stare.

We chatted and laughed and got to know each other. Lissie was a schoolteacher; she taught tenth-grade math. She had her master's in teaching. She was twenty-nine years old. I knew Loch and Alex were twenty-seven.

We sat enjoying each other's company. Their father had made dinner, tomato-basil soup. He made up his wife's bowl and fed it to her. He drank from her tea, chatting away with her like nothing had changed and no time had ever passed between them.

Eventually Alex leaned over to where I sat in front of the hot fireplace, "Want to take a walk?"

I nodded. Lissie had left with promises to be back early to help with Thanksgiving dinner.

We left the house and I sobbed, leaning against the truck in the driveway. I covered my face in hateful shame.

Alex rubbed my back,

"It's a lot to take at first. I'm sorry Loch never told you. I honestly don't think he notices sometimes."

I shook my head, "He treats me the same as her and I got mad at him. I told him to stop making my fucking plates of food and drinking my drinks. I never knew…"

He wrapped himself around me, "How could you have known?

We've seen it for almost a decade? Well, almost six years anyway."

He took my hand in his and pulled me along. I sniffled and nearly heaved. I'd never felt worse in my life.

"I feel so bad."

He nudged me, "You shouldn't. We've been exposed to it for so long, it's just regular for us. Dad refused to put her in a home when it happened. She was young, jeez, fifty-years old. We were on the road to success. Loch had just finished his MBA. I was in university, taking too many courses, and Lissie had finally made it off the substitute list. She had her first full-time job. We were all so busy. Loch decided not to take the job he'd gotten. He sang at the bar nights and spent the days with Dad. The two of them got her to where she is now. She's as good as it gets. She can swallow normally, breathe normally, and she understands us. If we ask her questions, she can blink her eyes as answers. Loch spent a lot of time with her."

I frowned, "What made him do the show?"

He got a grim look on his face, "We forced him. We knew what an amazing singer he was, and Lissie and I were stable. We hired help for Dad and forced Loch to do the show."

I laughed, "I'm sure you didn't have to completely force him."

He laughed too, "He was made to do this."

I had never imagined it was anything like this—never. I shook my head, "No wonder he's always going on about living everyday to the fullest and trying new things. He's inspired by her."

He gave me a look, "That's his ADHD. He's always struggled with it and oh, Mom and Dad, they tried medicating him when he was little. But he became a zombie. He lost the passion and the flare that is Lochlan. His eyes glazed over and he said yes to everything in a monotone. No sarcasm, no joie de vivre. Mom wouldn't hear of it. She took him off the meds and shit. She made him take music, started with piano. It helped him focus. So when he would be having a fit or a hard time focusing, she would make him play. He took singing lessons. The music saved him."

I was dying inside, "Oh my God, he never told me that either."

He nodded, "I assumed. If it's too much for you, all of this, I can take you to the airport. I know he's a lot to handle, and Mom, well she's hard to watch. We are all watching her die, slowly. Dad has a bad heart, high cholesterol, and blood pressure. They won't go into a home, and we won't let Loch put his life on hold for them. They don't want it. They want this for him. Our family is a mess, so if you need to bail, I will make him understand."

I felt sick, "You think I'm that shallow?"

He grabbed my hands, shaking his head, "No, my God, no. But he never told you any of this, and he might not ever have. There are things he might not ever tell you. That's something you have to live with. It's not deviousness; he isn't like that. It's truly that he sees things his way. He is stubborn as shit, and refuses for the flaws to bring him or anyone down. He still believes, in his crazy way, that she might recover." He sighed, "If there is ever anything you need to ask me, I'll always tell you the truth."

I held his hands tight, "Why did he beat that guy up on the show?"

His eyes twitched with the memory, "Okay, the truth on anything but that. That he has to tell you himself."

"Do you think I should go to the airport?"

He shook his head, "No. Lochlan used to need music and now it seems like he just needs you. The music has finally become a joy and not a release."

I felt my cheeks blush, "He seems so normal and together. He's smart and funny and outgoing. He doesn't seem broken."

His grip tightened, "He's not." His tone changed.

I jumped, "Sorry, I'm thinking aloud. I just mean that he's like... well you know...the darkness sometimes it's... like a demon."

He glared slightly, "Erin, you have to see the strengths, not the weaknesses. I didn't tell you this so you would judge him. I told you so you would be fair with him and see the whole picture."

I swallowed, "I'm not judging him, I swear. I just see so many things making sense; it's all just my brain working. I have to say it out loud. It's my own ADD."

He pulled me into his embrace.

I rested my head on his chest and sighed, "You sure you're gay?"

He laughed, "Unbearably gay."

I laughed and then I cried some more. "Want to watch the show?"

He shook his head, "No. Let's wait for Mom. Dad will be putting her to bed now."

I nodded and we walked back, hand in hand. I tried to convince him to run away with me, and let me be his beard.

He never caved once, just smiled at me with his sparkly-blue eyes that never once turned into a dark look.

He led me to Lochlan's bed. I curled up in the sheets and tried not to be creepy about smelling his pillow. It was bad enough I was in his boxers and tee shirt.

I woke to Lochlan sleeping on the bed over the covers. He was still dressed. It was light out. I kissed his cheek and crawled from the bed. He was passed out so I got dressed and went down the hall, to find Al giving Judith a type of sponge bath on her face and neck.

"Good morning. Can I help with anything?" I smiled at Judith.

He shook his head, "No. I was just going to watch the boys' show from last night. I recorded it. It makes her happy, but they were playing too late."

I smiled, "Can I get you anything, Al?"

He glanced at me, "Cup of the coffee that's made, if you don't mind. One sugar and one cream."

My Side

Judith gave him an evil look. He chuckled, "One milk. No cream for me."

I laughed and patted her on the shoulder, "I've got your back, Judith." I wished his family were my family. They were amazing and sweet, and everything a person wanted in parents. I'd seen kids with ADHD act out. I couldn't imagine being so brave as to take him off his meds and have the patience to suffer through his music lessons. I got us both a coffee and sat on the couch. I sipped as he started the recording.

It was the same sort of set up as the one the night before it. They were on a small stage, ready to start playing their instruments. I sighed seeing him. They played my favorite song, Hold My Heart Tonight. It was amazing. His vocals were the best in that song. Mid-way, a young woman came on stage with her microphone. She sang the lyrics with him. He laughed, beaming at her. He wrapped an arm around her waist and sang with her. She was beautiful, long red hair and a stunning face. The way she looked at him was intense.

Al pointed, "That's Mikayla, the girl who was on the show with him. She was in the final four with him."

I hadn't watched the show, except for searching his performances.

The two of them were amazing together. They finished the song. She stood on her tiptoes to kiss him. The cameras zoomed in. She kissed him with tongue. He kissed her back. The crowd cheered. The kiss lasted long enough that I was down the hallway, pulling the ring off my finger and placing it on his pillow before the talking started. I left it there and grabbed my suitcase. I closed the door and walked to the living room, "I'm so sorry, Al. I need to leave."

He was breathing heavily. He gave a sorrowful look, "I didn't know. I'm so sorry, Erin. I won't even try to defend his actions."

I shook my head, "You are lovely. Never be sorry." I kissed his cheek and knelt next to Judith. Tears were streaming down her cheeks. It broke my heart. I kissed her damp cheek, "It was lovely to meet you. You have a beautiful home and the best family I've ever met."

She gripped my hand. I nodded, "I know. I'm sorry about the whole thing. I don't want to have this here, making you uncomfortable." I kissed her and hugged her and Al again. I left out the front door, dialing for a cab.

He picked me up on the side of the road, walking and pulling my carry-on. I climbed in, "Airport, please."

He drove off. I slapped myself in the forehead, "Stupid, stupid, stupid."

I walked up to the counter, sunglasses covering my puffy eyes and paid for a ticket home. He was killing my cash flow.

I walked slowly to the gate. My phone was buzzing non-stop. Finally angry, in a way I couldn't contain, I answered, "WHAT?"

Danny started talking fast, "Holy fuck. We asked Alex not to let you see it, until we got to talk to you. She kissed him. He wasn't ready for it. He didn't want to shove her off on camera. He kissed her, and the minute we were backstage, I honestly had to contain him. He was pissed. He tried calling you, but I wouldn't let him. I knew if you saw the kiss you'd flip out and not know the whole story."

I sighed, "You suit your new job, Danny." I hung up the phone. He called back, so I turned it off. I boarded the plane in dead agony. I was flat and emotionless. It was the only thing that saved me from my fear of flying.

Chapter Sixteen
Drama Llama

I heard him enter the apartment. My heart was pounding, but I couldn't get a breath to save my life.

Danny walked into my room. He looked bad but I sighed when I saw it was him. He wrapped his arms around me, "I'm always your brother first. Always."

I cried into his chest.

"I don't expect you to forgive him, but I need you to go back, Erin."

I pulled back, confused, "What? Fuck you, Danny. He's not my kid. I don't have to coddle him."

He started to cry, "Gerry and I were sleeping in the basement in the guest rooms. We heard the screaming; he was so mad. She took another stroke. She's in the hospital and his dad's almost there too. They're scared his dad is going to have a heart attack."

I grabbed my wallet and phone and we ran from the apartment. I didn't need anything else as an explanation. In the cab, I sobbed, "This is all my fault. I should have come with you. I didn't want to mix that life and this one. I wanted the other him, not the star."

Danny shook his head, "It's that bitch Mikayla's fault. She's an asshole. He fucked her on the show; she's obsessed and sees him succeeding and wanted to latch on to the rising star." He gave me a grim look, "I actually phoned her and told her that this morning. Told her exactly what happened and how she was responsible for almost killing his mom."

I'd never seen Danny get so emotional. "Is Gerry with him?"

He nodded, "And Mike."

I turned on my phone, ignoring the constant stream of messages and voicemails. I pressed his name and held the phone up to my ear. We jumped out at departures and starting running for the counter.

"Hey."

I stopped running when he answered and let Danny get the tickets.

"Hey."

He sighed, "I'm so sorry. I get it. I know I fucked up. Just don't leave me. We can go back, we can just be friends again. I deserve whatever judgments you have of me, princess." His words were a whisper. It was devastating.

I shook my head, "I'm sorry. I should have kept our drama to myself. Her stroke… it's my fault. I immediately assumed the worst of you. I did it in front of her. I'm an asshole. Baby, I'll be there in a couple hours."

He paused for a minute, "You're coming back?"

I nodded, even though he couldn't see me, "I'll be there in a couple hours."

"Thank you." He hung up. I felt sick and dialed Gerry.

"Erin, we need you. He won't leave his mom's side. His dad is on oxygen and they're monitoring him. Oh shit, he's coming out of the room. He looks like death. Are you coming back here?" He was whispering.

"Yeah, we'll be there in a couple hours. Is she bad?"

He whispered, "No. She's hanging in there. They have her stabilized and said it was a very minor one. She's being released tonight or tomorrow. She didn't suffer any worse than last time. Some kind of fucking miracle or something. It depends on his dad and how he's doing." He paused and then spoke again quietly, "If you could have seen his face. Danny took his phone and made him calm down. I thought he was going to trash the dressing room. He was angry, like I've never seen before. Danny made us stay till he was calm and we nearly missed the flight."

I glanced at my brother and nodded, "He's a good guy."

"Erin, he'd be on a plane if his mom wasn't sick. He's taking all the blame. His brother and sister are trying to calm him down. His dad is livid with him—said awful things to him."

I sighed, "I'll message you when we land." I hung up and followed Danny to the gate. He wrapped an arm around me, "You're going to fuck this up with your bad-boyfriend juju. You assume shit and treat him like the sucky guys you dated as a kid."

I looked at him, "I didn't make him kiss her."

He laughed bitterly, "You made him overreact about it and act like a spaz. You've got him so wound up about you leaving him that he's like suicidal once a week. I'm going to find him cutting himself and listening to all your favorite songs one day, I'm convinced."

I swallowed, "He's just so hard to trust. He acts so nuts."

He grabbed my arms and held me tight, "Erin, that is your fault in a small way. Your self-absorbed bullshit has to end. He's already stressed to the max about the band, the record deal, finding new members and making sure they fit in, and suddenly being handed all the responsibility of the band. You're so fucking selfish and wrapped up in your own little problems that you don't ever look at his side."

We walked fast. My chest was tightening but he kept on going.

"You can't keep him this wound up. So fucking what? Some slut kissed him on a stage. That's bound to happen to any guy who leaves his house. It happens to me every other day, and I'm me. Fucking Lochlan's seen his dad give up his whole life for his wife. He took early retirement from his job—he had a cool job. He was an air-traffic controller. How cool is that? Al was a badass dude before his wife got sick. Now he's a fucking housewife and a caretaker, and Loch has seen that for a lot of years. To him love means sacrifice. Our parents aren't like these people. Neither was willing to bend, so they quit. We're quitters and Loch's people are the type who hang in there till the last bitter drop of blood is squeezed. He is never going to cheat on you. He's had opportunity like a mother fucker. I'm not kidding. He gets chicks begging him to suck hi..."

"STOP!" I stopped walking and shook my head, "I get it."

He released me and pointed, "You're doing it now. You can't control every aspect of his work life. You have to let him out of the yard and off the leash. He needs to not worry about getting dumped every time you don't like a girl giving him her number. He never takes the offers up and he never even checks out the girls. The minute he can stop being center stage Lochlan, he does. For fuck's sake. Either be with him the way he is, or let him go. And get some self-esteem. What the fuck is that? It's so annoying to see a pretty girl see herself as not worthy. You know what it makes us guys think you aren't worthy? We see you how you see you. You're pretty and funny and smart. Stop being such a douche-canoe."

I looked at my brother, shaking and ready to slap him hard. Instead, I nodded, "We need to catch the plane."

He laughed, "Picking up bad habits from Lochlan, little sister." The difference was that I heard every God-damned word.

We boarded our plane and I had to think about everything he'd said. It took over for me in the fear department. It consumed me. I was the evil bitch from the alley.

Danny was right. When had he gotten so smart? I thought about the childhoods we'd had. Everything about mine had been easy. Every minute was given to me. Even my older brother stopped me from ever being picked on. The one stalker boyfriend seemed like nothing compared to the things Lochlan had faced.

I hated myself more and more with every mile we flew. We landed and I sprinted for the entrance. He was standing alone with sunglasses and a hoodie on. I would have known him even with the hood pulled up. I ran across the wide space and leapt into his arms. He held me tight to him. Lochlan took deep breaths of my neck.

Danny dragged us out, Lochlan carrying me and all. I looked up and sobbed, "I'm so sorry I made her stressed."

He shook his head, "Just don't leave me. Please, stop doing that."

I shook my head, "I won't leave. And you can plate my food. It's weird but I see why you do it."

A tear rolled down his cheek, "She's doing really well. Dad has her at the house again."

I frowned, "So soon?"

He nodded, "She might not say much, but what she does communicate is not missed. She's never going to forgive me, and she wanted her own bed."

I kissed his lips softly, "I'm sorry, baby."

"I'm more sorry."

We got into the truck that had been in the driveway. Lochlan drove like a nut. We didn't talk.

When we got to the house, I was fading fast. I was beat but I wanted to see Judith desperately. Gerry opened the door as we arrived. I kissed his cheek, walking past him to the living room. She wasn't there. I turned and walked out, ignoring Mike, Lissie and Alex. I opened the door at the end of the hall, knocking lightly as I did it. Al beamed when he saw me. I shushed him, trying not to cry, "I'm so sorry for the drama I brought into your home."

He pulled me back, "No. Our son is the one…"

I put my finger to his lips, "He has never been anything but a good boyfriend. He's never given me a reason to doubt him." I shrugged and stole my brother's line, "I come from quitters. They're not like you people. My parents don't support each other the way you do. They would never understand your marriage. Or your compassion. They're selfish people. I'm selfish and self-absorbed. I see the light inside of Loch, and I know how big it is. I don't think I'm big enough to be a part of it. It's me not deserving him, not him straying on me. He would never and I know it. But I see the darkness in him and I assume the worst. Even though, he has never done anything but love me and protect me from it all. It's a flawed version of love because it's unique to him. But everyone has the same circumstances. We all love something or someone according to our ability to love. Loch is crazy and passionate and weird and intense and giving and funny. His love reflects all those things. He gets those amazing qualities from you both. I am sorry for whatever problems I have caused."

He hugged me, "Thank you. You caused no problems, but thank you for seeing him. Seeing the light and the dark."

I pulled from his arms and knelt at her bed. She was sobbing silently. She made a noise. I gripped her hand, "I am truly sorry."

She blinked out of control.

"She wants to tell you something."

I looked at Al, "How?"

He grabbed a pen and paper, wiping a rogue tear from his face, "Okay, baby."

She looked at him and started a series of blinks. I didn't understand anything, but assumed he was counting blinks and putting down the letters that matched the number of blinks.

It went on for a couple minutes. He read it and smiled, "She said 'be his shelter from the storm, whether it's inside or out.'"

She gave me a peaceful look, and I knew she was giving him to me. He would be mine to protect and keep safe. We would learn to love each other like his parents; I could learn how. I gripped her hands and fought my sobs, "I will. I'll always keep him safe in my heart." I kissed her hand and rose, "Get some rest."

She blinked twice.

"That means yes."

I nodded, "I assumed. Goodnight and happy Thanksgiving from the other day."

Al nodded, "We're thankful for you."

I shook my head, "Not as thankful as I am for you." I hardly knew them and yet I'd never felt more welcomed and loved.

I walked out of the room. He was standing in the hall looking dark. I stood on my tiptoes and brushed my lips against his, "Your turn."

He looked down and walked in. I walked into his room, not going into the living room. I was humiliated and sickened by my actions. I wanted a time machine to go back and change it all.

Gerry walked into the room with a huge sandwich.

He handed it to me, "You okay?"

I shook my head, "I'm a petty asshole."

He tilted his head, "Girl, if I saw Dean do that on TV, I would burn the fucking production set to the ground. You're not petty, you're insecure because women of the world wanna dry hump your man."

I sighed, "Isn't there a saying about the brighter the star, the hotter the fire?"

He laughed, "Yeah, something like that. You feeling scorched?"

I laughed, "No, just the heat maybe." Danny came in the room, "Hey. You okay?"

"Ya."

"How's Judith?"

I nodded, "She's good."

He took half of my turkey sandwich and ate a big bite. "You know we should have just gone to Mom and Dad's this weekend. They wouldn't have even noticed the drama."

I smiled, "I'm glad we came here. I feel sick about Judith getting stressed and having a stroke, but I'm glad I met them, and I see it all now."

Danny shook his head, "I feel sick too. I'm glad I phoned Mikayla though. She was bawling and apologizing. It was awesome."

Gerry gave him a look, "You did?"

Danny nodded and chewed. Gerry was about to say something, but Lochlan came in. He looked at us all with a confused stare. I smiled at him. He walked over and took my half sandwich that was left. He took a huge bite and sat back. We sat in silence. It wasn't awkward; it was exhaustion. We were tired of our petty selves.

Chapter Seventeen
I want my MTV

I curled into him, sucking the warmth from him. He wrapped a huge arm around me, pulling me in, "Princess, you awake?"

I nodded, "Sort of."

"I love you."

I turned around to face him, "Loch, I don't how it happened so fast, and I don't why it's taken me something like this to say it, but I want to."

He kissed my nose and then my cheek. I whispered into his scruffy face, "I love you."

He pulled back, "You do?"

I nodded, "More than I can explain or understand. It goes against every natural and reasonable thing I believe, but I do. In three and a half months you have won me, body and soul."

He smiled, the sexy one that made me inhale funny, "Marry me."

I laughed, "I can't."

He pulled back, "You love me and I love you. Why not?"

I laughed, "Because, we've known each other for three and a half months. That's crazy."

His eyes sparkled, "I'm crazy, crazy about you and sort of crazy on my own."

I nodded, "Yeah, you are. Tell me what happened on that show."

His eyes narrowed, "Me, Andrew, Mikayla, and Ben were the final four. Ben found out that Andrew was gay. Andrew was in first place, as far as stats went. Being gay would hurt his chances of winning. It would also hurt his chances of being a successful pop star. You have to be like George Michael and build the fans and then come out, maybe not in a public washroom though."

I snickered but his face stayed dark.

"Ben came to me, not knowing my identical twin was gay, and told me of his plan. I was tied for second place with Ben, not giving a shit about the show. I just wanted it to end. I hated it. It wasn't art; it was drama. Anyway I told him no, I wouldn't help him, and if I found out anyone heard Andrew was gay, I would kick his head in." It was starting to make sense.

"So the night of the second-to-last show, Andrew and I went first and did our performances. Best ones ever; we rocked it. Ben was scheduled last. I came off stage and heard him telling the producer that Andrew wanted them to have a gay pride thing on there in support of him and his coming out. He'd told his family and was coming out. Of course, that wasn't true. Andrew never told anyone. I flipped out. I beat him up. I went black. I don't even remember it. But he never performed and ended up being 'the poor guy that psycho Lochlan beat up'. He won the show and I took the rap, to stop anyone from knowing about Andrew."

I kissed him, "Why didn't you tell me?"

He shook his head, "It's not my secret to tell, but I'm more scared of losing you than I am of protecting him."

I grabbed his face hard, "You will never lose me. I'm done with all of that. I don't want to be like my parents. I don't want to run away every time I'm scared or hurt. I want to find a way to be with you and not lose me. I want to be part of both Lochlans. I want to come with you and be with you."

He frowned, "What about law school? I don't want you to give up your dream. That is you."

I shrugged, "I'm twenty-three years old. I have loads of time. Who knows how long this is going to be happening for you? Stardom is fleeting, but law school is permanent."

"What about your plan?"

I laughed, "You've been fucking with my plans from the minute I met you. I was supposed to unpack my apartment, go for a run, come back and make dinner in my new kitchen. I wanted to set up my Netflix account, eat, and watch TV alone. My plan only ever involved me. It was a selfish plan for a selfish person. Now I want to support you. I want you to relax, and not worry about us, and not worry about losing me. Make it about the music. I want to finish this semester and then I'll take a leave."

He smiled and kissed me, "I want you to come with me. I hate being away from you." I closed my eyes and laid my head in the crook of his arm.

When I woke up, he was passed out. It was light out. It felt like I was in the movie Groundhog Day, and I was waking up with my second chance at everything. I pulled on clothes and stumbled down the hall. Danny grinned at me, "You always have been such a beautiful morning person."

I flipped him the bird and poured a cup of coffee. Al was setting the table and Gerry was flipping bacon. Al looked at me, "Go wake his ass up. He's going to be upset if he misses breakfast."

I laughed, "Okay." I poured him a coffee and glanced at Al, "How does he like his coffee?"

A grin crept across his lips, "One cream."

I nodded and added it to the coffee. I carried it down the hall. I put it on the bedside table and bent forward, kissing him good morning. He smiled against my lips, "It feels early still."

I took a deep breath, "Smell anything you might be upset about missing?"

He inhaled, sniffing the air, and nodded, "You."

I shoved, "You're going to have to do better than that."

He opened his bright-blue eyes, giving me the look, "You want me to start trying?"

I laughed, "No. I don't think we'll leave the room if you start trying. I want you to get up because Al said you have to."

He glanced at the mug of steaming coffee, "Did you make my coffee?" He sounded skeptical.

Crossing my arms and looking hurt, "Don't act like I never do things for you."

He wrapped his arms around me, "I know you do, just not things like that." He sat up, dragging me with him. He sipped the coffee and nodded, "You know how to make my coffee?"

I winked at him and shot him my cheesy grin, "I'm full of all kinds of surprises." I got up and walked out of the room with swagger, "Hurry up."

"Yes, ma'am."

My heart melted. No one on earth could say 'yes ma'am' the way a boy from Tennessee could.

We stayed for two more days. I lost my job and got my first warning email about missing classes. But I laughed harder than I ever had. I smiled bigger than I could imagine doing, especially considering the circumstances. And I relaxed into the crook of his arm, like I belonged there. Danny, Gerry, and I stayed with Judith, so Alex, Lissie, and Loch could all go out for dinner with their dad. When they got home, Loch never looked freer.

We got back to Boston mid-afternoon the next day. I went for a run and he, Gerry, and Danny went to deal with band stuff. When he got back, I was working like a slave to catch up on the papers I needed to finish, and definitions I needed to memorize. He kissed the side of my face; I waved him away. He laughed, "Nice. I come to tell you we have been invited to replace another band and perform live at the MTV music awards in the Netherlands, and you swat me."

My Side

My jaw dropped, "What?"

He nodded, "There was a series of terrible storms, so it got switched from November to December. It's next week and we got invited. One of the other bands had to back out. Lead singer had to have vocal surgery."

I looked at Danny who was eating yogurt from the big container in the fridge, "Shut the front door!"

Danny nodded, "I'm going to get laid so much."

I grimaced, "Not if you eat like that."

I jumped up, grabbing Lochlan. He wrapped around me, "Can you come?"

My stomach sank, I shook my head, "All my finals are next week and the week after. It's from the 6th to the 13th of December. There is no way I can miss them; I'll blow the entire semester."

He looked like he might... but he didn't flip out, he stayed calm and nodded, "I'll get the guys to record my every move."

I shook my head, feeling like I was the old ball and chain. "Baby, have fun. When the fuck does this happen to anyone? I'll see the performance live and enjoy every second of it. If you kiss a celebrity or let girls maul you, I'll make my drink extra strong and try to take it like a man. When you get home you'll be given a few minutes to explain. If your explanation is 'oh man, I was so drunk'—I mace you."

He looked amused, "Funny."

I shook my head, "Not funny, deal or no deal." I put my hand out.

He gave me a hesitant look, "You ever been sprayed by that shit?"

I tilted my head. He sighed and took my hand in his, "You're sort of mean, you know that, right?"

I nodded, "And yet, I won't lose any sleep over it."

Danny shook his head, "I wouldn't agree to shit with her, not shit like that. Her brain works in evil ways."

Lochlan gave me the smile, making my heart race, "I'd agree to anything."

Danny flopped into a chair, "That is because you are a sucker, my friend."

I gave him a look, but Lochlan just shook his head, "You wait. I was like you until August 12th."

I poked him, "You picked a chick up on the way home from the restaurant that day."

He winked, "That was the last one. I swear. I thought about you the entire…"

My hand shot up, covering his mouth, "Oh my God, do not finish that sentence. And you forget about the girl at Costco."

He laughed, "Okay, that was the last one, I swear. Besides she doesn't count, Gerry went all mean-ass ho on her. Mocked that lovely tattoo on her back that looked like a bullseye." He winked at Danny who was howling and leaning against the counter for support.

I shuddered, "What the heck? I need a bath and a whiskey. Gross." I stopped and looked at him, "Why the hell all the bets and the bravado if you weren't sleeping with other people?"

He blushed, "I never worked so hard to get laid in all my life. You had me thinking constantly of new ways to impress you, or how I would be able to spend time with you. I just knew I had to make you mine."

I nodded and slumped back down on the couch. He was killing me. I forced myself to pick my book back up. He sat beside me and turned the TV on and passed me his iPod and Beats. I pulled them on and turned on the playlist he'd made for me. They watched something about people who lived in a swamp or girls with gators.

Somehow, I got lost in the books and the music and when I surfaced, he and Danny were passed out. I stole the remote and turned on my favorite movie on Netflix, The Jane Austen Book club.

When Loch woke, it was the scene where the teacher was standing at the intersection, looking at the boy across the sidewalk. I shuddered with a sob.

"Are you crying?"

I shook my head, "No."

He wiped my tears, "What's wrong?"

I shook my head, "Nothing. I love this movie."

He looked horrified, "That is something I will never understand about girls."

He pulled me in, passing me some tissues. When the movie was over, he was out cold again. I climbed off the couch and crept to bed. I lay there for a minute, thinking and feeling the things I had pretended to be okay with. Things like I was settling with the belief that his magic was bigger than my own. God blessed his purpose, whereas mine was run of the mill. There was a terrible whisper in the back of my mind that taunted me. It told me I would tire of being second fiddle and less important. I would tire of his love when I didn't see myself in his eyes anymore.

I pulled up my big girl panties and scolded my low self-esteem. I knew none of that would ever happen. Well… I hoped. When I fell asleep, I was certain we would be together forever.

Chapter Eighteen
The passing

I finished the last exam and knew I'd fucked myself. Law school took a serious commitment, and I had barely given fifty percent. If I passed it would be some kind of miracle. My phone vibrated as I left the exam. I looked at yet another picture of a massive beer and Danny smoking a huge joint. I laughed and shook my head. The MTV music awards had been mind blowing. The show was insane, and they rocked it like they'd been doing it for a hundred years, like the Rolling Stones. They were staying in Europe for a few extra days to do some last-minute shows. I spent the entire week he'd been gone watching the live performance over and over like a freakshow.

Dean caught up with me in the hallway, "Hey." He grabbed my arm.

I smiled, "Hey, how's it going?"

He shook his head, "I marked your tests, and I'm confused. Are you blowing this on purpose?"

I shook my head, "No, I've just been caught up in all of it, ya know."

He linked his arm in mine, "Let's go get a coffee. You need a peppy speech and I happen to rock those like a boss."

I rolled my eyes, "You're starting to sound like Gerry and them."

He snorted, "At least I'm not giving up my dreams to be with them."

"Dean, he's not a normal guy. My dreams barely register with his lifestyle."

He gave me a bizarre look, "You mean because he has ADHD and his mom is dying? You think there aren't a thousand like him in this state alone?"

I met his challenging look, "Are they performing live and having every second of their bad behavior scrutinized like he is? I'd say he's one in a billion."

He ran his hands through his hair, "Erin, you have to have something that's yours. Every relationship needs that."

I shook my head, "My parents both have something that's theirs, and they don't have each other anymore. They wanted their own things too much. If you watch celebrity couples, one always hangs back a bit, lets the other one have the lime light."

He rolled his eyes, "You aren't exactly a celebrity couple."

I laughed, "Harsh, I mean... I'm cool with pulling back and supporting him."

"So you're okay with blowing all that money and the semester, because he's a dramatic rock star?"

I shook my head, "I'm not okay with it. I just want to be there for him. They start tours next year; they're already booked into seventeen. That's a lot of shows. Three are sold out. He is going to need me."

He crossed his arms, releasing me, "Why? Are you a magical pill or are you just trying to convince him that he needs you, so that you feel justified in your suspicions of him?"

Guilt tore into me, "No offense sir, but screw you."

He laughed bitterly, "We aren't doing the teacher-student thing right now and you know it."

"I made a mess of our relationship. I made him feel like he had to choose me or the music."

He grabbed my shoulders, "Honey, the solution isn't him or your career. It's trusting him and letting him rock. I'm not stressed about Gerry. If he doesn't want to be with me anymore or finds someone new, I'll be devastated, but I'm worthy of someone who wants to be with me as I am. Gerry isn't the only man in the world and he's not the reason I'm happy. I'm happy on my terms. He makes all the good things better." His words resonated. "Don't drop out. You'll have to pull your grades up next semester but don't drop out. I'll help you."

I nodded. It was the choice I wanted. If I was honest with myself and standing at the crosswalk like the teacher, I would choose my dreams—not let guilt and a lack of trust get me down. "Thank you."

He shook his head, "It's my job."

I went home after coffee and took a hot bath. My phone rang, just as I was getting settled. I sat up and dried my hand.

"Hello?"

It was Alex, "Hey, Erin."

I smiled, "Hi. How are you?"

"Not good."

My stomach dropped.

"What's happened? Is it Judith?"

He sighed, "No. Mom is good. She's doing great. It's Dad, if you can believe it."

"Fuck off."

"Not even kidding. He's had a massive heart attack. The doctor sad it was just a matter of time, and this whole year has been so stressful for them. He's getting stabilized and then they're doing surgery."

"His cholesterol?"

"Yes, and blood pressure, and diabetes, and whatever else he has going on that he hasn't warned us about."

I closed my eyes, "Have you called Lochlan?"

"Mom doesn't want him called. She wants him to focus on himself and the band. She wants him to stay in Europe and do the shows."

I gasped, "His dad is about to have surgery. He needs to come home."

"I know. They feel like a burden and like they're holding him back. And you know him, he's going to say that him leaving Dad to care for her himself and the stress of his career is what caused this."

I felt something I'd never felt before, "You know that's not true." I would protect him from anything, including them.

"I know. But you know what he's like. He's going to say this was his fault, and quit music. Erin, he'll quit the band, just like he did the job he had lined up."

I pulled the plug on the tub, "I'll be there as fast as I can." I called my Dad and begged for him to book my flight. I was nearly broke. I turned on the water works; it was easy.

My back was aching, and I was flooded with memories of the article I'd read about radiation on planes. I ate my salted peanuts and drank my ginger ale, trying not to rock and think about plane crashes. At least the flight was only just over two hours.

Lissie picked me up. She looked rough. I hugged her, letting her cry on my shoulder.

"He's not strong enough for surgery. They can't do anything."

I closed my eyes and just breathed. I didn't know what to say. My phone started ringing. I pulled it out and answered, still holding her, "Hey."

I smiled, "Hey." He sounded good. I hated that I was about to ruin that.

"We just got home, and you're not here. I saw your carry-on was gone. You okay?"

I nodded, "No." I couldn't lie to him. Lissie pulled back and nodded, "Tell him."

I handed her the phone, "Do you want to?"

"Is that my sister? What the fuck is going on?"

She shook her head, "It's better if you do it."

I placed the phone over my ear, "I need you to calm down and listen to me. Do not overreact and do not stop listening until I get it all out, okay?"

"FUCKING TELL ME WHATS WRONG!"

I stayed calm, "Put Danny on if you can't stay calm."

He sounded savage, "I'm calm."

I would have laughed if it had been any other circumstances. "Your dad had a heart attack. He's in the hospital and they're trying to stabilize him. Your mom is fine. Alex has her in the hospital so she can see him. She's in her wheelchair and completely fine. He is being stabilized."

"Are you done now?"

I frowned, "Yeah."

"Be there in three hours. We'll meet you at the hospital."

He hung up the phone, and I couldn't help but wonder what he was smashing.

I sighed and gave his sister my weakest smile, "They'll be here in a few hours."

She hugged herself and showed me the way to the car."

The hospital was silent until they arrived. I was giving Judith a sip of water when we heard his voice. Her eyes opened wide. She looked at me with daggers. I gave them back, "He was done with the show. He doesn't have another performance now until after Christmas."

She blinked twice. I nodded, "Okay, then."

He bent, kissing her face and then mine. His eyes were black when he stood back and looked down on me. "How is he?"

I shook my head, "Nothing has changed."

He pointed down the hall and clenched his jaw, "I just talked to his doctor and he's under the impression that we understand they can't do anything for him."

I felt my gaze weaken. His weakened with it. He didn't fill with fury the way I thought he would. He looked destroyed. He walked into the room and laid his face on his dad's stomach. My heart broke.

I took Judith for a walk. We sat in the window of a breezeway, enjoying the flash rainstorm outside. I didn't look at her. I just spoke softly, "I think that I have learned more from your family in the weeks I've known them than I have in the decades with mine."

She blinked fast. I pulled my cell phone out and nodded, "Okay. I can do this."

She blinked, 9 times, 12 times, 15 times, 22 times, 5 times, 21 times, took a break, 4 times, 1 time, 21 times, 7 times, 8 times, 20 times, 5 times, 18 times. I counted them out in my head and smiled. ILOVEUDAUGHTER, was what it said on my cell phone screen. I leaned into her, "Thank you. I love you too." And I did. No amount of time was needed to make me love them.

We sat in the silence and watched the rain and held hands. Danny came running down the hallway. I knew by his face what had happened. He stopped when he saw me looking. His eyes shone. He turned around and walked back.

I looked down on her. Her face was covered in tears. They were silent. I didn't belittle the fact. I knew she had felt him leave. There was no way she saw Danny. She was watching the rain. She gripped my hand a little bit tighter. We sat there until she squeezed, "Ready to go back?"

She blinked twice. I wheeled her back to the room. Lochlan was gone; Danny, Gerry, and Mike were sitting on the seats outside of the room. I wheeled her to the door. Lissie took her from there. I whispered, "I'm so sorry."

She shook and wheeled her mother into the room to say her

goodbyes. I turned and ran. I didn't know where he would go. I never memorized him the way he did me. I ran hard until I reached the window showing one side of the courtyard. It dawned on me. I knew he would be in the rain. I pushed the door open and walked out. He was there, sitting on a stone bench amongst large trees and bushes. He was hunched over. I stood in front of him for a moment, getting completely soaked. He grabbed my hips and pulled me into his lap. He buried his face in my neck, as I wrapped my legs around him. He folded around me completely. I closed my eyes and let the rain wash all over us.

I kissed the side of his face, "I'm sorry, baby."

Chapter Nineteen

November rain brings December pain

My parents flew in, taking up all the room in everyone's minds. Mom doted on Judith like it was her job, not that Judith minded the crazy distraction. At one point, I whispered into her ear, "You see what I'm saying?"

She gave me the two blinks and we moved on from the conversation. My dad went for a couple runs with Lissie. He never stopped talking about her. I was ready to strangle him. Danny and Gerry made arrangements for the band to move to Nashville. It was better for them anyway.

I lay on the bed beside him, staring at his lost face. "Mike and Gerry, and the new guy Leon, they're moving. Gerry bought a house, and he, Danny, and Mike are thinking about sharing it.

His eyes flicked on me, "I can't ask them to do that."

I shrugged, "It's done. No one wants to see Judith in a home. Your dad worked hard to keep her here. Everyone wants to be here."

He bit his chapped lip, "I'm the newest member. They can't move and lose Lenny."

I smiled, "Lenny sent a huge bouquet of flowers and a long letter, basically saying he was leaving Thin Ice in your capable hands. He wanted your mom to have you, and he wanted you to have your dreams."

He closed his eyes, "I need some more sleep."

I grabbed his jaw, "Look at me, Loch."

He opened his eyes.

I shook my head, "No. You need to get up and help your family. Your mom lost her husband and his support. She's scared, and she doesn't need to add you to the things she needs to worry about."

He kissed my nose and climbed out of the bed, "Okay." He left the room, leaving me there.

Danny came in the room and closed the door. He lay on the bed next to me, "How the hell did this many things go wrong, all at once?"

I shook my head, "I don't know, but damn."

He nodded and looked at me, "Did they used to live under power lines? How the hell are they so sick and so young? Look at our mom and dad in comparison?"

"I know. In some ways I think our parents have done a couple things right. They've been selfish, but they take care of themselves. Yeah, they've always been number one their books, but at least that involves health. We can at least give them that."

He snorted, "Yeah, the fucking line draws there. Mom has been a complete psycho about Judith. She even talks to her like Judith doesn't speak English. And Dad was chatting up some young thing on the road when I went outside for a minute."

I grimaced, "I swear he hit on Lissie."

He scowled, "I'm gonna hit him. He needs to remember he's fifty-seven."

I sighed, "Maybe they are doing the right thing by acting young. They look young and live young." I glanced at him, "Do you see yourself getting married, having kids, and adding to the stress and shit in your life? Or do you see it as more enjoyable to be like mom and dad, and just have fun and be carefree?"

He sighed, "I don't know."

I snuggled into him, "Me either."

"What about Loch?"

I shrugged, "We can be young and fun together maybe. He can show me how."

"Fat chance. You won't ever be fun. Let's face it."

I slapped his belly and closed my eyes.

The funeral was lovely. His old friends and workmates came with their wives. Lissie had put Judith in a beautifully elegant dress she'd bought for her. She looked beautiful.

Lochlan stood, stoic. He didn't cry; he hadn't since the courtyard at the hospital. He didn't hold my hand or even stand near me. He'd shut me out, except in his sleep. He needed me then. He whispered things, like begging me not to leave.

We got back to the house, all exhausted and ready to sink into a pit of despair. I pulled off the heels I had to get my mom to buy me, along with the dress. I didn't have anything that was worthy of a funeral in my tiny bag. The kitchen was where I lost it. I made coffee and slumped against the counter. The kitchen was Al's domain. He made the coffee and the snacks. He made the meals and catered to everyone. He had never done it in all their years of marriage until he had to. Then he learned how to cook. How to make everything the way she liked it. How to guess on the things he didn't know and how to make everyone in his home comfortable, regardless of the fact that his life was hard.

He was mother, father, and friend to his children. I knew him for a couple weeks and I loved him like he was my family. I felt warm hands on my back. I looked back at Gerry, wiping my face, "Sorry." He took a tissue and wiped away my tears and mascara.

"Wanna go for a walk?"

I nodded.

We left the house. Danny and Mike came. We left the Barlows to grieve alone. Mom and Dad had gone to their hotel rooms.

We didn't tell them we were leaving. We just did. We walked, the four of us, looking too fancy and dark for the peaceful neighborhood.

Gerry walked up to a huge, fancy house in the new area. It had a sold sign. He produced a key, "Want to see it?"

I smiled, "You bought into the same neighborhood?"

He nodded, "Yeah. Alex and Lissie are too. Everyone has agreed that we should all be as close as possible. This is my close." He turned the key and stood back, impressed. It was a huge home, double-car garage, two stories and a basement. I frowned, "What are you going to do with all this room?"

He grinned and opened the huge door. We stepped into the grand front entry. The floors were slate and maple hardwood, with a slightly reddish stain. The kitchen was slate and marble with stainless everything. Two sinks and a huge island. It was spectacular. The master bedroom was the size of our entire apartment and the ensuite was worthy of royalty. Gerry grinned, "It's nice, huh?"

I shook my head, "Nice is like insulting this home."

He patted Danny on the back, "The best is downstairs." We followed him to the unfinished basement. He held his hands out at the drywall and framework. "This is going to be a state-of-the-art sound room. It will be soundproofed and finished for us to record and rehearse, and whatever we need it for. It's only a block from Judith's, so we don't have to worry about being far from her while we work."

Danny beamed, "That's awesome." None of us could get very excited, and honestly, he didn't even sound impressed with himself. Mike sat on the stairs, "Our first concert isn't until March, so we'll have plenty of time."

Danny shook his head, "No. We have a new keyboard player to get used to, we have three new songs that we just bought, and we have to get the rest of the album cut. There is zero time. How long till this is complete?"

Gerry thought for a second, "They said three weeks, first week of January."

I wondered how much money they all had suddenly? Even Danny seemed flush.

I looked around, "This will be perfect for you guys. Good choice,

Gerry."

He grinned, "You are welcome to stay anytime you want—you know that, right?"

His tone made my stomach feel like it fell. I nodded, "Of course. Thank you." I pointed, "I'm going to head back."

They stayed at the house, plotting or avoiding. It didn't matter which.

I entered through the backyard and sat on the huge, sofa-like deck swing. I curled up and watched the fluffy, white clouds. The skies in Nashville were bluer and clearer than Boston's. It was more like North Dakota. I missed home. I closed my eyes and fell asleep.

I woke to voices. I opened my eyes and looked through the dark yard. The sun had fully set and night had claimed the sky. Lochlan and Alex were standing in the yard.

"You owe her more than that." Alex said. I was about to come to Loch's defense, assuming it was about his mother.

Lochlan crossed his arms, "I want her to go home. I just want her gone. I don't want to have to think about this anymore."

Gerry's comment about me staying with him made me instantly sick. Was I the last to know I was being dumped on the day Al was buried? I stayed perfectly still.

Alex shook his head, looking down, "You haven't changed at all. Everyone is always focused on poor Lochlan, Brave Lochlan, Sad Lochlan, ADHD Lochlan, Successful Lochlan. Everything is always about you." He walked past him, leaving Loch staring at the backyard.

Silent tears streamed down my face. What had I done? Why did he want me gone? I wanted answers but I could see the darkness in him from there. Provoking him seemed like a... oh fuck it. I sat upright. He turned. I could barely see his eyes in the dimly-lit yard.

"I just want to know why. Alex is right; you owe me that."

He didn't walk to me. He looked down, "I just want you gone. I don't want to do this anymore. I have to focus on my mom and Thin Ice and I don't have room. You're too much work."

I got up and slowly walked to him, "You're making a decision for me?"

His face stayed frozen, "Just run away, like you always do. I'm giving you permission to go this time."

I looked up at him, "I always saw you as so brave and strong. You overcame so many things and saved that Andrew guy." I nodded, "You had me fooled. I have to give it to you. I always believed you were the better one. I thought that I wasn't worthy because I couldn't shine as bright as you." I turned to leave but he grabbed my arm and spun me.

He looked desperate and angry, "I need this."

I shoved him, ripping the mace from my dress pocket and holding it out, "YOU RUINED MY FUCKING LIFE!" I pulled my other arm free and wiped my face, "I NEVER WANT TO SEE YOU AGAIN! I WISH I NEVER MET YOU!" I took a deep breath and calmed my fury, as I backed up with my mace still out, "I hate you, Lochlan Barlow. I hate you."

I turned and left the yard. I ran as fast as I could to Gerry's house. I knocked on the door. Gerry answered, his face broke. He wrapped around me but I shook my head, "I just need a ride to the airport and my shit from Judith's."

Danny looked psycho. I pointed at him, "You stay here. You get it under control. I'm your sister first, and this is the best you there has ever been. So you stay and make it work with him. You make it work."

He looked sick. I looked at Mike, "Get him drunk and don't let him go to Judith's. Don't let him fight with Loch."

I walked with Gerry back to Lochlan's, "How did you know?"

He gave me a sideways look, "I could see it on him. He was shutting you out. I've played those cards before."

My Side

We got close. I stopped, "I'll wait here."

He nodded weakly.

It was Alex who came in his BMW. I shook my head, "You need to be with your family."

He laughed, "I'm going to strangle my fucking idiot of a brother if I stay there another minute. So get in and stop being a pain in the ass."

I relented when I saw Lochlan running towards us and climbed in. I ignored his screams and his face as we drove past him.

"I called and booked your flight for you. I imagine this has cost you a lot of money."

I gave him a disgusted look, "I don't want anything from you."

He looked hurt, "I may look like him but I'm not him." His jaw trembled. "He's doing this, pushing you away, because..." I put a hand out, "Stop. He's a big boy, he's made his choice. He has to live with it. I am done with him."

He snorted, "You're both so selfish, it's insane. You can't see that he's trying to spare you."

I looked at him with daggers, "Spare me from what? Being part of his life? Dealing with the awful things that happen to people? Fuck that. He asked me to marry him. That would mean good times and bad. You know how close I was to saying yes? Had he asked a second time, it would have been a yes. I am against marriage and giving up your life for another person; it was bred into me. But for him, I would give it all up. I already had my email written to school, telling them I wouldn't be returning because Judith needed me and so he could go on the road. Don't you dare call me selfish. Fuck you. You should have quit dental school and helped take care of her and Lissie too. She should have stayed a substitute but she didn't. Your poor father worked himself to death, trying to keep her comfortable and alive. Only Loch stayed and took care of her, you two took care of yourselves. Don't call us selfish."

He nodded, "I'm sorry. I didn't know. I just thought this was you running away again."

I bit my lip, "You expect me to beg him to let me stay? I have just a smidge more pride than that. I'm sorry."

"No, I'm sorry."

I looked out the window, "It doesn't matter anyway. He isn't ever going to be able to juggle Judith, his career, and a relationship."

He looked like he was going to say something but he didn't.

I hugged him when we got to the airport, "I'm sorry I said that about you and Lissie. I don't believe that. I think you did exactly what Al would have wanted you to do. He was so proud of all three of you."

He nodded, "Thank you. I'm sorry I called you selfish."

I shook my head, "I am. If I write her letters, will you help her read them?"

He started to cry and nodded.

I didn't cry. I kissed his cheek and left dry-eyed. I was done crying for all of them. Well, except Judith. I would visit her on spring break. I would just make sure he was gone on a concert or something.

I took a deep breath and prepared for my flight, another one alone and scared. That would be fun to add to my broken heart.

Chapter Twenty
When we were young

"Erin, I really think you should consider coming to our firm for the summer practicum. I'm recommending you." His smug face made me angry. He was so full of himself. I used to think rock stars were the egotistical men of the world... Matthew Price was the example of how wrong I was to assume they owned the franchise. He was suave, handsome, and a complete fucking tool.

A tool I smiled at, with all my heart. I had been for two months. He was a partner in a successful, corporate law firm. I had once wanted to put away bad guys. That dream ended, along with a few others.

I nodded, "Thank you, Mr. Price. I was thinking of it. Dean has told me all about it." Dean gave me a look and twitched his head no. I smiled at him, "He speaks very highly of you."

Dean laughed and patted Mr. Price on the back, "Yes, well... we are old friends."

Matthew scoffed, "Speak for yourself—I am in my prime." He crossed his arms and gave Dean a serious look, "You will ensure she ends up in my hands, won't you?"

Dean swallowed, "Well, we have some excellent placements for students. I'm sure she will pick your office, but you never know."

I smiled, "Of course, I will. If you'll have me." I regretted the words as I said them. I watched Matthew's face change to that of a wolf and Dean's eyes darkened with a furrow. I stammered, "I-I-I mean, I'm sure there are plenty of great candidates, but your firm interests me the most."

He nodded, "Excellent. We will be in touch at the end of May." He smiled at Dean, "We need to meet up for some racquet ball."

Dean nodded, "Yes, that would be lovely."

Matthew took my hand in his, "Until we meet again." He delicately stroked his fingers along mine and walked away.

I gave Dean a look as the classroom emptied, "He's so creepy, but I want that job."

He shook his head, "I forbid it."

I laughed and handed in my paper with a smug look. Dean shook his head, "I liked you better when you were struggling." I laughed, "I liked you better when I still had a faint hope that you were straight, and possibly going to hit on me."

He whacked me on the head with a paper and pointed, "Go, smart ass. I'll see you in an hour for coffee?"

I nodded.

Dean was the only old piece left of the old me, him and the apartment. I wasn't leaving the apartment though. It was my chance to finally make it mine. I boxed up the asshole's shit and burned his sheets and mailed the ashes of the sheets along with the boxes, to Nashville... C.O.D. Then I went out and I bought new sheets and made the room pretty.

January and February in Boston were cold, but March was worse. My heart was colder as the time went on too. I was quickly becoming the stone fox I needed to be. Thanks to the boy I never named, my womanly wiles were found. I used them to manipulate like a boss. The apartment looked the way I had always wanted it to. It was clean, white, and shiny, like my straight hair. When I looked in the mirror, I didn't see myself in my eyes. I saw a girl who scared me, but that was good for the job I wanted to have.

Was the job ever going to be enough? I didn't know that for sure. It would never be enough to make me forget being with him. There was never going to be anything that was enough to fill the void. Nothing could compare to him. It was a pity I never fully realized it until after he'd pushed me away. I regretted the time I'd spent running from him. It could have been so much better spent.

I sat in the chair at Starbucks and sipped my coffee.

He came in smiling, "How are you since I last saw you fawning over Mr. Price?"

I grinned, "Good. "I'm taking that summer term if I get it. Anyway, enough of that. I got a letter from Judith today, well Gerry translated it for her. He said we had to read it together." I pulled it from my purse and laid it down. Dean lifted it and smelled it. He smiled, "Still wearing Dirty English."

I laughed, "It probably reminds him of you."

He stuck his tongue out. His accent was so faded, no one ever really noticed it. I certainly hadn't, until we got drunk on New Year's. Gerry had sent him over to rescue me after I spent Christmas alone. I had been ready to board my flight home when I discovered that Danny wasn't going home alone. I'd had a bad feeling Danny might bring the one person I couldn't see... and he had. When I cancelled, Danny ratted me out to Gerry for not going to North Dakota. Gerry had to be with his family in Seattle and hadn't been able to come to my rescue, so he sent the next best thing. Dean took me to a gay and lesbian bar, and I could truly say I'd had a blast.

Dean gave me an odd look, "Where were you just now?"

I shook my head, "Just lost for a second."

He smiled, "Want me to read it?"

I nodded and sipped my caramel macchiato.

He opened it, smelling it once more, and began to read.

"Dearest, we miss you more than anything. The boys miss you. All of them." He stopped and smiled knowingly. I remained stoic. He took the hint and continued, "When I was young and in love, I wanted to be a flight attendant. I even went to school for it. I met Al at the airport the day we were given our assignments. I got New York. I had done well. Al asked me out and I agreed. I never expected to love him immediately. He was charming and slightly crazy as all controllers were. He begged me to stay with him and see where we could go with our relationship. I turned him down, chasing my dreams. He showed up in New York a few weeks later, begging me to come home. I saw the look in those eyes; they got so intense and frightened when faced with the possibility of losing me. I switched with a girl in Nashville and took the lesser posting. I have never regretted that decision. He knew from the minute he met me. It took me longer to see, but he always knew. I am writing you from my new home. Gerry and Alex helped me move here. Lissie is convincing Lochlan it is a good idea. You see I never cared about being home after the stroke, I only cared about being where Al was. He was my home." Dean stopped reading and fanned his damp eyes with the letter, "Oh wow."

I held my stiff upper lip until I saw the tear slip from his eye. We dabbed our eyes. Dean's voice broke as he read, "I am happy to be in a home so my children can live their lives and find love and happiness for themselves. No parent wants to be a burden. My children are brilliant and beautiful, and it's just like you said: they love each love in their own special way. I am glad that Lochlan found you, and I hope to God that he will earn his way back into your heart one day. Thank you for seeing him and being his shelter." Dean stopped, "I can't fucking do this here."

I sobbed into my napkin and laughed, "Jesus Christ. She is the queen of manipulation. She's doing that from a wheelchair with a blinking letter."

He put the letter down, "Wow, that was bad. She is good. Don't you agree?"

I shrugged, "I need to worry about me. I can't fall into that trap again."

He sipped his coffee and wiped his eyes again, "Oh, I don't know. I think you might, if given the right opportunity."

I sneered at him, "Worry about your own backyard. You forget your boyfriend is hanging with Satan's gay twin."

He shrugged and played with the smile crossing his lips, "I trust Gerry." His eyes narrowed, "Stop being such a bitch. Besides, Alex is dating someone."

I leaned forward, "What?" I snatched the letter, skipping the rest of the part that was Judith's diction, and went to the mushy shit intended for Dean. I gasped, "He's dating a dental hygienist?"

He smiled, "I won't lie. That makes me feel better."

I laughed, "It should. Alex got all the good things in the womb. He is the perfect version of you-know-who."

He swatted me, "Stop."

I laughed and began to finish my coffee. I swallowed, seeing how badly my hand was shaking. I put it down.

He nodded, "Going back to the letter, Judith's right. Love is love. I used to think love could be found anywhere. I see now though, I was wrong. If Gerry didn't love me anymore, I would die inside."

My tears started again. I knew that death.

He gripped my hands, "There is no letting go once you find it and it's real. There is no set amount of time it takes to see it either." He pulled a ring from his jacket.

I gasped, putting my hands to my mouth.

"I'm sorry if this is bad timing on your broken heart, but mine is so full I can't contain it. I'm going to ask him to be mine."

I smiled, "Oh my God, Dean. I'm so sorry for joking about Alex." I gripped his hands and cried the first good tears I'd cried in ages.

He laughed, "It was perfect timing for some delicious irony." His eyes twinkled, "Do you think he'll say yes?"

I shook my head, "I think he'll say I do."

He blushed, "I am very excited they're home this week. I'm going to ask tomorrow night. Will you go to the show with me?"

I gulped, "Thin Ice is playing this week?" Of course, I knew that.

He nodded, "Yes."

I shook my head, "No."

He pulled two backstage passes, "Yes, you are. Danny, Gerry, and Mike want to see you. I will need moral support for my huge life-altering decision. You will come and be my bestie. Stop acting like you lost Gerry and Mike as the kids in the divorce. They're as devastated as you are."

I shook my head, "I'm not devastated. I'm happy."

"You feel strong and healed then?"

I sighed, "I feel as good as I can. My heart was broken, I can't deny that. But I chose to move on and so has he, so there you have it."

He nodded, "Then you should be strong enough to be near him, I mean, if you're healed enough."

I sighed, "Not even funny. Don't you think one manipulation a day is enough?"

He shook his head, "No, and I feel like the second one is always the more effective one."

I stuck my tongue out at him, "Fine, pick me up."

He smiled, "You're sort of bad at the whole hag thing. I'm proposing in a country where gay marriage is not entirely legal. You need to be more fun and supportive. You need to be more into shopping and having fun. You're all about the school work and the deadlines now."

"Well, you should be into checking out hot, young men and going to gay bars with me, and instead, you are marrying the best man I know."

He snorted, "Thanks, I've had my share of Y.M.C.A."

I laughed and sighed.

Chapter Twenty-One
Full Circle

He got there early the day of the show. I was miserable, trying to stuff my considerably-bigger breasts into my push-up bra. He leaned on the door of the bathroom and sighed, "I thought women lost weight when they were stressed."

I scowled, "It's my winter weight. I gain it every winter and lose it every spring. It's from the lack of running."

"It's from the whole coconut-cream pie you bought at that scary-ass restaurant you made me take you to last week. Did you, or did you not, eat the entire pie?"

I moaned, "I'm not going. I don't fit anything."

He rolled his eyes, "It's ten pounds, and it's all tits and ass. Put on a dress. It'll hide the weight."

"You find something; I have to powder my face again. I'm blotchy." I looked like a stressed-out mess. I sat on the toilet, trying to find my Zen. I'd started taking hot yoga when the depressive blanket of fog landed on Boston and rained snow and sleet down on us for months. The heat made me feel better.

He came back with a gleam in his eye. "This is perfect. It'll show off the new tattoo."

I looked at it and drummed my fingers against the counter. I pulled off my push-up bra and slid the backless halter dress on. I turned to see my new tattoo. It was a harmony flower, the petals were made from hearts. I'd seen it at the yoga studio. It was to draw harmony into my life. I didn't want anyone thinking it was for him. It wasn't. It was for me. The tattoo sat on my left ribs, close to my heart. No one would ever see it unless I wore a backless dress like the one I was wearing. I looked in the mirror. The brown dress sat a bit short compared to before. My larger butt lifted it a bit. "Is it obscene?"

He smiled, "It's perfect. You look stunning. I would molest you if tits and ass were my thing." I smacked his arm, "Stop saying that."

The front hung in baggy ripples, preventing anyone from being able to see my nipples, but the side-boob made it obvious I was not wearing even a cup. The dress sat just below my butt cheeks. I shook my head, "I can't do it." My entire back was exposed. I would never make it.

He grabbed my hand and dragged me from the house. He grabbed my purse on the way and locked the door. I stood there, "Seriously, I can't do it."

"See him or the dress?"

I shook my head, "Both, neither."

He laughed and flipped me over his shoulder, "Let's go. You'll make him pay in this. Trust me, he'll suffer. He deserves that, at least a bit."

I wiggled, "Put me down. My underwear is showing."

"You're wearing cotton jockeys; no one is going to look."

I laughed and suffered through the ride down the stairs. He stopped part way, "Whew, that ten pounds is feeling more like forty."

I smacked him, "I weighed this morning. It was only ten. This dress is a six. That's only fat if you're making the mistake of shopping at Abercrombie and Fitch."

He laughed, "Imagine the legal damage control after that."

I chuckled as he placed me on the floor. He pulled me to his car. I was instantly freezing, "I need a coat."

He rolled his eyes, "It's going to be a thousand degrees in there. Stop being such a whiny bitch."

My Side

I snarled as he drove off.

He was giddy, Gerry had been in town for a day so far. That always meant Dean was excitable.

"Lise is going to be in the front row," he mentioned.

I nodded, "Good. I might need to go hang with her."

He nudged me, "Backstage is going to be incredible. You'll have fun if you let your hair down."

I shook my head, "I don't think that's going to help."

I took a deep breath and remembered I was strong and confident, and Asshole Barlow didn't stand a chance at making me doubt that. I was fabulous.

He parked in the restricted spot and put something in his window. He got out and came and dragged me from the car. He held my hand. I tried to ignore that my hands were sweating all over his. He walked up to a bouncer and handed him the tickets and a paper. He opened the door and handed us both a pass. I wrapped mine around my wrist and walked in.

It was dark and everything was black. People were bustling and going crazy. It was their first show at The Bank of America Pavilion. It was a huge deal. I was excited for them and hating that I cared.

Danny came running up. He looked so different that I hardly knew him. He was dressed in business casual and looking respectable. It brought an instant smile to my lips. He ran and scooped me into his arms.

"Who's the hottie, Danny boy?"

Danny spun me around, "This is my little sister, Erin."

When he set me down, I noticed the dimply smile of a dark-haired, tall drink of water. He put a hand out and flashed me the 'I'm with the band' smile, "I'm Leon." My heart beat a mile a minute. Status checks were revealing that I was still a groupie, and now I was even dressed like one. He glanced at Danny, "She doesn't look so little."

I scowled as Dean nudged. Danny stepped in front of me, "She's off-limits to the band."

I waved at him as Dean dragged me off, "Bye, Leon." Gerry mauled me when I got to where he was talking to someone. He shrieked and attacked me and Dean. "My two favorite people in the whole world." He pulled back, "What, Danny has to dress nice, so you decide to take his place as the family whore?"

I clenched my jaw. Dean looked hurt, "Hey, I picked that out."

Gerry gave him a knowing look, "We want Lo…" Dean slapped his hand over Gerry's mouth, "We say his, or him, or sometimes Satan. Never the name."

I swallowed and looked at Dean, "I want to go home."

He gripped my hand, "Who is the strong woman I know who is literally wearing some very big-girl panties and kicking some butt at law school?"

I took a huge inhale and nodded. I smiled and looked at Gerry, "Thank you for the letter." I was giddy about the night he was going to have, but I reined it in and kissed his cheek before I walked past him. I grabbed Danny's arm, "I want to go to the front stage area. My friend Lise is there. I don't want to be back here. I don't even want to be here."

He looked upset, "Stay. Please stay back here. We told him you were coming, and he's been better."

I hardened my heart, "I don't give a fuck."

He nodded, "Still mad, huh?"

My eyes narrowed. He put his hands in the air, "Alright, I'll be back in a minute."

I wrapped my arms around myself, wishing I had a jacket or a snowsuit.

"Princess?"

I turned like a well-trained seal, even though it wasn't my name. Lochlan...shit I thought his name... looked rough, sexy rough. It suited his bad boy of rock and roll look. His dark hair was still in the fohawk-mullet thing and his look was dark as sin.

"You got a tattoo?" He looked devastated.

I nodded. I wanted to say his name again. I wanted to hear it roll off my tongue or around in my mind.

He looked like he was going to take a step towards me but I spoke quickly, "Congratulations on the show. This is huge."

He smiled bitterly, "It ain't no Fargodome, but it's a step up from the bar circuit."

I laughed. I couldn't help myself.

"My mom is in a home now." He looked like he didn't know why he said it.

I nodded, "I know. She writes me letters."

He smiled the most broken smile I'd ever seen on his face, "Yeah, Gerry has a new way for her to press a letter and make words. She uses the iPad he bought her."

I smiled, "Good. The blinking made me tired, and I was only writing down the numbers."

"You staying backstage?"

I shook my head, hating the look on his face, but I was about to buckle and jump him. I needed to be away from him, "No. My friends are in the front row."

He bit his lip and winced, "Well, will you stick around after?"

I shook my head with the last of my self-preservation, "No. I have a lot of homework."

Dean came to my rescue, earning himself an evil look from Lochlan. His name was starting to fit back into my mind. It would be so easy to start saying it again, regardless of the fact that it burned me to do it.

He ignored Lochlan and pointed, "Danny said they are holding the seat, and some girl who is screaming right now and freaking out is taking your place backstage."

I smiled and nodded, "Have a good show."

His eyes got worse, "Don't leave." His words were a whisper.

I turned away quickly and waved, "See ya 'round." I followed Dean to the edge of the curtains. He rubbed my back, "You did so well."

I looked at him and Gerry, "I think I can do this. I can see him if I have to, you know, 'cause of you, Danny and Mike."

"ERIN!" I turned to see Mike running for me. He picked me up, smelling my neck, "Girl, how have you been?"

I smiled, "Good." I looked behind him to see the dark blue eyes still watching me. I hugged Mike again and blushed when he gushed, "You look hot."

Dean nodded, "That is the response I was looking for."

"You been lifting weights or something?" Mike grinned, not noticing Lochlan getting closer and closer behind him.

I shook my head, ignoring that he had joined the conversation. I spoke softly, "Hot yoga. When the shitty weather is over, I'll be running again."

Gerry smacked me in the butt, "Dean said she's been living on coconut-cream pies from some hole in the earth dive, so she has some extra junk in her trunk. I think it looks good though. You're curvy now. Kind of sexy. I bet you look good in the business suits now."

I shot him a look.

Mike nodded, "You do look good. The coconut-cream pies are doing you some good."

When I looked back at Mike, Lochlan was smirking from behind him. I looked down, "I better go. It was nice seeing you guys."

Mike hugged me again. I kept my eyes down, so I wouldn't have to see the dark blue eyes staring at me. I waved again as I turned and walked away. I went to where a bouncer was standing. He moved and I sat. Lise smiled at me, "Oh my God, I didn't think you were coming. I asked you like a month ago and you said no. I love your dress."

I laughed, "Thanks. Yeah, Dean changed my mind. I wanted to see everyone."

She winked, "Your brother is looking fine."

"Yeah, he is in his element. This is him."

She smiled, "This is everyone's. Anyone would want this life."

I was about to tell her how wrong she was, but I decided to keep my mouth shut. Let her have her fantasies. Everyone needed a dream.

The girl on the other side of me whispered, "So the girl who had your seat is the one he's gonna fuck tonight. Lucky, huh? Every show, Lochlan picks a girl from the audience and she stays with him backstage."

I felt sick, but I made myself remember how strong I was. I smiled, "Poor thing. I heard those musicians can't get it up, 'cause they do too much coke."

She made a face, "Ewww, really?"

I nodded.

"Yikes, I was all jealous, but damned if I'm suffering through some limp biscuit. God love her for getting picked."

I laughed. Lise hit my arm, "You are wicked."

I shrugged, "Whatever. She got to go backstage because I didn't want to be."

Lise winked, "The best part of the show is up front."

I never thought about that.

The opening act was good. They were indie sounding and fun.

The songs were toe tapping almost. They did a great show but we all knew why we were there.

They left the stage after receiving a good cheer.

Lise looked at me with an animated smile, "Eeeeeek." she squealed. I laughed until the lights went black, then my heart raced.

Lights flashed onto the crowd. We could see smoke above our heads.

His voice sang softly from the dark of the stage. A light flicked on to Leon. He played the keyboard softly. Another light flicked on revealing Gerry. He was lightly hitting the cymbals. The next light was Mike with the bass. With each light being switched on, the crowd screamed.

When the light hit Loch, they lost their minds. He sang softly until the light flicked onto him. Then he rocked. The crowd was on their feet. I was shoved forward instantly. My hands shot into the air, and I clapped along with everyone. The song was intense and fast. His jumped to life, using the whole stage. Song after song, my wall crumbled. I screamed along with the fans. They were still amazing. His control over the crowd was ridiculous. He was still the puppet master.

Lise and I gripped to each other, screaming and shouting the words to the songs. The girl next to me cried.

I was in a trance, a Lochlan trance, shit. But then I felt an elbow in my back. I shoved back. We were pressed into the stage. They did their last song of the night. I was deaf and voiceless but it was bliss; the best thing that had happened to me in a long time.

My heart was full.

Until...

"We want to thank y'all for coming to the show. We love Boston!" He threw a hand in the air. The crowd screamed and shoved forward again. I winced. I was going to have stage bruises later.

My Side

He waved, "Night y'all!" he pointed at me, "Don't leave."

My jaw dropped. Lise screamed.

The girl next to me made a face, "Oh God. He wants to invite you for the limp biscuit too."

I started to laugh, but the crowd pushed forward again. The lights shut off and then on. The band was gone.

I grabbed Lise's hand. It was getting chaotic in there. Danny came to the front of the stage and put a hand out for me, "Come with me."

I hesitated but I was again pushed forward. I put Lise's hand in his, "Her first."

He hauled her up like she weighed nothing. I put my hand in his, but I was pushed into the stage. I almost fell under the people. I heard Lochlan shout and grab my arm. He hauled me onto the stage, just as the bouncers were getting everyone back and forcing people out the doors. I looked out over the sea of people and then felt myself get picked up and dragged to the back. I slapped his arm, "Put me down, Loch."

He hesitated for a second. I could feel his heart beating against my squished arm. He put me down. His face softened, "Are you okay?"

I slapped his hand away when he tried to touch my cheek, "I'm fine."

Lise was smiling at Danny like he was her savior.

Gerry brought out trays of champagne, "To celebrate our Boston concert!" He seemed to miss my near death.

The guys all grabbed one. He handed one to me and Lise. Leon gave me a sly grin. I scowled at him. Mike backhanded him lightly in the stomach. He nodded at the darkened face stalking me like I was prey.

Leon looked confused, and then I literally watched the light bulb come on.

Lochlan held up his glass, "To Danny and the band for the amazing job you all do. I feel like the luckiest guy ever."

The glasses clinked. I sipped the champagne. He walked in front of me, pushing me back with his presence, "Don't leave me. Let me try to explain."

I shook my head, "I can't do this."

He took my champagne and put it down on the table next to us. He took my hands in his. The smell and warmth was too familiar. It made me feel sick almost. His eyes burned down on me. I pulled away, "I have to go."

I looked at Dean. He nodded and gave Gerry a kiss, "See you at home."

I smiled at them all, "Excellent show." I looked at Lise, "You coming?"

She looked at Danny, 'No. I'll get a ride home with him."

I smirked, "Eww. Okay. Night all." I walked away, feeling their eyes burning into my back. We had to drive with the other people out of the parking lot. It took forever to get back on the main road.

He stopped the car outside my apartment, "You okay?"

I nodded slowly, "I am okay. I feel conflicted about him, but I feel strong about my decision. I've seen him, we've touched hands, and I didn't falter. I think I'm safe from the thing we had."

He sighed, "That's too bad."

I frowned, "Why?"

He shrugged, "I don't think I've ever seen him look more in love with you. Gerry agreed. It was the best they've played in months."

I shook my head, "Don't be such a bitch."

He smiled, "See you Monday."

I laughed, "Thanks for making me face my fears."

He nodded, "That's my job." I got out and went upstairs.

I was in the kitchen drinking from the carton, when someone walked out of the hallway, "Hey."

I ripped my mace from my purse and sprayed before I realized what had happened. Seeing it was Lochlan, I dropped it and rushed to him. "Oh my God, baby. Are you okay? Never mind, dumb question. Come on." Tears streamed down his face. "Jesus, Erin, you trying to blind me for real?" He blinked and looked at me, his eyes were completely red. I winced and got the eye-wash station from the first aid kit. I pulled him to the sink and started to flush his eyes.

He blinked some more, "Is this stronger than the last time?"

I laughed, noticing my eyes were burning too. "I don't know." I filled the cups and started the eye washing. He cleaned his face. I opened all the windows and doors.

I came back into the kitchen feeling slightly justified, "I'm sorry, but why are you here? How did you get in?"

He held up his key. I had forgotten to ask for it back. Technically, the apartment was still his. He never had stopped paying for half.

"How did you beat us here?"

He chuckled, I think at himself, "I ran some of it and had a car pick me up. I knew you would be stuck in the traffic. I couldn't let you slip through my fingers again."

He ran across the city for me? Even the evil, man-hating bitch inside of me had to give that some credit.

He looked at the floor, "I didn't think it was fair to you, the band, and mom. They all saddled me with the band and everyone's success. Gerry bought a house, and everyone was buying cars, and there was no way I could back out. Their success was based on me being in the band. My dad was dead and everything felt too big. My mom needed help and I never thought about what she wanted. I wanted things to stay the way my dad had done it."

I took a step closer to him, "You don't need to tell me this."

He looked at me, "I needed you to see my side. You never see it." He sighed, "So I wanted you gone, because I had obligations. I never wanted you to feel like one of them. I wanted your life to be better than always waiting for me to have a free minute. I knew if I pushed you away, you would come back here and finish school, and I could try to win you back later. Then Gerry told me Dean said you seemed like you were over me. He said you had been flirting with some lawyer who was talking about your summer job being at his firm. I panicked. I came here, and I saw you at school."

I started to feel the desperation that was all over his face. He had been watching me?

"You were laughing with a guy. He was older than you. He was dressed like a lawyer and he suited you. You were so clean and shiny and perfect together. He was your kind of guy. You looked alive again. I didn't know what to do. You looked so professional and he touched your hand and you let him."

He gave me a look, "But you came tonight." He hopped off the counter, "It gave me some hope." He walked to me. I almost wished I had my mace again.

I shook my head, "Don't."

He ignored me and walked right up against me. My braless breasts squished against his abs. He looked down on me, "Seeing you tonight made me realize…" he bent and kissed my cheek, wrapping his arms around me. He kissed the other side of my face, "I don't have to be a singer. I don't have to be in a band. I don't have to do anything in this whole world. But I do have to make you love me again."

He lifted my chin and pressed his lips against mine. "That's all I want, baby. I don't even care if you love me back. Just let me try again." His hands slid down my body, lifting my dress. He cupped my ass cheeks and lifted me into his arms. I wrapped my legs around him. He walked to the bar and sat me on it. He cleared the shit off with a swipe of his arm.

Instantly, our lips moved against each other hungrily. His touch lit me on fire, worse than before. His hands got between my legs. He grabbed my underwear, ripping them, pulling them off of me. He pulled back my dress and unzipped his jeans in one movement. I was still wet from the show. He pushed himself into me. I gasped as he shoved into me hard. There was no controlling him. He was long past that. I gripped to him as his fingers bit into my hips. He thrust hard and fierce. His lips never left mine. We breathed each other in, in moans and sharp inhales.

He pulled me into each thrust, filling every bit of me. He held me so tight, I could feel the desperation in his fingertips. I could taste it in his kisses. I came hard, leaning back, letting him have me. He spread my thighs more and he came inside of me with an explosion. Breathless and confused, we clung to each other. He placed out-of-breath kisses on my stomach.

I watched him. He glanced up at me, "I missed you."

I smiled, "Me too."

He lifted me off the counter, "Let's go have a shower. I'm sweaty from the concert."

I put a hand on his chest, "Wait."

He shook his head, "Not another minute, princess."

After the shower, we lay in each other's arms, wrapped tight and constricted.

"I like the effect coconut-cream pie has on your body."

I laughed, "Are you saying you like my new fat?"

He lifted my breast like he was weighing it, "It makes you look fuller, like a woman." He sucked my nipple, "Makes me want to touch you more than before, which was a lot."

I laughed, "I remember."

He stroked a finger down my cheek, "I'm sorry I hurt you. I hate myself."

I shrugged, "I understand and I don't. I just... don't... can't forgive you. That's going to take time and we can't just be together like living together, like before, until I can get there."

His eyes burned, "I'm not leaving."

I laughed, "You have your work and I have school. We can finally take it slow. Take those trips you take all the time as a way to go slow."

"You want to take it slow? We just fucked and showered together, and I'm about to buy you breakfast at that all-night dive where we got the eggs Benny."

I smiled, "Yeah. I expect you will buy me breakfast, and then you'll frig off, so I can study and write my paper. I also expect that you'll text me as soon as you get wherever the hell you're going to next, and maybe even a few times in the cabs and shit."

He kissed my belly, "Okay, slow it is, but I ain't leaving."

Chapter Twenty-Two
Slow it ain't

98.8

Perfectly normal.

I frowned at the thermometer and put it down on the counter. It had to work; it was brand new.

I looked at the other thing that was brand new and sighed. If the throwing up wasn't the flu, it was something else. I walked, defeated and sickened, to the bathroom to try package number two.

There are things you should never do alone. This was one of them. I peed, holding it under the stream. I capped it, wrapped it in toilet paper, and washed my hands. I paced, feeling hungry and sick at the same time. I wanted some more pie. I looked at the clock, two more minutes. I went over the things in my bag one more time. I had everything. I was ready to go. This couldn't be happening.

One minute.

I ran into the bathroom and picked it up. The second line was faint. I squinted and shook my head, "That's not a line." Of course as I said it, the line filled in. I dropped the pee stick and dropped to my knees. I leaned into the bathroom counter, gasping for air.

Instead of breathing, I vomited again. I clutched the toilet and tried not to die. I was heaving when I heard the horn for the second time. I wiped myself down and grabbed the pee stick. I shoved it in my purse and grabbed my bags.

I ran to the car and jumped in. Dean gave me the disapproving-teacher look. Lise was in the back seat, grinning away.

I rolled my eyes, "Would you stop." My heart was pounding.

She shook her head, "I can't. I can't wait to see him."

Dean frowned, "We can't be late. Jeez. It's a wedding, Erin. Not a normal day. Her, I expect to be late. You—not so much."

I frowned, "Sorry." And I was. I was very sorry. I didn't even know what I was going to do. The wedding would be an awesome distraction at least.

We ran when we got to the airport. We just made our flight and the customs guys were pissed. They like two hours for international flights, not twenty minutes.

I was just about to start a full-fledged panic attack when we finally landed in British Columbia, Canada. Dean was a friend of a lawyer who had bought a winery in the Okanogan Valley. He was excited to have a wedding there.

I was exhausted. The time change was deadly. Gerry, Danny and Loch met us at the airport in Kelowna. It was hot and sunny. I looked at Dean, "This is Canada in May?"

He laughed, "This is actually part of the same desert as Nevada. The North American desert comes up into Canada. That's why the wine is so amazing, the heat."

The guys walked up in tee shirts and shorts. I pulled my parka off, "Seriously, Canada's hotter than Boston in May? There was a frost warning when we left."

Lochlan smiled and pulled off his sunglasses Seeing him was making it all worse. He was being so sweet and I was in the midst of trapping him. He nodded at me, "Want to see something cool?"

I frowned, "Hi to you too."

He waved at a group of young girls. They looked confused, then instantly recognized him. They waved back and walked away. I was stunned, "They never tried to take any of your clothes or pictures."

Gerry nudged my arm, "They're so nice. You know you always hear it, but oh my God. I have been left alone completely."

I gave Loch a look, "Can we live here?" We would have a new

reason to hide away from the screaming fans.

He nodded, "Fuck yes."

Danny was already taking Lise's bags and kissing her hands. We three couples, yeah, I know—barf, walked to the van. The driver took our bags. I nestled into Lochlan's arm and took a deep breath of him in.

He made a peaceful sound and did the same to my head. "You smell good." I felt my stomach twist into knots. He smiled, "It's going to be fun."

I frowned, "I know."

"You look worried."

I shrugged, "Jet lag."

We got to the inn next to the vineyard. It was huge, right on a massive, bright-blue lake. The hills were desert-like and rolling. It was cool. He carried my bags to the room. I flopped onto the bed.

"Turn on the AC."

He chuckled, "You hot already? I like it here. Come swim in the pool with me."

I shook my head, "Sleep." I closed my eyes and I was gone.

I woke later to the sound of tapping.

I opened my eyes. Gerry was tapping something on the desk.

"What are you doing?"

He raised an eyebrow, "What are you doing?"

I frowned, "Huh?"

He held up the pee stick, "Really?"

I sighed, "I peed on that."

"I know the science behind it, ass. It's one of the reasons I am so grateful to be gay."

I sighed, "Fuck me, Ger. What am I going to do? Everyone is

going to think I trapped him with this."

"They already think that; remember that picture from the day he bet you that you couldn't eat a whole pizza?

I groaned, "Oh my God. They have that picture too? What am I going to do?"

"Uh, I don't know. Tell him... since it's his." He gave me a look, "It's his right?"

I flipped him the bird.

"Well, you never know. As far as the media goes, you're kind of a mean-ass ho." I lifted my other hand to give him a second finger, and buried my face in a pillow. He came and laid beside me, "I came for you to tell me I'm doing the right thing."

I shot him a look, "And to snoop in my purse."

He stuck his tongue out, "I was looking for lip gloss. My lips are chapped. It's fucking hot here."

I nudged him, "You're making the right choice. I've spent the last five months trying to convince Dean to run away with me, and he never even wavered."

He grinned, "You think so?"

I smiled, "He loves you so much."

His face turned red, like the glasses he was wearing, "I know right?" He pointed down to my belly, "What's the plan for that?"

I shook my head, "I have no clue. I never wanted one of those. I wanted a condo, a BMW, and my own money. I had a goal and it wasn't this." My eyes shone, "This is your weekend though and I wasn't going to tell you or him."

"You brought the pee stick."

I laughed, "I had to keep checking it. I just didn't believe it. Although I will say, I'm glad it's just that. I thought for a minute that it was cancer. Google doctor said cancer or pregnancy but I was on the pill. So I assumed cancer. I hoped for flu."

He laughed, "Well, that's a pink line my friend."

"Let's just do your wedding and worry about my uterus later."

He smiled, "Okay. Eeeeek, me!"

That was easier said than done though. I didn't stop thinking about it. It plagued every second of my night. When Lochlan came to bed, he frowned at me, "You okay? And don't say jet lag."

I looked at him and nodded, "How do you see this all panning out, me and you? What's your vision for it?"

He yawned, "It's like three in the morning back home."

I shook his shoulder, "I need to know."

He sighed, "You and your damned plans. How about we just take it one day at a time, like you wanted to."

"So, one day at a time forever."

He gave me a look, "I'm not getting away without a 'let's talk about our relationship' moment, am I?"

I pinched him. He laughed and yawned again, "Baby, I see you as a successful lawyer and me as a musician, and we live wherever makes you happiest. I'll bring you weird things from the places I see and you can come on the road, anytime you want. How's that sound? We'll be free as birds."

I instantly started bawling. I didn't even know why. He wrapped around me, "Erin, you're scaring me. What's wrong?"

I climbed off the bed and tossed the pee covered pregnancy test at him. He held it for a second and then dropped it with a wrinkled nose, "Is that a joke?"

I laughed and then cried again. I stalked into the bathroom and slammed the door.

"Babe, let's talk about this. You can't throw a pregnancy test at a man. That's just wrong. You peed on that. And you gave me no warning."

I sat in the empty tub, rocking back and forth. Weird sounds ripped from my lips. They were high-pitch sobs.

He knocked again, "Baby, you're scaring me. You set me up with the whole what's our future talk, and then the pee stick. Erin, don't make me break down the door."

I managed a couple words, still very high-pitched, "Just give me a minute." I was having a panic attack, and I knew he would break the door down.

"Yes, ma'am."

I crawled out of the tub and dropped onto the floor by the door.

I heard him slide down the door too.

"You don't seem happy," he said after a minute.

I shook my head, "Yeah, not so much. I'm scared and wondering why I my birth control didn't work, and how we're going to have a baby? We have had the weirdest year ever. How do we add a kid to that?"

"We love each other, have a great income, and don't have drug problems, or drinking problems, or weird addictions. Well, except mine for you."

"What if I get fat and all the girls are hitting on you, and you have to come home to a sweaty, fat wife who pees when she sneezes and shit?"

He laughed, "Oh baby, you have to open the door, so I can be excited about this."

I swallowed, "What if we fuck this up?"

"We won't. We already fucked it up. We did that part. Now we have to enjoy the rewards of ruining everything, and putting it back together. It's lucky actually that we're in the rebuilding stage; we have loads of flexibility for a baby. I know I love you. I know I want to be with you. I know I'll spend the rest of my life trying to make you happy, in my special, frustrating way."

I turned the lock on the door. He pushed it open and scooped me up. He carried me to the bed. He kissed my belly, "Just think. All the love that we have for each other, we put it in this safe place here." He kissed my belly again.

I still couldn't breathe properly.

He looked up at me, his eyes were the clearest blue I'd ever seen them, "I want to give you something."

I laughed, "You already gave me something."

He laughed, "Funny."

He pulled out my ring from his pocket. He dragged me down the bed and knelt between my legs, "It's not even close to how I wanted to do it. I've been carrying it for weeks, just trying to find the right way or right moment. I wanted it to be so romantic and whatever. And right now, I can't think of anything that trumps what you're giving me. There won't be a better moment in my life than this one. Marry me."

I gave him a hard look. I gave him my right hand, "Until they're married, I don't want to steal the show with babies and engagements."

Lochlan cocked his head, "You never said yes."

"Yes." I challenged him with my stare.

He cocked an eyebrow, "Yes?"

I laughed, "Yes. I will marry you, before I get fat."

He laughed, "Good. Mom and I were talking and she'd really like to see the wedding in the next couple months. She's been really weak lately and she doesn't want to do it when it gets too hot."

I shoved him, "You have not been talking about this with your mom."

He pulled me into his arms, "I have, I swear. We've been planning it. She gave me this." He pulled out a wedding band, "It was my Dad's. She told me to give it to you when I was ready, and we could maybe have it made into a ring I would like."

I breathed out fast, "I think you just trumped what I'm giving you."

He grinned, stealing my heart all over again, "No way."

The next day we all stood and watched our best friends get married. They declared their love for each other in the sweetest of ways. Dean had gotten a ring made with his favorite line from one of their songs, "Save my soul from the seconds we're apart"; Gerry got the band to perform a song he wrote for him. I cried way too much and waited for the bottom to fall out of our perfection like it always did.

Chapter Twenty-Three
Bunnies and brownies

The moment it all changed happened in front of everyone. The doctor rubbed the wand over my bare belly, pushing into it. The jelly he had rubbed on there was cold and sticky.

The rapid beat filled the room and everyone burst into tears and gasps. We did it in Nashville at the home where Judith was. She cried and punched letters like crazy.

Alex read it, "I am so proud of both of you for finding your way back to each other."

I sniffled and felt the beat within my body.

"I think we got us a drummer!" Gerry laughed.

Mike scowled, "No way, bass for sure."

I closed my eyes and felt Loch's hand on mine. He squeezed hard, "I love you, baby."

The doctor smiled, "I'll say you're about fifteen weeks along. How much have you gained?"

I shook my head, "None yet."

Lochlan nodded, "She's been a crazy woman about her food."

The doctor shook his head, "The first three months, it's common for women not to gain anything, but from here on out, I need you to maintain the calories on the piece of paper I've got here, and make sure you're getting those food groups. Okay?"

I nodded.

"The less fat in your diet, the less brain development in your baby."

"Okay." I knew nothing about babies, and the books scared me. I couldn't read them. I didn't even really want sex anymore after what I'd read in the last one.

He wiped me down and let me get up. "Everything sounds normal, but your sonogram at 19 weeks will be the photo shoot."

I smiled, "Thanks for doing it here."

He nodded, "Anytime."

I got off the table and let everyone hug me. Lochlan wrapped his arms around me, "You ready for tomorrow?"

I nodded and looked back at him, "I am."

He attacked his mom, "You're gonna be a grandma." She smiled. She was gaining back little bits of movements. Living in the home was helping tremendously. She had full physio every week and constant care.

I kissed her goodbye and left with Dean, Lise, and Lissie. We went to the hotel room while Alex, Mike, Danny, Leon, and Gerry went with Loch to take his mom back to her room.

We had done everything in the few weeks we had to organize. Having money helped a lot. When money was no object, people just said yes.

Dean looked at me, "Did you ever hear why Lochlan beat that guy up on the show?"

I nodded, "Yeah."

"It came out to the press yesterday. Look." He laid down his iPad. I read the article, "Wow. That Andrew guy really thinks a lot of Loch."

Dean nodded, "I do too. I never knew that was why he did it."

I nodded, "I only just found out. He let me believe he was jealous of the guy winning."

He shook his head, "Wow."

Lissie nodded "Yeah, we were sworn to secrecy on it. I hated listening to everyone talking shit about him when they didn't have clue."

Lise shrugged, "I always thought it made him hotter to be so crazy and unpredictable."

I smiled at her, when Dean and Lissie gave her a confused stare.

A knock on the door interrupted their judgments. Dean answered and was instantly cougar-attacked by my mom, "Oh myyyy. You must be in the band."

I rolled my eyes, "Mom, this is professor Dean. He's married to Gerry."

She blushed, "Ohhhh right. Of course he is. How is young Gerry?" She got a predatory look in her eyes. Dean stepped back. I laughed, "He's married and happy."

She smiled, "Well, anyway. Congratulations. And how is the bride to be?"

I smiled, "Good. Little tired, but I'm good."

"How is my little grandbaby?" she actually talked to my belly, or even my vagina, depending on the angle you were at.

"Good. We heard the heartbeat today."

She looked up from my low, low abdomen, "Was it high or low? There's some old wives tale about that."

I shook my head, "I don't know. It sounded fast."

Lissie nodded, "To me, it was really fast."

Dean nodded, "Yeah. I know, right."

Lise laughed, "I thought that too, but then he said it was normal."

My mom stared at us like we were insane, "Of course it's faster. Iou didn't know that?"

We all shrugged and shook our heads. We slept in the room, all of us, but mom. She was oddly fast to leave, for her. She usually hovered and it got awkward.

I heard a light knock at the door. I slipped out of the bed and answered. Lochlan stood there, looming in the doorway. He looked down on me and smiled, "I needed to see you two."

I smiled back, "Hi."

"Did you eat?"

I nodded, "Just some room service."

He pulled a brown bag from behind his back, "I brought you fudgy-brownie swirl!"

I closed the door with a shoe in it, not mine, and sat in the hallway with him. We sat beside each other. He pulled off the lid and passed me the spoon. I dipped it in and took the first bite. I closed my eyes and let the flavor of the fudge ice cream melt across my tongue, "Mmmmmmm. I wuv yew."

He laughed and took the spoon, "I know you do."

I looked at the ring on my finger and nodded, "You're cool if I just keep it a sapphire right?"

He smirked. My smile dropped right off my face, "Was it ever a sapphire?"

He shook his head, "I was seriously going to ask you that night. I know your ex had tainted the insta-love for you, but I wanted you to be mine. Your face when I pulled out that box was sheer horror. So I came up with a super-fast lie. You bought it and I got my ring on your finger."

I stole back the spoon, "No fudgy-swirl for you."

He laughed, "You can't get mad about old shit."

"I can and I will. I can even overreact, thanks to the baby bunny."

He gave me a look, "Baby bunny?"

I felt my face burning, "Yeah. So?"

He bent down and kissed my belly, "I love you."

I smiled and let him kiss the small roll we were both pretending was baby, but was more like coconut-cream pie from before.

I leaned into him when he sat up, "You see the news article about Andrew?"

He nodded, "Yeah. He called and told me he was doing it. I told him not to worry, but he said he had taken the coward's path or some crap. Anyway, he came out to his family."

I smiled, not looking at him, "At least he got the chance. At least that wanker never got to out him."

"Agreed."

"You nervous about tomorrow?"

He looked down on me, "No. You?"

I shook my head, "No. It's bizarre, but I'm not. I should be. I didn't want any of this, and now it feels like I always wanted it."

He kissed my temple, "Maybe you just didn't know you did."

I nodded, "Maybe." I sighed, "Maybe it just needed you in the equation, to make me want it."

He lifted me off the floor and kissed me sweetly. I wrapped my arms around his neck and kissed him like I meant it. He growled, "Not here."

"Fine." I kissed him goodnight, getting lost in his eyes. He pushed me inside, "You need sleep for you and the baby bunny."

I closed the door and sighed against it. My heart was full from him and some ice cream, and a hallway. I never knew I was such a simple person.

The next day, swathed in a princess-cut, strapless wedding dress and a huge grin, my dad gripped my arm. He kissed my cheek,

"You ready, kid?"

I nodded.

He beamed, "You look beautiful."

I laughed and rubbed my still fairly-flat stomach, "Can you tell it's a shotgun wedding?"

He shook his head, "No. It's not anyway, he asked me for my permission last November. He's had it since."

I frowned, "He did?"

He nodded, "You two belong together. Just like me and your mother do."

I made face, "You're back together?"

He nodded, "Yeah. Something about visiting Nashville affected us both. We saw how selfish we were being. We compromised. Winters in the city, summers in the country, and spring and fall is whatever."

I laughed, "Wow. Is that my wedding gift?"

He laughed, "No."

The music started and my dad frowned, "You're walking to Bob Dylan?"

I nodded, "Shelter From The Storm has special meaning for us."

"Weird, I guess, though musicians are different."

I kissed his cheek, "Let's do this."

We walked down the aisle slowly, I never really noticed though. I was stuck on the dark-blue eyes in front of me. His expression was getting darker with every step I took. His face was all I saw. He shook my dad's hand as my dad kissed my cheek. I took Loch's hand and let him pull me to the minister.

I barely recalled the words I spoke. The eyes had me mesmerized. The next thing I knew he kissed me. I melted into him. He dropped to his knee and kissed my stomach, whispering things to it. I smiled at him.

As we walked down the aisle, he whispered, "Mrs. Barlow, how are you feeling?"

I smiled, "Good. I'm married to this super-cheesy guy, but it's good."

He kissed my cheek.

Epilogue

I finished setting up the kitchen, and everything was where I wanted it. I wondered how long it would stay that way.

"Come see."

I looked up. He was standing in the hall in cargo shorts and a baby-blue tee shirt. I sighed looking at his tattoos and muscles. I looked down at my belly and rubbed it.

"Erin, I swear to God, you have to see this."

I followed him, waddling out into the hot, summer night. Kids were playing on the cul-de-sac and people were mowing their lawns. It was the furthest thing from a condo in Downton New York that I could imagine. It was a house in the burbs, down the road from Alex, Lissie, Gerry, Danny, and Mike. We had become those barbecue people who were exhausted by ten at night.

I got out into the yard and snarled, maybe even hissed like a vampire, when I saw what he wanted to show me. It was hideous. I covered my mouth, about to cry, but he wrapped his arms around me, "Just give it a chance. I swear I'll buy you the sports car, one day, but for safety features, this is the shit. I mean who knew BMW made a minivan?"

I shook my head, "I'm twenty-five, not forty. I hate it. Take it back."

He pulled me back, "Princess, you have to check it out before you hate it. There's a damned movie theatre in there."

I tilted my head, "You are a liar."

His voice rose, "I swear to God, it's a fucking movie theatre."

My hand shot out, pointing at him, "What did I say about swearing?"

He put his hands out, "Deep breaths. Just take deep breaths." He dragged me to the van and opened the large, sliding door. He shoved me inside gently, since I was liable to burst. I climbed into the seat. He started the van and turned on the air conditioning. It blew down on me from the roof. He pressed buttons and instantly Fear and Loathing in Las Vegas started to play.

I gave him a look. He shrugged, "We don't have kids movies yet."

I watched the movie and nestled into the chair. I sighed and gave him a look, "This is pretty cool."

He leaned in for a kiss, "So when I leave tomorrow for London, you'll take it for a drive. Get used to being in a mommy mobile?"

I sneered, "Don't call it that."

He laughed, "Baby steps."

I pointed at the screen, "That I like."

He nodded, "I told you. I'm having a rockin' week. Double platinum for our first non indie album and now this sweet ride." I rolled my eyes but he leaned in, brushing his lips against mine, "Did I also tell you how pretty you are and how lucky I am?"

I shook my head, "Not today."

His eyes narrowed but I could see myself in them still. I had a feeling, I always would. He got that sexy grin and I shook my head again, "Not in the minivan. The kids are going to sit back here. Ewww."

He laughed, "Kids? You already planning the next one?"

I nodded, "Yeah. We can't have one, they're always, well look at Leon. He's so... no. I need at least two, but then I was thinking since you, Alex, and Issie are so sweet together, we should have three."

He kissed my nose, "One day at a time. You and your plans. Now come in the house, so I can show you how pretty I think you are before we take this minivan for a spin."

I followed him inside. I would have followed him anywhere.

My Side

That's my side

The end

Other books by Tara Brown

Cursed - (Book #1 of The Devil's Roses)

Bane - (Book #2 of The Devils Roses)

Hyde - (Book #3 of The Devils Roses)

Witch - (Book #4 of the Devil's Roses)

Death - Book #5 of the Devil's Roses)

The Light of the World - Light Series

Blackwater- The Blackwater Witches

Vengeance - The Blood Trail Chronicles

The Lonely

The End of Me

Born – (Book #1 of the Born Trilogy)

Born to Fight - (Book #2 of the Born Trilogy)

Reborn – (Book #3 of the Born Trilogy)

Imaginations

The Long Way Home

My Side

My Side

ABOUT THE AUTHOR

Tara Brown is the bestselling author of the controversial novel The Lonely, the completed series The Devil's Roses, and the exciting Science Fiction Trilogy Born…only to name a few.
Her WIP is always a list of about ten books and her ideas range from psycho thrillers to science fiction futuristic worlds to vampires with a bad attitude and a penchant for reality TV.
She lives in Canada with her husband, daughters, beagle, and a pair of saucy felines.
She can always be reached at her blog http://tarabrown22.blogspot.ca/
Or facebook page https://www.facebook.com/TaraBrownAuthor

Made in the USA
Charleston, SC
29 October 2013